The
History
of Our
Future

The History of Our Future

Fletcher Hopkins

ISBN: 979-8-234-05052-6
Library of Congress Congrol Number: 2026909561
First Edition: May 2026

Published by Fletcher Hopkins
Madisonville, Kentucky
www.fletcherhopkins.com

Disclaimer
This is a work of fiction. Names, characters, businesses, places, events, and incidents are either the product of the author's imagination or used fictitiously. Any resemblance to actual persons, living or dead, or real events is purely coincidental. While certain real-world locations or political offices may be mentioned, all characters, organizations, and events involving them are entirely fictional. Any similarities to actual political figures, past or present, or to specific historical or current incidents are unintended and purely coincidental.

The
History
of Our
Future

curated playlist inspired by the book

Follow You to Virgie
Tyler Childers, OurVinyl

Take Me Home, Country Roads
John Denver

8 to inifinity
Nic D

Runnin' (Lose It All)
Naughty Boy, Beyoncé, Arrow Benjamin

Go!
Soft Swells

Am I Okay?
Megan Moroney

Finding You
Kesha

Little by Little
Patrick Droney

Restless Mind
Sam Barber, Avery Anna

30,000 Ft
We Three, M Humble, B Zimmerman

The Best
Nicotine Dolls

You Are In Love (Taylor's Version)
Taylor Swift

Hey Driver
Zach Bryan, The War And Treaty

Not How I Want To
Zach Seabaugh

This Too Shall Last
Anderson East

One Life
James Bay

Meet Me in the City
Adam Doleac

Poetry
Wrabel

Not Ready to Make Nice
The Chicks

Look At Us Now (Honeycomb)
Marren Morris, Marcus Mumford,
Daisy Jones & The Six

Spotify Playlist

ONE

> "Some men see things as they are and say why. I dream things that never were and say why not." — Robert F. Kennedy

History is full of men who believed the future belongs to them.

I wrote the sentence across the whiteboard a few minutes before the hour, the marker dragging faintly against its surface as the first students filtered into the room behind me. Vanderbilt in late August carried a heat that seemed to settle into the walls themselves, lingering even indoors. By the time I stepped back, a thin line of perspiration had already formed along my wrist.

It was my first lecture of the semester. My first lecture anywhere beyond Johns Hopkins. My first time teaching this close to the place I had once called home. I stood there a moment longer, looking at the sentence as if it belonged to someone else.

It was a simple idea—almost obvious. But it had shaped the better part of my professional life, this quiet fascination with people who looked at the world as it was and believed, with varying degrees of conviction or delusion, that they could bend it into something else.

Behind me, chairs shifted softly as more students settled into their seats. A few opened laptops. Others flipped through notebooks with the practiced resignation of people who had already accepted the rhythm of a long semester brewing. I had always liked this moment—the brief pause before a class truly began, when the room still belonged equally to possibility and uncertainty.

As I turned slowly to face them, a dozen unfamiliar faces looked back, expectant in that cautious way students tend to be during the first week—curious, but not yet committed. I rested one hand lightly against the edge of the podium, grounding myself before I began.

"Political history," I said, gesturing toward the board, "is often the story of people who believed the future was theirs to shape."

A few heads tilted. That was usually enough.

"The Kennedys are frequently used as examples of that kind of political optimism," I continued. "John Kennedy's 'New Frontier'—the idea that a younger generation might move the country in a different direction."

A photograph flickered onto the screen behind me—Robert Kennedy leaning into a crowd, sleeves rolled, expression intent.

"But by 1968, it was Robert people were watching," I said. "If you read the coverage from that year, you can feel something building. Crowds getting bigger. People starting to believe—really believe—that something might shift."

I let the image sit briefly before continuing.

"And the strange part is that no one in those crowds thought it was temporary. That's the problem with studying the past—we know how things end long before the people living them ever do."

A few students nodded.

"In the moment," I added, "it just feels like something's opening."

An hour later, I crossed campus toward my office, the lecture already beginning to blur into the rest of the day.

The building itself was unremarkable—brick, functional, easy to overlook. My office on the second floor looked exactly like what it was: temporary. Boxes stacked along the wall, books half unpacked, a desk that hadn't quite decided where it belonged in the room.

I set my bag down and glanced at the clock. That evening, I was scheduled to join a panel discussion hosted by the Department of Political Science and the Nashville Metropolitan Council—The New South: Politics, Identity, and Power. It was the kind of conversation I had spent most of my career engaged with in some form. The South had never lacked for political reinvention—only for agreement about what that reinvention meant.

My phone buzzed against the desk.

Marcia Carrington—my PhD advisor at Johns Hopkins turned colleague who encouraged me to pursue the fellowship year at Vanderbilt.

"Hey, Marcia."

"Well," she said immediately, "that sounded exhausted. How did the first lecture go?"

"About how they always go," I said, leaning back in the chair. "Half the room looked interested. The other half looked like they'd made a mistake."

"Those are promising numbers."

"I did my best to keep them a little on edge."

"Good," she said. "It keeps them paying attention."

I smiled.

By the time evening settled over Nashville, the air had cooled just enough to make the walk across campus comfortable.

The lecture hall was already half full when I arrived. Students clustered in small groups near the back rows while faculty gathered along the aisles, continuing conversations that had likely begun earlier in the day. At the front of the room, a long table had been set with three microphones and a row of placards marking the speakers.

I took my seat and glanced down at the name beside mine: Representative William Beau Hale II. The name felt familiar in the way certain influential families tend to be—recognized without being fully known.

A few minutes later, the door at the back of the hall opened. The shift in the room was subtle, but noticeable. Conversations dipped, then resumed at a lower volume. A few heads turned.

The man who stepped inside moved with the kind of ease that suggested he was accustomed to being watched, even when he wasn't trying to be. He was tall—noticeably so—and broad-shouldered in a way that made his presence difficult to ignore without being overtly imposing. His jacket was draped casually over one arm, the sleeves of his white shirt rolled neatly to his elbows.

His hair caught the overhead light as he moved. Red—not dull or muted, but warm. Copper-toned, the kind of color that held attention a second longer than expected. He paused near the door to shake a few hands, offering easy smiles that didn't feel rehearsed, before he made his way toward the stage.

When he reached the table, he extended his hand almost reflexively.

"Professor Whitaker."

"Nate's fine," I said, standing to meet him.

A quick, easy smile. "Then you'd better call me Beau."

The discussion began a few minutes later.

"When we talk about the New South," Dr. Alvarez, the moderator for the evening said, "what exactly do we mean?" He gestured toward me. "Professor Whitaker?"

I adjusted the microphone slightly.

"Historians are usually a little suspicious of phrases like that," I said.

A few people smiled.

"Mostly because the South has been described as 'new' every decade or so for the last hundred years."

That earned a small ripple of laughter.

"But the idea itself isn't meaningless," I continued. "It usually reflects a moment when people believe something is changing—politically, culturally, economically."

"And the challenge?" Alvarez asked.

"We already know how the story ends," I said.

A few heads tilted.

"When we look back at earlier moments of optimism—Reconstruction, the civil rights era—we see both the progress and the resistance that followed. So, historians tend to approach optimism with a little caution."

Alvarez nodded and turned.

"Representative Hale?"

Beau leaned forward slightly, resting one arm on the table.

"I think that depends on whether you see the job as explaining the world or trying to change it."

A few murmurs of approval moved through the audience.

"I don't have the luxury of waiting fifty years to see how things turn out," he added. "We're expected to make decisions now. And sometimes those decisions come from believing things can be better than they are."

His tone was steady and unforced, but not arrogant as is often the case with those of the political class.

"It may be naïve," he said with a slight shrug, "but optimism comes with the territory."

"I don't think optimism is naïve," I said.

He glanced toward me.

"But history suggests it's fragile," I added.

"That may be true," Beau said easily. "But fragile things are still worth building."

By the time the panel ended, the room had filled with the familiar post-event shuffle of chairs and conversation.

I was gathering my notes when someone stepped beside the table.

Beau.

"Well," he said, "that went about as expected."

"Expected?" I asked.

"You didn't seem too unnerved," he answered.

"The life of the past is my comfort zone."

Beau smiled. "You think I was pushing too hard?" he asked.

"No," I replied.

He studied me for a moment. "What did you think?"

"I thought you meant what you were saying."

"Well," he started, his smile returning. "I did."

Time seemed to slow as the last of the room emptied around us.

"You been in Nashville long?" he asked.

"About a week."

"And how's it treating you?"

"Better than I expected."

He nodded once. "It grows on people."

"I've heard that."

"Give it time," he said.

The last of the crowd thinned around us. Beau slipped his jacket over his shoulder, pausing just long enough to extend his hand again.

"Well, Professor Whitaker—"

"Nate."

"Right," he said. "Nate." His handshake was firm but unstudied, the kind that felt more like acknowledgment than performance. "Good to meet you."

"You as well."

He gave a small nod before turning toward the aisle, stopping once or twice to exchange a few final words with people on his way out. Even in motion, he carried the same easy awareness of the room—never hurried, but never lingering too long.

I gathered my notes more slowly than necessary, waiting for Beau to clear the auditorium before making my way toward the exit. Outside, the night had steadied into something softer, the heat of the day finally giving way to a breeze that carried the distant sound of music from somewhere beyond the edge of campus.

At the bottom of the steps, I paused—not for any reason, just long enough to realize I was replaying the conversation in my head. His answers. The ease of them. Nothing he said had felt rehearsed, even when it probably should have been. Most politicians I'd encountered had mastered a certain kind of performance. Beau Hale didn't feel like he was performing. I wasn't sure whether that made him admirable or dangerous— probably both.

The walk to my slightly-off-campus apartment was unrushed. Campus had begun to empty, the cadence of the day giving way to scattered movement—students crossing the lawn in small groups, the occasional car along the outer roads. A warm breeze whistled through the trees, carrying the faint smell of cut grass and something else just beyond it—distant, indistinct, like sound carried farther than it should.

By the time I reached my apartment, the quiet felt immediate. I dropped my bag onto the table and loosened my collar, standing there as the stillness settled in. Academic life was a constant exchange of ideas—lectures, panels, conversations that stretched longer than they needed to—but it often ended like this: alone, quiet, the day lingering just beneath the surface.

I crossed to the desk and opened my laptop. The glow of the screen filled the room as my inbox loaded. Department emails. A handful of questions about the syllabus. A message from a colleague debating a point about Reconstruction voting patterns that could wait indefinitely. And then—

Beau Hale.

I stared at the name for a second before opening it.

Nate—

Enjoyed the conversation tonight. Historians and politicians probably won't agree on everything, but I'd argue that's half the fun.

If you're settling into Nashville and want to continue the discussion sometime, there's a place I usually take people who are new to the city. The Bluebird Café has live music most nights, and it's about as close as you'll get to a proper Nashville welcome.

They've got a show next week that's usually pretty good.

No pressure—just thought I'd offer.

—Beau

I read it twice. It wasn't an unusual email. Friendly. Casual.

The kind of invitation people extend without expecting much in return. Still, I found myself lingering there, the cursor blinking idly at the edge of the screen.

Part of it was curiosity. I had met plenty of people like Beau before—public figures who understood how to make a conversation feel personal without actually giving much away. Charm, in that context, was often just another form of strategy. But that wasn't quite what this felt like.

He hadn't seemed guarded. Not exactly. If anything, there had been a kind of openness to him that didn't quite align with the version of politics I was used to studying.

"Optimism is kind of the job description," he'd said. The line surfaced again without invitation. I glanced back at the email—the Bluebird Café. It sounded exactly like the sort of place someone would recommend to a newcomer. Still, there was something about the invitation that felt slightly more deliberate than that—not calculated, but intentional. I leaned back in the chair, rubbing a hand across the back of my neck.

Historians spend most of their lives trying to understand people they can no longer question. Letters, speeches, fragments of conversations preserved just long enough to suggest intention without ever fully confirming it.

In the present, the process isn't much clearer. Sometimes a person invites you to hear music. Sometimes they're curious about the argument you started in a crowded lecture hall. And sometimes—though history rarely marks the moment precisely— two lives begin to move, almost imperceptibly, toward the same point.

I closed the email without replying. The message would still be there in the morning. Outside, somewhere beyond the quiet streets surrounding campus, a guitar chord carried faintly through the night air before fading into something indistinct. I shut the laptop and stood, the room slipping back into shadow as the screen went dark. The boxes along the wall remained unopened. Books stacked unevenly where I'd left them. For a split second, I considered unpacking something—some small gesture toward settling in—but the thought passed as quickly as it came.

"Next week," Beau had written.

There was time. For now, Nashville moved quietly outside the window, and the future—like most things worth studying— remained just uncertain enough to be interesting.

TWO

"The past is never dead. It's not even past." — William Faulkner

Sunday morning found me in the reading chair by the window, a faint early-autumn breeze slipping through the narrow opening and moving lazily through the apartment. Nashville had begun its slow transition out of summer—the heat still present, but softened at the edges, as if the season itself was learning how to let go.

My phone buzzed against the arm of the chair:

Crossed into Tennessee. Forty minutes.

I smiled faintly. "See you soon," I typed back.

The apartment still looked like I'd moved in six days ago—which, technically, I had. Boxes sat half-opened along the walls, books stacked in uneven towers on the floor, and the coffee table had quietly taken on the role of temporary storage for anything I hadn't yet decided what to do with. Colt had seen worse.

The knock came exactly forty minutes later. When I opened the door, he stood there in jeans and a faded University of Kentucky T-shirt, one hand hooked casually through the strap of a duffel bag slung over his shoulder. For a beat, he looked exactly the same as he always had.

Maybe a little older. A little more settled into himself. But otherwise, unchanged—the same broad shoulders, the same easy confidence, the same quiet sense that wherever he happened to be was exactly where he belonged.

"Well," he said, stepping inside and glancing around the apartment. "You've gone full city on us."

"It's Nashville."

"That still counts."

He dropped the duffel near the couch and turned slowly, taking in the boxes, the books, the general lack of organization.

"You unpack yet?"

"Working on it."

He gave the room another once-over. "Looks like you lost interest halfway through."

"Not even halfway," I replied, gesturing towards the towers of unpacked belongings.

Colt laughed and clapped me once on the shoulder, the gesture as familiar as anything from home.

"Good to see you, man."

"You too."

We ordered lunch from a place down the street and ate it on opposite ends of the couch, the way we had when we were younger—close enough for conversation, far enough to feel like we didn't have to fill every silence. Colt carried most of it anyway.

He moved easily through updates from Kentucky—friends getting married, someone starting a business, the kind of small-town developments that continued whether you were there to witness them or not.

"How's Hannah?" I asked.

He leaned back against the couch, a grin settling in almost immediately. "Good. Tired. Hungry all the time."

"That tracks."

"She's about sixteen weeks now."

I nodded. "You picked a name yet?"

"We're working on it."

"That sounds diplomatic."

"You say that like you've done it before."

"I've observed from a safe distance."

Colt shook his head, laughing. "You're gonna be an uncle."

"So I've been told."

"You don't seem all that fazed."

I shrugged. "It's not my kid."

He let out a short laugh, shaking his head. "Alright, fair."

"I'm excited," I added, a little more honestly.

"You just don't look it."

"I contain multitudes."

That got a real laugh out of him, the kind that lingered a second longer than the joke deserved.

I glanced over at him. "So this is what—just a casual two-hour drive to evaluate my emotional range?"

"I drove two hours," he said, "because Hannah told me I needed to get out of the house before I reorganized the nursery again."

I smiled. "That I believe."

"I bought a label maker."

"Of course you did."

We spent the afternoon walking through the city. Colt wanted to see Nashville—something I hadn't quite gotten around to doing myself yet. We wandered through Centennial Park, cut across shaded paths beneath trees just beginning to shift in color, and eventually found our way to a bench overlooking the water near the Parthenon. A handful of paddleboats drifted lazily across the lake, their slow movement matching the pace of the afternoon.

For a while, we sat without saying much, watching people pass.

Then Colt spoke.

"So."

"So," I replied, mocking his slow cadence of the word.

"You seeing anybody?"

The question came out lightly, but not casually. Colt had always been careful like that—asking just enough to open the door without pushing through it.

"No," I said flatly.

He nodded once. "Okay."

I glanced over. "That's it?"

"What were you expecting?"

"A speech."

"I'm pacing myself."

I let out a quiet breath, my attention drifting back to the water.

Colt leaned forward, resting his elbows on his knees. "You've been in Baltimore how long now?"

"Six years."

"And this is just for the year?"

"Probably."

He repeated it under his breath. "Probably."

There was a pause before he spoke again, more quietly this time.

"You know I'm not asking to be nosy."

"I know."

"I just want to make sure you're alright."

I nodded. "I am."

He didn't answer right away. I could feel him looking at me, trying to decide whether to leave it there or push a little further.

"You don't have to do life alone forever," he said.

"I'm not alone."

He exhaled softly. "You know what I mean."

I did. I just didn't know what to do with it. Momentarily, neither of us said anything.

I still remember the night I called Colt from an emergency room in Boston. He hadn't asked many questions. He'd just shown up the next morning, helped me pack what mattered, and driven me across the city to Marcia's apartment like it was something simple—like it didn't require explanation to be understood. He only asks because he cares. My own history, though, has never been a subject I've had much interest in revisiting.

Colt leaned back again, stretching his arms across the bench, letting the conversation shift without forcing it.

"You can study history forever," he said after a moment. "Believe it teaches people something."

"That's the idea."

"But that doesn't mean your history gets to decide everything," he said. "Or what you deserve."

The words settled between us, quiet but deliberate. Colt didn't look at me after he said them. He just watched the water, giving me the space to respond—or not.

After a moment, I said, "Hannah put you up to this?"

"She suggested I check on you."

"That sounds right."

"I added the speech."

"I figured."

He smiled slightly. "You seem good here."

"I think I might be."

We sat there a while longer, the conversation settling into something easier again. Eventually Colt pushed himself up from the bench and stretched.

"Alright," he said. "You've shown me the calm, reflective side of Nashville. Now show me the part with bad decisions and loud music."

He left later that evening. True to form, he hugged me once in the parking lot, tossed his bag into the backseat of his truck, and pulled away with the same easy wave he'd been giving me since we were kids.

The apartment felt quieter when I stepped back inside. Not empty. Just still. I made coffee, sat down at my desk, and opened my laptop. My inbox hadn't changed much—student emails, department updates, the usual background noise of academic life.

And then—

Beau Hale.

I opened it again. The invitation was still there, quiet and uncomplicated in a way I hadn't decided what to do with.

The Bluebird Café.

I leaned back slightly in the chair, reading it one more time. The panel came back to me first—the conversation, the ease of it, the way nothing he said had felt rehearsed. Then, unexpectedly, Colt's voice drifted back in behind it.

Your history doesn't get to decide everything.

I stared at the screen, letting the thought settle—then clicked reply.

THREE

"Not everything that is faced can be changed, but nothing can be changed until it is faced." — James Baldwin

My second week at Vanderbilt felt more settled than I expected. Classes were going well—students engaged, discussions easy—but by Thursday afternoon, my attention had already begun to drift elsewhere: the Bluebird.

The thought surfaced again as I crossed campus, catching me slightly off guard. Not dread. Not even uncertainty. Something closer to anticipation, edged with a kind of nervousness that felt out of proportion to what the evening actually was. On paper, it was simple—two people meeting for a drink, listening to music, talking.

Still, there was something about Beau Hale that had stayed with me. Most politicians I'd encountered carried themselves with a kind of careful polish. Conversations felt rehearsed, even when they were pleasant. Beau hadn't felt rehearsed. And since the panel, I had caught myself returning to that more than once. It was the kind of detail that lingered—the kind that made you keep reading longer than you meant to.

I paused in the doorway of my office. The room looked more like a place I intended to stay than one I was passing through. The last of the boxes were gone. Books lined the shelves. The desk faced the door. I stood there a moment, taking it in—aware of how easily Nashville had begun to feel like somewhere I belonged.

The clock gave me about an hour—assuming Beau's meetings ended when he said they usually did. Still, I found myself straightening a stack of papers that didn't need straightening before finally grabbing my jacket and heading out.

The Bluebird Café sat tucked into an unassuming strip of storefronts a few miles south of campus, the kind of place you might pass without noticing if you didn't already know what it was. From the outside, it looked almost too small to matter.

Inside, it was something else entirely. The room opened into a low-lit space that felt more like a living room than a venue. Wooden tables sat close together, chairs drawn inward toward a small circular stage at the center. The air carried the faint scent of beer and worn wood, layered with the quiet murmur of conversation that never quite rose above a certain level, as if everyone understood—without being told—that this was a place meant for listening.

Outside, the last light of the evening lingered just long enough to catch the edges of the parking lot. Gravel shifted softly beneath people's shoes as they made their way in, the sound carrying faintly through the open door before fading into the warmth of the room.

A waitress led me to a small table near the back wall.

"Someone meeting you?" she asked.

"Yeah."

"I'll check back in a minute, doll," she replied with a tender and familiar southern accent.

I thanked her and sat, letting my attention move across the room. A few musicians near the stage tuned their guitars, soft chords drifting through the air as they adjusted strings and tested microphones. No one spoke loudly. Even the anticipation felt quiet. I checked my watch. Seven fifteen—right on time.

My thoughts drifted, almost automatically, back to the panel. The way Beau had spoken. The ease of it. The absence of calculation I had come to expect from people in his position.

I was still scanning the room when I heard my name.

"Nate."

I turned.

Beau stood a few steps away, one hand resting lightly against the back of a chair. The setting softened him slightly—less formal than the panel, more at ease. The sleeves of his shirt were rolled to his elbows, the top button undone, his posture relaxed without losing the quiet confidence that seemed to follow him into every room.

"Hope I didn't keep you waiting," he said.

"Not long."

He pulled out the chair across from me and sat. "Meetings ran late," he added. "Which usually means we spent an hour arguing about something we'll pass anyway."

"That sounds familiar."

"Oh yeah?"

"Faculty meetings."

That got a quick laugh. "Fair enough."

A waitress appeared beside us. "What can I get you?"

Beau glanced toward me. "You want a beer?"

"Yeah."

"Two lagers," he said.

When she left, he leaned back slightly, taking in the room. "You been here before?"

"First time."

"What do you think?"

I looked around again, taking in the closeness of it, the way the stage sat almost level with the tables. "It's… quieter than I expected."

"That's kind of the point," he said. "You actually have to listen."

He nodded toward the stage. "Most of the people playing tonight have written songs you've probably heard. Just not like this."

"That feels unlikely."

He smiled. "Give it a minute."

The drinks arrived, and he lifted his bottle slightly.

"To Nashville."

I raised mine. "To Nashville."

For a while, the conversation stayed easy—Vanderbilt, the rhythm of the academic calendar, the steady influx of tourists that Beau insisted had begun to outnumber actual residents.

Eventually, he leaned forward slightly. "You settling in alright?"

"Better than I expected."

"That's good."

"My brother came down last weekend."

"Oh yeah?"

"From Kentucky."

"Family still there?"

"All of them."

"What's he do?"

"He's an engineer. Works at a bottling plant outside Bardstown."

"Useful skill set."

"He's the practical one."

"And you're not?"

"Not in the same way."

He smiled slightly. "I think my family would say the same about me."

"Oh?"

"My dad and granddad are both in real estate."

"That tracks."

He laughed. "Careful."

"I mean it in a good way."

"Sure you do."

He took a sip of his drink. "They weren't thrilled when I ran for office."

"That surprises me."

"They came around," he said. "But at first, my dad thought I'd lost my mind."

"That seems like a reasonable reaction."

"He wanted me to stay with the firm. Less public scrutiny. Fewer angry calls."

"And you didn't."

He shook his head. "No."

"What changed his mind?"

Beau shrugged. "I won."

I laughed. "That helps."

The room shifted as the lights dimmed slightly. The low hum of conversation softened, replaced by the quiet anticipation that moved through the space like a shared understanding.

A man in a worn denim jacket stepped onto the stage and tapped lightly on the microphone.

"Evenin,' everybody. Welcome to the Bluebird."

A few people clapped softly.

"We've got a good round for you tonight. Y'all know the deal—listen close, tip your servers, and try not to talk while someone's pouring their heart out up here."

A ripple of laughter moved through the room.

He glanced out across the tables, squinting slightly.

"Well now… I hear we've got a friend of the house with us tonight."

A few heads turned.

"Where is he—" His eyes landed directly on Beau. "There he is."

The room followed his gaze.

"State Representative Hale is in the house tonight."

A low wave of recognition moved through the crowd. Beau shook his head immediately, lifting a hand as if to wave it off.

"Don't act shy on us," the emcee said.

A few people nearby started clapping.

I turned toward him. "You didn't mention this part."

He leaned back slightly, clearly amused. "I was hoping it wouldn't come up."

"You come here often?"

"Not enough to expect this."

The emcee wasn't finished. "Now Beau's been known to play a song or two…"

The applause picked up.

Someone near the stage called out, "Come on, Beau!"

Another voice followed. "Let's hear it!"

Beau let out a quiet breath and glanced at me. "This is not how I usually introduce people to Nashville."

"I don't know," I said. "Feels pretty convincing."

He shook his head, smiling despite himself, then pushed his chair back.

"Well," he said, standing, "I guess I don't have much of a vote."

He moved toward the stage, the gravelly applause following him as he stepped into the light. Up close, something shifted—not dramatically, but enough to notice. The same confidence was there, but it settled differently. Less outward. More contained.

He accepted a guitar from one of the musicians, adjusting the strap over his shoulder before stepping toward the microphone.

"Alright," he said, a faint smile pulling at the corner of his mouth. "This wasn't the plan."

The room quieted almost immediately.

He strummed a chord—soft, steady.

"You ever get to a point," he said, "where you're not sure which way you're supposed to go?"

A few quiet murmurs of agreement moved through the room.

"This one's about that."

> *I was raised on certain answers*
> *Told me what a life could be*
> *What was worth the chasing after*
> *What was meant for someone like me*
> *There's a road they say is steady*
> *Where you don't have to ask why*
> *Where you follow what you're given*
> *And you don't look too far outside*
> *But I've been hearing something different*
> *In the quiet I can't explain*
> *Like a voice that keeps on asking*
> *If there's more than just a name*
> *Sometimes a road don't feel like living*

Even if it looks alright
Sometimes the thing that keeps you moving
Ain't the thing that makes it right
I don't know where it's gonna take me
I don't know what I'll become
But I know I can't ignore it
When it tells me there's more to come
Sometimes the path you didn't plan for
Is the one you're meant to find
Sometimes the life you never pictured
Is the one that's been there the whole time

The last chord lingered, then faded. Briefly, the room held still. Then the applause came—full, unprompted, the kind that doesn't need encouragement. I found myself smiling without meaning to. He looked different up there. Not larger. Not more polished. Just… clearer. Like whatever he kept slightly guarded in conversation didn't feel necessary when he was holding a guitar. Beau stepped back, nodding once toward the crowd before returning the instrument and making his way back to the table.

"Well," he said, taking his seat, "that was not part of the evening."

I shook my head slightly. "You left that out."

"Seemed like a minor detail."

"You wrote that?"

"Yeah."

"It was good."

He gave me a look. "Just good?"

I held it for a second. "No. It was better than that."

Something in his expression shifted—subtle, but there. "I'll take that," he said.

The applause from Beau's song faded gradually as the next songwriter stepped onto the stage. The rhythm of the room settled again—glasses clinking softly, chairs shifting as people leaned forward to listen. The Bluebird held that balance effortlessly, where conversation never quite disappeared but never competed with the music either.

Beau took a sip from his drink, glancing briefly toward the stage. "Well," he said, "that's out of the way."

"You say that like it was something to get through."

"Not exactly," he said. "Just… wasn't planning on it."

"You seemed comfortable enough."

"I grew up around it," he said. "Music was kind of always there. My mom plays, my sister sings. Holidays usually turned into something resembling a concert."

"That explains it."

"Or at least excuses it," he said, a faint smile returning.

We let the next song carry for a while before he spoke again.

"So, what'd you really think?" he asked.

"The song?"

"Yeah."

I considered it for a second, not because I didn't have an answer, but because I wasn't sure how much of it I wanted to say out loud.

"It felt honest," I said finally.

He nodded once, looking down at his glass. "That's usually the goal."

"Is it about you?"

"Parts of it," he said, then let the rest sit there without elaboration.

I didn't push. The restraint felt intentional, and for reasons I couldn't quite explain, I found myself respecting it more than if he had answered fully. We listened in silence for a few minutes, the music filling in the space between us without making it feel empty.

"You ever write anything that's not academic?" he asked after a while.

"No."

"Not even just for yourself?"

"I don't think historians are known for that."

"That's not true," he said.

"No?"

"You spend your time telling stories about people who lived before you," he said. "That's not that far off."

"It feels different."

"Maybe," he said. "But not by much."

The night moved easily after that. Conversation drifted from family to work to the kinds of small details that tend to surface when two people are still figuring out how much to say and how much to leave unsaid. Nothing felt forced. Nothing felt particularly significant in the moment, and yet there was an undercurrent to it—a quiet sense that something was unfolding just beneath the surface of it all.

By the time I checked my watch again, it was later than I expected. Beau noticed.

"You've got somewhere to be?" he asked.

"Early class," I said. "Eight a.m."

He winced slightly. "That should be illegal."

"It's character building."

"That's what they tell you."

"And you?"

"Committee hearing at nine," he said. "So, I can't judge too much."

"Different kind of punishment."

"Arguably worse."

We let the final song play out without much conversation.

When it ended, the room shifted almost immediately—chairs scraping softly against the floor, conversations rising back to full volume, people gathering their things as the night came to a close.

Beau reached for his wallet, setting it on the table. "Let me get this."

"You already got the first round."

He glanced up. "And?"

"I can handle one beer."

"You're new here," he said. "Hospitality rules."

"That sounds like campaign messaging."

He smiled. "Only a little."

Outside, the air had cooled noticeably.

The warmth of the day had given way to something softer; the kind of early autumn night that made the city feel quieter than it actually was. A few groups lingered near the entrance, still talking about the music. Somewhere off to the side, gravel shifted underfoot as people made their way across the lot, the sound sharp and brief before fading back into the stillness.

We stepped out beneath the low glow of the parking lot lights, neither of us in much of a hurry to move.

"Well," Beau said, slipping his hands into his pockets, "I'm glad you came."

"Me too."

"You survived your first Bluebird night."

"I think I did."

"And you got a free concert out of it."

"That part I wasn't expecting."

He laughed quietly. "I try not to make a habit of it."

"Why not?"

"Reputation," he said. "I've got to maintain some level of professionalism."

"Right," I said. "Wouldn't want people thinking you're

interesting."

"That would be a problem."

We stood there longer than necessary, the kind of pause that doesn't feel uncomfortable but doesn't quite resolve itself either. Eventually, he nodded toward the parking lot, and we started walking. The gravel crunched softly beneath our shoes, the sound carrying just enough in the quiet to make the moment feel more grounded than it might have otherwise.

When we reached the point where the rows of cars split, Beau slowed.

"Well," he said.

I glanced over. He caught himself, a small smile pulling at the corner of his mouth. "Nate."

"That's right."

He shook his head lightly, as if correcting himself. Then his expression settled, something quieter replacing the humor. "I had a good time tonight."

"So did I."

A brief pause. "We should do it again," he said. "If you're up for it."

"I am."

He nodded once. "Good."

Another pause—shorter this time. "Drive safe," he added.

"You too."

I watched as he turned toward his truck, unlocking it with a quick press of his keys before climbing in. The engine started a moment later, headlights cutting across the lot as he pulled out.

My drive back was quiet. Nashville at that hour had a different rhythm—slower, more deliberate. Traffic moved steadily but without urgency, headlights stretching into long reflections across the pavement. My mind drifted back through the evening in pieces—the conversation, the ease of it, the way nothing had felt forced. And then, inevitably, the song—that was the part that stayed.

There's a road they say is steady,
Where you don't have to ask why.

Steady.

For a long time, that would have been enough. More than enough. Something predictable. Something that didn't shift beneath you without warning. Something you didn't have to question every time it started to feel too good to last. I had spent years learning how to live without that. Or at least how to convince myself I didn't need it. I spent countless battered nights craving steady.

But the way Beau had sung it—it hadn't sounded like something he was searching for. It sounded like something he was willing to leave behind. That was the part I couldn't quite reconcile. Most people spend their lives trying to find something steady. Build it. Hold onto it. Beau seemed ready to walk away from it without hesitation. I wasn't sure what that said about him. I wasn't sure what it said about me.

By the time I reached my apartment, the city had established into a quiet that felt almost complete. I climbed the stairs slowly, the faint hum of distant traffic fading behind me. Inside, the room was still, the dim light from the street slipping faintly through the window.

I set my keys on the counter and paused there, my hand resting briefly against the surface as I looked out into the dark. The street below was empty—unmoving, steady.

FOUR

"For one human being to love
another: that is perhaps the
most difficult of all our tasks."
— Rainer Maria Rilke

I woke earlier than usual that Sunday morning. Not abruptly—no alarm, no sudden noise—just the slow awareness of morning settling into the apartment. Light filtered through the blinds in thin, uneven lines, stretching across the floor and up the wall. Somewhere outside, a car rolled past, a dog barked occasionally, and the laughter of children echoed faintly in the distance.

My mind returned, almost immediately, to the Bluebird. It wasn't just the music. The melody still moved faintly in the background, but what stayed with me more was the feeling of the evening itself—the ease of it, the conversation, the way Beau had carried himself without seeming to try.

I had known him only briefly. Still, something about him had unsettled the careful balance of my life in a way I hadn't expected.

Not in a way that felt exceptionally risky. Just noticeable.

The clock read 8:19.

I sat up and ran a hand across the back of my neck, letting the room come into focus. The apartment still looked like it belonged to someone passing through—books stacked unevenly, boxes half unpacked, the quiet disorder of a life not fully settled.

Colt's voice surfaced then, uninvited but not unwelcome: *your history doesn't get to decide everything.* At the time, I had brushed it aside. It had been easier to joke than to engage.

I moved into the kitchen and started coffee, following the routine without thinking. Grind. Pour. Wait. The kind of small, deliberate steps that usually gave structure to the morning.

That morning, they didn't do much of anything.

I stood at the counter with the mug in my hands, watching the courtyard through the narrow window. Leaves stirred slightly in the breeze, the muted sounds of the building carrying faintly through the walls.

For the past few years, I had built a life that functioned well. It was stable. Predictable. Full in all the ways that could be measured. And still—something about it felt incomplete. Not loneliness exactly. Just absence. A subtle realization nagged at me: I hadn't been inside a church in nearly ten years.

That surprised me more than it should have. Growing up in Kentucky, church had been part of the rhythm of life—Sunday mornings, midweek services, familiar hymns sung without needing to think about the words.

Back then, faith hadn't felt complicated. It had simply been there. Somewhere along the way—graduate school, Baltimore, the long stretch of years spent in classrooms and archives—it had slipped out of routine.

I set the mug down and reached for my phone.

The search felt deliberate, even if the decision wasn't: gay friendly church Nashville.

A list appeared almost immediately—photos, short

descriptions, promises of community and welcome. I scrolled slowly until one caught my attention. A small church not far from campus. The website was simple. No spectacle—just a quiet emphasis on presence, compassion, and inclusion—that felt like enough.

The church sat on a quiet residential corner, framed by old trees just beginning to shift into early autumn. The building itself was modest—red brick, narrow stained-glass windows, a white steeple that rose without drawing too much attention to itself.

A wooden sign stood near the sidewalk: All Are Welcome. Beneath it, a small rainbow banner moved slightly in the breeze. I parked along the street and watched for a while as people made their way inside. No rush. No urgency. Just a steady, unremarkable flow.

Inside, the sanctuary felt warm in a way I hadn't expected. Sunlight filtered through stained glass, casting soft color across the pews. A piano rested near the front. Conversations stayed low, easy.

I took a seat halfway down the aisle and let the space settle around me. The service began with a hymn. The melody came first—familiar, though it took a moment to place it. Then the words followed, surfacing almost all at once.

Prone to wander, Lord, I feel it…

I hadn't heard it in years. Still, the words returned easily. There was something grounding about it. Not overwhelming. Not emotional in any dramatic sense. Just steady.

The pastor stepped forward a few minutes later. He looked younger than I expected—early forties, maybe. His presence was calm without feeling rehearsed, his voice carrying easily without rising.

"Good morning," he said.

A few voices answered back.

"I hope you've had a week that gave you at least a moment to breathe," he added, a faint smile crossing his face.

A quiet ripple of laughter moved through the room.

"Life has a way of filling itself up," he continued. "Responsibilities, expectations—some we choose, some we inherit, some we don't even notice we've taken on."

He paused briefly.

"And sometimes," he said, "the busyness becomes a way of avoiding something else."

The room stilled.

"I've been thinking this week about the past," he continued. "About the way people carry it."

The word landed differently here.

"We talk about the past like it's finished," he said. "Like it's something we can place neatly behind us. But most of the time, that's not how it works."

He rested his hands lightly against the pulpit.

"The past tends to follow us. Not loudly. Not in ways that always draw attention. But in quieter ways—in habits, in assumptions, in the stories we tell ourselves about who we are and what we deserve."

I shifted slightly in the pew.

"Some of those stories are good," he said. "They ground us. They remind us where we come from. But others… we carry them longer than we should."

He let that settle before continuing.

"Moments that taught us something painful. Moments that reshaped the way we trust. The temptation is to treat those moments like conclusions. Like they get to decide what the rest of our lives look like."

A pause.

"But faith isn't about pretending those moments didn't

happen," he said. "It's about refusing to let them have the final word."

The sentence landed cleanly.

"Grace," he continued, "is the belief that your story is still being written. That whatever came before—however much it shaped you—doesn't get to define everything that comes next."

He glanced across the room.

"That's not always easy to believe," he added. "Especially if what came before taught you to expect something different."

Another brief pause.

"But part of faith—real faith—is the willingness to imagine that the future might not look like the past."

The service moved on after that, but the words stayed with me.

Not in a dramatic way. Just present.

The congregation filtered out slowly once it ended. Conversations picked up in the aisles, familiar and unhurried. I had just reached the aisle when a voice caught me.

"First time?"

I turned. Daniel stood a few feet away, hands resting easily in his pockets, his expression open but not intrusive.

"That obvious?" I asked.

He smiled. "Only a little."

"I'll take that."

"I'm Daniel," he said, extending his hand.

"Nate."

"Well, Nate," he said, giving a quick, easy shake before letting go, "I'm glad you came."

"Me too."

We stood there as people moved around us—quiet conversations, the soft shuffle of footsteps toward the doors. Daniel didn't rush to fill the space, which made it easier not to either.

"What brought you in this morning?" he asked.

The question was simple, but it didn't feel casual.

I considered it for a second. "Curiosity, I guess."

He nodded. "That's usually how it starts."

"I didn't overthink it."

"Probably for the best," he said. "Most people who overthink it don't end up coming at all."

I let out a small breath, glancing back toward the front of the sanctuary. "I almost didn't."

"What changed?"

I shrugged lightly. "Couldn't think of a good reason not to."

"That'll do it."

A couple passed between us on their way out, offering Daniel a quick wave as they went. He returned it with an easy familiarity, then looked back at me.

"You from around here?" he asked.

"No—Boston now. Kentucky first."

"Ah," he said. "Then this probably feels at least a little familiar."

"In some ways."

"And in others?"

I hesitated. "Different."

He studied that just long enough, not pressing.

"What changed?" he asked after a beat.

"Life," I said.

He gave a small nod, like that was enough of an answer for now. "That tends to cover a lot."

We stood there a second longer, the last few people making their way out into the sunlight.

"Well," he said, glancing toward the doors, "if you're not

in a rush, I was about to grab lunch down the street."

I looked back at him. "I don't want to take up your afternoon."

"You wouldn't."

"I'm sure you've got things to do."

"I do," he said. "But they'll still be there later."

There was something in the way he said it—easy, unforced—that made the offer feel less like an obligation.

"I'm not much for formal church follow-ups," he added. "This is just lunch."

That got a small smile out of me. "That's reassuring."

He nodded toward the door. "There's a café a couple blocks away. Nothing fancy, but it's good."

I hesitated just long enough to recognize that I didn't have a reason to say no.

"Alright," I said.

Daniel smiled. "Good." He nodded toward the door. "There's a little café about two blocks away," he said. "Best sandwiches in the neighborhood."

The café Daniel had mentioned sat on a quiet corner a few blocks from the church, tucked between a small bookstore and a florist whose front windows overflowed with late-summer arrangements. From the outside it looked unremarkable—brick façade, narrow windows, a chalkboard sign advertising soup of the day. Inside, though, the room carried the warm, lived-in atmosphere of a place people visited often and lingered in longer than they intended. The smell of coffee hung comfortably in the air. A handful of small tables lined the windows, most already occupied by people finishing brunch or lingering over second cups of coffee while the late-morning sunlight filtered through the glass.

Daniel greeted the woman behind the counter with the

familiarity of someone who came here regularly. "Good morning, Kinsey."

"Morning, Pastor," she replied with an easy smile. "The usual?"

"Tempting," he said. "But I should probably pretend to branch out once in a while."

She laughed. "Well, let me know when you figure out how to do that."

We ordered sandwiches and found a table near the window. Outside, the neighborhood moved slowly through the quiet rhythm of a Sunday afternoon—people walking dogs, a couple pushing a stroller past the café, the low hum of traffic drifting along the distant intersection. For a moment we simply sat there in comfortable silence while the waitress brought two glasses of water.

Daniel rested his hands lightly on the table. "So," he said, "Nate from Kentucky who wandered into church this morning out of curiosity."

I smiled faintly. "That's the short version of the story."

"What's the longer version?"

I considered the question. "I'm teaching at Vanderbilt this year," I said. "A fellowship program. I usually work at Johns Hopkins."

"A historian?" Pastor Daniel asked.

"That obvious?"

"You mentioned Kentucky, academia, and curiosity within the first two minutes of conversation," he said. "Those are strong indicators."

"Political history," I added.

"Ah," he said. "So, you spend your days explaining to young people why the world works the way it does."

"Or why it doesn't."

"That sounds like a complicated job."

"It can be."

At the café, the conversation unfolded more easily. When he mentioned his husband, it was casual—unremarkable in the way it should have been. Still, I felt something in me shift slightly, some quiet tension easing without needing to be named.

"You seem relieved," Daniel said gently.

"Maybe a little."

"Church hasn't always been easy for people like us."

"No," I said. "It hasn't."

He nodded once, letting that be enough.

We let the conversation drift after that. It moved easily—through the kinds of things that didn't require much at first. The church, mostly. How long he'd been there, what drew people in, what made them stay. He asked about Vanderbilt, about my classes, the students, the rhythm of the semester as it settled into something more predictable.

It wasn't anything particularly personal, not on the surface. But there was a steadiness to it—something unhurried. Daniel had a way of asking questions that didn't feel like questions so much as invitations. He didn't press. Didn't rush to fill silence. He let things land. And somewhere along the way, I found myself answering more honestly than I had intended to.

He set his coffee down and looked at me again, not sharply, just with a little more focus than before.

"Do you have someone back in Boston?" he asked. "A spouse, or anything like that?"

I shook my head. "No."

He nodded once, like that was enough on its own. From there, the conversation could have moved on—it probably should have.

Instead, I said, "There was someone." The words landed

quieter than I expected.

Daniel didn't interrupt. He didn't shift or lean forward. He just waited.

"It was a few years ago," I continued. "Back when I was starting out teaching."

I glanced down at my hands.

"At first, it felt normal. Good, even."

"And then?" he asked.

I exhaled lightly. "He needed control. Where I was. Who I talked to. What I was doing."

Daniel gave a small nod.

"And eventually," I said, "it stopped being questions."

I looked up at him.

"It turned into something else."

He held my gaze. "He hurt you."

A pause.

"Yes."

Daniel didn't rush to fill the silence.

"I'm sorry," he said finally.

"Me too."

The rest of the conversation moved carefully, without pressure.

"You don't erase the past," he said at one point. "But you don't let it decide everything either."

I leaned back slightly, considering that.

"You carry it," he added. "But you also choose what comes next."

We stayed longer than either of us intended.

By the time we stepped back outside, the afternoon had settled into something quieter.

"I'm glad you came," he said.

"So am I."

"You're welcome back."

"I might take you up on that."

"I hope you do."

The drive back to my apartment felt quieter than usual. Not silent exactly—Nashville traffic moved steadily through the streets, the low hum of engines and distant horns blending into the familiar background noise of a Sunday afternoon—but quieter inside my head.

The conversation with Daniel stayed with me, not as a single thought but as a series of small shifts. The way he spoke about the past. The way he refused to treat it as something final. For most of my adult life, I had approached history as something external—events, movements, people whose decisions shaped the world long before I arrived in it. It was easier that way. Cleaner. But personal history didn't work like that. It stayed with you. It shaped the way you trusted people, the way you guarded parts of yourself, the way you imagined the future might unfold.

When I reached my apartment, I sat in the car letting the quiet deepen before turning off the engine. The street was quiet. A few leaves drifted across the pavement in the breeze. Inside, the room was still. Sunlight stretched across the floor, catching the edges of the books I still hadn't unpacked. I set my keys down and stood there before reaching for my phone.

Daniel had been right about one thing: the past mattered. But it didn't necessarily get to decide everything that came next.

I found Beau's number and opened a new message.

Hey.

It's Nate Whitaker. Have you ever been to the Frist Art Museum?

I paused, then added:

I was thinking about going sometime this week.

I read it once, then pressed send. For the first time in a

long while, the future didn't feel like something I had to analyze before stepping into it.

FIVE

⸻ ◆ ⸻

"I am made and remade continually. Different people draw different words from me." — Virginia Woolf

Beau didn't respond immediately.

After sending the message, I set my phone down on the kitchen counter and tried—with little success—to stop thinking about it. For the next several minutes, I moved through the apartment with the vague intention of being productive, straightening a stack of books that didn't need straightening, rinsing out a coffee mug I had already rinsed once before.

Eventually, the phone buzzed. I picked it up a little faster than I meant to.

"The Frist?" Beau wrote. "I haven't been in years." A second message followed. "When were you thinking?"

I hesitated briefly, considering how deliberate I wanted to sound.

"Thursday afternoon?" I replied.

The typing indicator appeared almost immediately.

"Works for me."

Then—

"Are you giving me a tour, Professor?"

I smiled despite myself.

"I make no promises."

Thursday arrived with the quiet certainty of something I had been looking forward to without fully admitting it. The morning passed quickly—two lectures, a brief meeting with a graduate student, and a stack of reading I only half absorbed. By the time I stepped outside, the afternoon had settled into that early autumn light Nashville seemed to do particularly well— warm, slanted, unhurried.

I drove downtown and parked across from the museum. For a moment, I stayed in the car, looking up at the building. The Frist had once been Nashville's main post office, built in the 1930s as part of a broader effort to modernize federal infrastructure. The architecture still carried the unmistakable influence of Art Deco design—clean vertical lines, geometric detailing carved into pale stone, tall windows that caught the light in a way that made the façade feel both deliberate and enduring.

Buildings like this always held my attention longer than I intended. I had spent years studying history through documents—letters, legislation, speeches preserved on paper— but being inside the places where history had actually unfolded always carried a different weight. The scale of it. The permanence. The quiet reminder that decisions made in rooms like these had once felt immediate, uncertain, unfinished.

Inside, the museum carried that familiar stillness— conversation softening without instruction, footsteps echoing faintly against polished floors, the space itself encouraging a kind of quiet attention.

Arriving at the museum before Beau, I wandered toward the main gallery entrance, studying the exhibition placard posted on the wall. The largest collection currently on display traced the development of Impressionism across several decades—Monet, Renoir, Degas, and Matisse arranged in a loose progression of light, color, and movement. It seemed like a reasonable place to start. I was still looking at the gallery map when I heard someone say my name.

"Nate."

I turned.

Beau crossed the entrance hall toward me, slipping his phone into his pocket as he approached. There was something slightly unguarded about him—like he had arrived quickly and hadn't quite settled yet.

"Sorry," he said. "I didn't mean to keep you waiting."

"You didn't."

He glanced around, taking in the space. "I forgot how big this place feels."

"It's easy to underestimate from the outside."

"Yeah," he said. "It doesn't look like much until you're in it."

I nodded toward the gallery entrance. "Ready?"

He gave a small smile. "Lead the way."

The first gallery opened into a softly lit room; the far wall lined with Monet paintings. We stopped almost immediately. A water garden stretched across the canvas—muted blues and greens layered in loose brushstrokes, the surface of the water shifting subtly depending on where you stood.

"I always forget how large these are," Beau said.

"That's a common reaction."

"In photos, they feel smaller."

"Photographs flatten everything."

He nodded slowly, studying the painting. For a few seconds, neither of us spoke. Then he glanced toward me.

"So how long have you been waiting to bring someone here and explain all of this?"

I let out a quiet breath. "That obvious?"

"A little."

I gestured toward the canvas. "The Impressionists were trying to capture something that doesn't really hold still. Light changes too quickly. So, they painted the impression of a moment instead of the moment itself."

"Which means it's already gone by the time you finish it."

"Exactly."

He looked back at the painting.

"Seems like a strange thing to chase."

"Why?"

"Because you know you're not going to catch it."

I considered that. "Maybe that's not the point."

He tilted his head slightly. "What is?"

"That you noticed it at all."

We moved slowly through the gallery, stopping where something held his attention long enough to ask a question, or mine long enough to answer one. What struck me most wasn't the art. It was how easy the conversation felt. At the Bluebird, I had been aware of everything—the proximity, the unfamiliarity, the quiet sense that something was unfolding without a clear direction. This felt different. Not less significant. Just steadier.

The next gallery shifted tone entirely. The colors deepened. The subjects grounded themselves in something more tangible—small towns, open land, ordinary people rendered with quiet attention.

Beau slowed as we entered.

"This feels different."

"It is."

"How?"

"Less about light," I said. "More about people."

He studied a painting of a small-town street—a church steeple rising above low storefronts, a handful of figures moving through the space as if nothing about the moment required attention.

"It feels familiar," he said.

"That's intentional."

I stepped slightly closer. "American artists were trying to capture something about identity. Not just beauty—recognition."

"Recognition," he repeated.

"The idea that ordinary life carries meaning."

He nodded.

"Like history," he said.

"In a way."

He glanced at me. "That's your section, isn't it?"

"Is it that obvious?"

"Just a little."

We moved deeper into the gallery.

A painting of a railroad cut through an open landscape, the tracks stretching toward the horizon. Beau stopped.

"That feels like something," he said.

"How so?"

"Progress. Expansion."

"That's how it was often used."

"And was it?"

"Sometimes."

He smiled faintly. "That sounds like a historian answer."

"It's an honest one."

"You ever notice," he said after a moment, "how much of this country is built around the idea of what comes next?"

I looked at him. "What do you mean?"

"Everything points forward. Growth, expansion, the next

version of things."

"That's part of the national story."

"And you don't believe it?"

"I think it's more complicated than that."

He nodded. "That seems to be your answer to most things."

"It usually is."

When we left the museum, the city had shifted into early evening.

The air was cooler. The light softer.

Beau gestured toward his car. "I've got one more stop, if you're up for it."

I looked at him. "Should I be concerned?"

"Not yet."

"That's not reassuring."

"It'll make sense when we get there."

I hesitated just long enough to recognize that I wasn't going to say no.

"Alright."

I slid into the passenger seat, still slightly amused by the mystery of it. Beau circled the front of the car and climbed into the driver's seat, starting the engine as the radio came to life briefly before he turned it down.

For several minutes we drove through the streets of downtown without speaking much. The sun had begun its slow descent toward the horizon, and the light across the city had shifted into something softer than it had been earlier in the afternoon. Long shadows stretched across the sidewalks while the windows of the taller buildings caught the fading gold of the evening sky. The Tennessee State Capitol sat on the highest hill in downtown Nashville, its pale stone façade catching the fading light of the evening as Beau pulled the car into a small lot beside the building.

I gazed appreciatively at it through the windshield. From a distance the structure had seemed imposing. Up close it felt something closer to deliberate—a building constructed with the quiet confidence of people who believed the institutions inside it would matter long after they themselves were gone.

"I've always liked places like this," I said as we stepped out of the car.

"Yeah?"

"I can read about history all day," I said, glancing toward the stone façade, "but being in the places where it actually happened… it's different."

"How?"

"It feels less distant," I said. "Like the decisions weren't inevitable. Like they could have gone another way."

He watched me considerately. "That sounds like it would make things harder to study."

"It does."

The air outside had cooled slightly as the afternoon drifted toward evening. A light breeze moved across the hilltop as we walked toward the entrance, the sounds of the city below rising faintly through the trees surrounding the grounds.

Inside, the Capitol felt almost reverent in its quiet. Most of the day's activity had already ended, and the corridors carried the low stillness of a building temporarily between purposes. Marble floors reflected the soft glow of overhead lights while portraits of former governors watched silently from the walls.

Buildings like this always carried a strange emotional gravity for me. History didn't live in textbooks nearly as much as it lived in places. In hallways where arguments had once unfolded. In chambers where voices had risen and fallen across decades of debate. In rooms where people had tried—sometimes successfully, sometimes not—to shape the future of a country larger than themselves.

The climb to the tower was longer than I expected. We passed through a narrow corridor and up several flights of worn stone steps before Beau pushed open a small door at the top of the stairwell. The evening sky opened around us immediately. The view from the tower stretched across nearly the entire city.

Downtown Nashville spread outward below us in layers of glass, brick, and fading sunlight. Streets cut through the city in long diagonal lines while the Cumberland River curved quietly beyond the cluster of buildings near the center of downtown. Farther west, the towers of The Gulch rose into the skyline— sleek glass high-rises catching the last golden light of the day.

"You ever think about what skylines actually are?" he asked.

"What?"

"Markers," he said. "Every building is someone deciding they want to leave something behind."

I followed his gaze.

"And you decided not to?"

He shook his head slightly. "I decided I wanted to leave something different."

"The rules instead of the buildings."

"Something like that."

A soft breeze passed us as we stood quietly beside one another, watching the sun drift lower toward the horizon. The light across the skyline shifted gradually, the same slow transformation we had talked about earlier in the museum. Monet had spent entire seasons chasing moments like this—trying to capture the way the world looked when light began slipping toward evening.

"You were right earlier," Beau said.

"About what?"

"The paintings."

I glanced at him.

"They're not really about holding onto something," he said. "They're about noticing it while it's happening."

I let out a quiet breath. "That's a better way to put it."

The sun slipped lower as the skyline softened to a silhouette of progress. For a moment, neither of us said anything.

"I'm glad you asked me to come today," he said.

"So am I."

He nodded slightly, like that was enough. Something shifted then—not suddenly, but enough to notice. Beau stepped a little closer. Not enough to be obvious—just enough that the space between us changed.

"Can I tell you something?" he asked.

"Yeah."

"I wasn't sure how today was going to go."

I smiled slightly. "That makes two of us."

He shook his head. "No, I mean…"

He hesitated, then let out a quiet breath.

"I was hoping it would feel like this."

I looked at him. "Like what?"

"Easy," he said. "Like I didn't have to think about it."

That landed. I knew exactly what he meant because I felt it too. For a long time, I had learned to measure everything— words, reactions, the subtle shifts in a room that signaled when something—someone—was about to turn. Nothing about this felt like that.

He reached for my hand then. Not quickly. Not uncertainly—just with a quiet confidence I didn't feel any need to resist. When he leaned in, it felt inevitable in a way I hadn't expected. The kiss that followed was quiet, uncomplicated—the kind that doesn't need to prove anything to exist. When we stepped back, the city had fully settled into evening. Lights stretched across the streets below, steady and distant.

Beau smiled slightly.

"Well."

I let out a quiet laugh. "Yeah."

Standing there above the city, watching the last colors of the sunset fade into night, I realized something I hadn't allowed myself to believe for a very long time. The future I had begun to give myself permission to imagine—an acceptance of possibility—was no longer something distant or theoretical.

It had already started to bloom—and Beau Hale was standing right in the middle of it.

SIX

> "There is a crack in
> everything, that's how the
> light gets in." — Leonard
> Cohen

Saturday mornings in Nashville arrived more slowly than the rest of the week did, as if the city allowed itself a little more time to become itself again. The urgency that defined weekdays—the steady movement of traffic, the clipped pace of people moving from one obligation to the next—gave way to something quieter, less insistent. Cars moved, but without impatience. Sidewalks filled gradually, not all at once—people walking dogs, carrying coffee, lingering outside cafés like they hadn't yet decided what the day required of them.

I sat near the window of a small coffee shop a few blocks from campus; my hands wrapped loosely around a mug that had already begun to lose its heat. For several minutes, I let myself do very little beyond watching the movement outside—people passing in fragments, conversations half-heard, the quiet rhythm of a city not yet fully awake.

It had only been two days since the evening at the Capitol tower, and the memory returned with an ease that suggested it hadn't gone anywhere at all. The skyline still held that last stretch of fading light. The breeze moved just enough to be noticed without interrupting anything. And Beau—his hand closing around mine with a kind of quiet certainty that hadn't felt hesitant or calculated, just present.

What stayed with me, though, wasn't the moment itself so much as what hadn't followed it. For years, closeness had carried with it a kind of underlying tension, subtle enough that it didn't always announce itself, but constant enough that I had learned to expect it. There was always a sense—quiet but persistent—that something could shift without warning. That whatever felt steady might not stay that way for long.

When I thought about Beau, that tension never surfaced. There was no instinct to pull back, no quiet calculation about how something might unravel. The absence of that feeling was almost unfamiliar in itself. In its place was something steadier— not certainty, not yet, but something close enough that I found myself recognizing it before I could fully explain it—possibility.

The vibration of my phone against the table pulled me back.

"Morning," Colt said.

"Morning."

I could hear his kitchen in the background—the soft thud of a cabinet door, the low hum of a coffee maker finishing its cycle. The sounds were ordinary, but they carried a kind of familiarity that made the distance between us feel smaller than it was.

"You sound awake," he said.

"I've been up for a bit."

"That's concerning."

"Why?"

"You're not usually a Saturday morning person."

"I'm evolving."

He laughed quietly. "I'll believe that when I see it."

We stayed in the easier part of the conversation for a while—talking about things that didn't require much thought or explanation. The weather back in Kentucky had started to turn. Hannah was tired more often now, which, according to Colt, meant everything was progressing exactly as expected. He mentioned the nursery—half-finished but already reorganized twice—and I could picture it without needing to ask.

Eventually, though, the conversation shifted.

"So," he said, and there was just enough of a pause before it to make the change noticeable, "how's Nashville?"

"Good," I said.

He didn't respond right away.

"That sounded like you answered out of habit."

"It's still accurate."

"Try again."

I leaned back slightly in the chair, my attention drifting briefly to the window. A couple passed by with a dog that seemed far more interested in the street than in wherever it was supposed to be going.

"It's good," I said again.

"That's better," Colt replied. "But it's still not the whole answer."

I let out a small breath, a faint smile settling in despite myself.

"You've gotten more persistent."

"That's what younger brothers are for."

There was a brief pause, and when he spoke again, his tone had shifted—subtle, but intentional.

"You sound… lighter."

"Lighter?" I repeated.

"Yeah."

"I'm drinking coffee."

"That's not what I mean."

I didn't answer immediately. Outside, the dog had stopped walking entirely, and the couple stood there, negotiating with it in the quiet, patient way people do when they know they're not actually in control of the situation.

"What do you mean?" I asked.

Colt hesitated, and I could almost hear him choosing how much to say.

"You just sound different," he said finally. "Not like the last couple of years."

The words settled without force, but they didn't need it.

Colt had always known how to ask questions without pushing too far—how to leave space for an answer without demanding one. He had seen enough to understand that some things couldn't be rushed into clarity.

I watched as the dog finally gave in, the three of them continuing down the sidewalk as if nothing had interrupted them.

"I met someone," I said.

Saying it out loud made it feel both more real and less complicated than I had expected.

There was a pause on the other end of the line—long enough to register, but not long enough to feel uncertain.

"Someone?" he asked.

"Yeah."

"What's his name?"

"Beau."

Another brief silence.

"And?"

I smiled faintly. "You're not even trying to be subtle."

"I gave subtle a chance."

I traced the rim of the mug with my thumb, watching the faint line it left in the condensation.

"He's good," I said after a moment.

"Good," Colt repeated. "That's a very carefully chosen word."

"It's an accurate one."

"For now?"

"For now."

He let that sit for a second. "How long have you known him?"

"Not long."

"But long enough to call him someone."

The silence that followed wasn't uncomfortable. It never had been with Colt. It was the kind that allowed a conversation to settle rather than forcing it forward.

Then he asked the question I knew he had been working toward. "Is he good to you?"

The answer came more easily than I expected. I thought about the Bluebird, about the way conversation with Beau never felt like something I had to manage or anticipate. I thought about the museum, the way he moved through the space without trying to define it. And I thought about the Capitol—the way his hand had found mine, not hesitantly, not carelessly, but with a kind of awareness that made the moment feel understood without needing to be explained.

"Yes," I said quietly.

On the other end of the line, Colt exhaled, the sound carrying something close to relief.

"Alright," he said. "That's what I needed to know."

I felt a small, almost reluctant smile.

"That's it?"

"Oh, no," he said. "I've got plenty more questions."

"I'm sure you do."

"I'm just choosing not to ask them all at once."

"That's generous of you."

"Don't get used to it."

We both laughed, the conversation easing back into something familiar.

After a moment, his voice softened again. "I'm proud of you."

"For what?"

"For not letting everything that happened before decide what happens next."

The words landed more quietly than the others, but they carried more weight.

"Thanks," I said.

"Just… be happy, alright?"

"I'll try."

"That's all I'm asking."

We said goodbye a few minutes later, and when the call ended, the quiet returned almost immediately.

I set the phone down beside my coffee and sat there longer than I meant to, the café gradually filling around me as the morning moved forward. Sunlight had begun to stretch farther across the floor near the entrance, catching the edges of chairs and shoes as people came and went, settling into their own versions of the day.

Be happy.

The phrase stayed with me, not because it was new, but because of how easily Colt had said it. As if it were something straightforward. As if it didn't require negotiation or caution or the quiet recalibration I had grown used to over the past few years.

For a long time, happiness had felt less like something I

was moving toward and more like something I observed at a distance—recognizable, but not entirely within reach. It belonged to other people's lives. Other versions of mine that hadn't quite materialized. But sitting there, in a city that still felt new in ways I hadn't fully processed, I found myself considering the possibility that it might not be as distant as I had assumed. Not guaranteed. Not fully understood. But no longer out of reach.

Daniel's invitation arrived the evening before, just as I was finishing sorting through lecture notes at my desk. His name stood out immediately in my inbox, though for a second I couldn't place how he would have found my email. Then I remembered—faculty pages were rarely as private as people assumed. The message itself was simple.

> *Hi Nate—*
>
> *I hope you're settling into Nashville well. Elijah and I were planning a quiet dinner tomorrow evening and wondered if you might like to join us. No pressure at all, but we enjoyed meeting you last Sunday and thought you might enjoy the conversation.*
> *—Daniel*

I read it once, then again, not because it required clarification, but because I found myself hesitating in a way that had become familiar.

For the past few years, declining invitations had been easier than accepting them. Not out of disinterest, but out of habit—a kind of quiet self-containment that had gradually shaped itself into routine. It was simpler not to step into spaces where something might be expected of me, even if that expectation was only conversation.

Still, the memory of the café lingered. The way Daniel had listened—not with curiosity that pressed for answers, but with an attentiveness that left room for them to exist without being explained. It hadn't felt invasive. It hadn't felt performative. And if I was being honest, there was something else beneath that. Not curiosity about them, exactly. Curiosity about what their life represented: a pastor and his husband. A life structured around something steady—not perfect, not idealized, but intentional. Not defined by avoidance or recovery, but by something built deliberately over time.

That was the difference. It wasn't a life I had imagined for myself. It was a life I hadn't allowed myself to consider. I closed the laptop for a beat, then opened it again before I could reconsider.

I'd love to. Thank you for the invitation.

Daniel's house sat on a quiet residential street not far from the church, the kind of neighborhood where the evening seemed to settle more completely than it did closer to campus. By the time I arrived, the last of the daylight had already begun to fade behind a row of tall trees, their leaves just starting to turn at the edges. Warm light spilled from the windows of the house, soft and steady against the darkening street.

He opened the door before I had the chance to knock twice.

"Nate," he said, his expression easing into something genuinely welcoming. "I'm glad you came."

"Thanks for inviting me."

"Of course."

The warmth of the house was immediate—not just in temperature, but in the way it held itself together. The scent of something cooking drifted from the kitchen, garlic and rosemary layered into the air in a way that felt both familiar and unhurried.

"Elijah's finishing dinner," Daniel said as I stepped inside. "You're arriving at exactly the right time."

As if on cue, a voice carried from the kitchen, followed by

the sound of movement. A moment later, Elijah appeared, holding two glasses of wine with the casual confidence of someone who had done this a hundred times before.

"Elijah," Daniel said, "this is Nate."

Elijah handed me one of the glasses before extending his hand. "Nice to meet you. I've heard a little about you."

"That's concerning."

He smiled easily. "Nothing you need to worry about. Mostly good things."

Daniel shook his head, though there was no real correction in it. "Please ignore him."

"I wouldn't recommend that," Elijah said. "It tends to backfire."

The kitchen opened into a space that felt lived-in rather than arranged—chairs pulled close to the table, a pot simmering quietly on the stove, the kind of environment where conversation didn't need to be initiated so much as continued.

For a while, that's exactly what we did.

We stayed near the surface at first—Nashville, the slow transition into October, the way university schedules managed to distort time so that weeks passed quickly but individual days stretched longer than expected. It was easy conversation, but not empty. The kind that allowed people to find their footing without needing to define themselves too quickly.

Eventually, Elijah leaned back slightly in his chair, studying me with a kind of open curiosity that felt more observational than intrusive.

"So," he said, "how are you finding the city so far?"

"I like it," I said.

"That's a promising start."

"It's been… good for perspective," I added, after a moment.

Daniel nodded, not as agreement, but as recognition. "Nashville has a way of doing that."

"How so?" I asked.

"It's a place where different lives intersect," he said. "Music, politics, academia, faith. You see people moving in very different directions, often in the same spaces."

"That sounds right."

Elijah gestured lightly toward him. "He prefers to believe the spiritual side of that is the most important."

Daniel's smile was faint, but it held. "I didn't say that."

"You didn't have to."

I laughed quietly, the exchange settling into something familiar—an ease that came not from trying to impress, but from not needing to. The room quieted as Elijah moved back toward the stove. Then Daniel looked at me again, the shift in his attention subtle but noticeable.

"How have you been since last Sunday?" he asked.

The question was simple, but it carried more weight than it appeared to.

"Better," I said.

"Better how?"

I considered the answer more carefully than I had expected to.

"More open," I said finally. "To the idea that things don't have to stay the same."

Daniel nodded slowly. "That's not a small shift."

Elijah glanced between us as he returned to the table. "Something happen?"

I hesitated, not because I didn't have an answer, but because I wasn't sure how much of it belonged in the room.

Then—

"Yes," I said.

"What kind of something?" Elijah asked, though his tone suggested he wasn't expecting anything dramatic.

I looked down briefly at the glass in my hand, watching the light catch along the surface before answering.

"Do you know Beau Hale?"

Daniel's expression changed slightly—not surprise, exactly, but recognition.

"The state representative?"

"That's the one."

"I know of him," Daniel said.

Elijah leaned forward with interest. "Now that sounds like a story."

I felt a small, almost reluctant smile. "We met at a panel at Vanderbilt."

"And then?"

"And then we kept talking."

Daniel didn't interrupt, but his attention remained steady.

"And now?" he asked.

I exhaled lightly, searching for something that felt accurate without overstating it.

"Now we've spent some time together."

Elijah glanced at Daniel. "That feels like a very calm way to describe something that is probably less calm than that."

"It didn't feel rushed," I said. "It felt… natural."

Daniel rested his hands lightly on the table, considering that.

"And how does that feel?" he asked.

The question lingered longer than the others.

"For a while," I said slowly, "the idea of being close to someone again felt like something I needed to avoid."

"Because of what you've been through," Daniel said, not as a question.

"Yes."

He nodded once, as if that alone explained more than anything else needed to.

"There's a passage in the First Letter of John," he said after a moment.

Elijah smiled faintly. "There it is."

Daniel didn't look at him. "Perfect love casts out fear."

The words settled into the room without emphasis, which made them land more cleanly.

"It doesn't mean fear disappears all at once," Daniel continued. "But it does mean it doesn't get to lead anymore."

I sat with those words as they lingered delicately in my mind.

"That sounds… different than how I've been approaching things," I said.

"It usually is," Elijah added, lifting his glass slightly. "But for what it's worth, most relationships start exactly where you are right now."

I glanced at him. "Which is?"

"Not entirely sure what this is," he said, "but pretty sure you want to keep finding out."

I let out a quiet laugh. "That's accurate."

Dinner lingered longer than I expected.

Not because anything in particular demanded it, but because the conversation never required an ending. It moved easily—through small stories, quiet disagreements, moments of humor that felt unforced. Elijah told a story about a parish event that had gone predictably wrong, embellishing just enough to make it better, while Daniel offered occasional corrections that only made it more convincing.

There was no sense of performance to any of it. No careful shaping of how things should be said or received. The evening held together on its own, the way certain spaces do when the people inside them aren't trying to manage them.

When I stepped outside, the air carried the edge of October—cooler now, the neighborhood settled into a quiet that felt complete. Streetlights pooled along the sidewalk, and something moved faintly in the distance without ever quite reaching me.

Standing by my car for a moment, I felt myself absorbing the shifts in my life recently. The past few weeks arranged themselves almost without effort—the church, the café, the Bluebird, the Capitol. And now this. An evening that had asked nothing of me beyond showing up and being present.

It wasn't that those moments were connected in any obvious way. It was that they didn't feel separate. I wasn't sure what Beau and I were becoming, and I found I wasn't particularly interested in forcing an answer. The uncertainty had shifted. It no longer felt like something to guard against—it felt like something worth following.

Wednesday arrived easily and the rhythm of the week had settled back into place. Classes filled the morning, followed by office hours that lingered just long enough to delay leaving. When the last students filtered out, the hallway fell quiet.

I gathered my notes, slipped them into my bag, and stepped outside again. The light had sharpened with the season, the air cooler but not yet cold. Walking across campus felt slower—not from hesitation, but from the absence of urgency. My phone buzzed just as I reached the steps.

Coffee?

I paused, reading it once before responding.

You sound like someone who just escaped a meeting.

The reply came almost immediately.

Three of them.

I smiled, a reflex I didn't bother to question.

Then yes. Coffee seems appropriate.

The café sat just off the edge of campus, tucked between a narrow bookstore and a record shop that let its music drift out onto the sidewalk, soft enough to blend with passing conversation. The street carried that familiar, unhurried energy—students lingering a little longer than they needed to, cups in hand, the late afternoon light settling gently against the storefront windows. It felt less like a destination than something you happened into and stayed.

Beau was already there, seated near the window with two cups of coffee on the table, leaning back in his chair with an ease that made it seem like he belonged to the space. The late afternoon light filtered in softly, settling along the floor and the edge of the table before catching on him in pieces—his sleeve, his hands, and, when he tilted his head, the auburn in his hair, briefly brighter where the light held it.

"You're late," he said as I approached.

"I teach undergraduates," I replied, taking the seat across from him. "Time becomes less precise."

"That sounds like an excuse."

"It's a consistent one."

He slid one of the cups toward me without comment. For a moment, neither of us spoke. The café carried the low, steady murmur of conversation—students moving in and out, the quiet rhythm of people passing through without lingering too long.

"So," Beau said eventually, resting his forearms lightly against the table, "how's the week treating you?"

"Mostly grading papers and trying to convince people that Reconstruction is more complicated than they want it to be."

"That sounds exhausting."

"It's surprisingly dramatic."

He glanced up. "In what way?"

"Turns out rebuilding a country after a civil war involves a lot of disagreement."

"Yeah," Beau replied. He shot me a grin. "We couldn't even agree on the best name for bill during judiciary committee today."

I took a sip of the coffee, still too warm to drink comfortably.

"What about you?" I asked.

He exhaled lightly. "Committee meetings. Campaign calls. I got invited to a ribbon-cutting for a parking garage."

"That feels like a career highlight."

"Free parking," he said. "I'm considering it a win."

I smiled, the conversation settling into an easy rhythm that didn't require much effort to maintain.

After a moment, he leaned back slightly, his attention shifting—not away, but inward, as if deciding whether to say something before doing it.

"My nephew's turning six this weekend," he said.

"What's his name?"

"Caleb."

"And he's already orchestrating events?"

"Demanding cake," Beau said. "The rest is negotiable."

"Firm in principle," I replied. "I respect it."

Beau laughed after a brief pause. "My family's doing something out at my grandfather's place," he continued. "Nothing formal. Just everyone showing up and letting the kids run around."

"It sounds nice."

"It usually is."

He paused then, not long enough to disrupt the conversation, but long enough to change it. "You should come."

The words were casual, but not careless. I didn't answer instantly. Instead, I found myself thinking back to Saturday—to Daniel's voice, steady and unforced, offering something that hadn't felt like instruction so much as permission: fear doesn't get to lead.

"Are you sure that's a good idea?" I asked.

Beau tilted his head slightly. "Why wouldn't it be?"

"I don't know," I said, more honestly than I intended. "Meeting family feels… significant."

"They're not interviewing you."

"I assumed there would be at least a small panel."

That earned a quiet laugh.

"The only person you'll need to impress is Caleb," he said. "And that mostly comes down to chocolate frosting."

"That's reassuring."

He studied me for a moment then—not in a way that felt evaluative, but attentive. As if he were gauging something I hadn't said.

"You don't have to come," he added. "I just thought you might want to."

There was no pressure in it. No expectation hidden beneath the invitation. Just the same quiet sincerity that had defined every interaction I'd had with him so far. And somewhere in that absence of pressure, something shifted. For a long time, my instinct had been to step back from anything that carried the potential to matter. To keep things contained, manageable, defined before they had the chance to become complicated. But sitting there, in the middle of an ordinary afternoon that didn't feel particularly significant on its own, I realized that instinct wasn't the strongest thing in the room anymore.

Something else had taken its place. Not certainty, not even

confidence. Something quieter—willingness.

I looked back up at him.

"Alright," I said.

He blinked once, like he hadn't expected the answer to come that easily. "Alright?"

"I'd be happy to share some cake."

A slow smile settled across his face—not exaggerated, not surprised, but genuinely pleased.

"Good," he said.

The moment passed without needing to be acknowledged further, the conversation slipping back into something lighter as if it had never shifted at all.

"Someone's going to need to keep Caleb from eating an entire cake," he added.

"I feel like I'd be more of an accomplice than a deterrent."

"That's a risk I'm willing to take."

Outside, the light had begun to lower, stretching longer shadows across the sidewalk. The day was slipping toward evening in that gradual, almost unnoticed way it often did this time of year.

"This Saturday?" I asked.

"That's the one."

"That gives me time to prepare."

"For what?"

"Your family."

He smiled slightly. "You'll be fine."

Maybe he was right. And maybe, I thought as we sat there finishing our coffee, stepping into someone else's life didn't have to feel like something you braced yourself for. Sometimes it could simply be the next place you chose to go.

The walk back to my apartment felt slower than it had that morning, though nothing about the distance had changed. The air had cooled further, settling into that early evening balance where the day hadn't fully let go, but the night had already begun to take hold. Lights came on in windows as I passed, one by one, small contained worlds unfolding behind glass.

Inside, the apartment was quiet in the way it always was when I returned to it alone. Not empty, exactly—just still. The kind of quiet that didn't demand attention, but didn't offer distraction either.

I set my keys on the counter and stood there thoughtlessly, letting the space settle around me. The same half-unpacked boxes lined the walls. Books remained stacked where I had left them, their placement more temporary than intentional. Nothing had changed since I'd left that afternoon.

And yet—

Something had.

It wasn't anything visible. Not something that could be pointed to or explained in a way that would make sense outside of the moment itself. But it was there, in the way the day lingered—not as a series of events, but as a shift that hadn't fully resolved yet.

I moved toward the window and rested a hand lightly against the frame, looking out over the quiet street below. A car passed once, headlights cutting briefly across the pavement before disappearing at the end of the block. Then stillness again.

For a long time, I had thought of my life in terms of what had already happened—something to be understood, analyzed, placed into context. It was easier that way. History, even when it was personal, could be studied at a distance if you were careful enough about how you approached it.

But the past had a way of lingering in places you didn't always recognize at first. Not just in memory, but in expectation. In the quiet assumptions you carried about how things would unfold, about what was likely to last and what wasn't.

That had been the steadiness I understood.

Not something dependable.

Something expected.

I thought about the way Beau had described his song at the Bluebird—the idea of a path that looked right from the outside, steady in all the ways people are taught to value. For a long time, I had wanted something like that. Not because it was meaningful, necessarily, but because it was predictable. Because it suggested a kind of permanence that didn't require constant attention.

But standing there, watching the faint movement of the street below, I realized that what I had mistaken for steadiness in the past hadn't been stability at all.

It had been limitation.

A narrowing of what I allowed myself to expect.

The difference, now, was subtle.

Nothing about my life had suddenly become certain. There were no guarantees in any of it—not in Beau, not in whatever we were becoming, not in the version of the future that had only just begun to take shape.

The uncertainty no longer carried the same weight. It didn't feel like something waiting to collapse or something to fear. It felt like something still being built—a history still being written.

Outside, Nashville moved on without noticing the difference. Inside, for the first time in a long while, I wasn't trying to anticipate how things might end before they had the chance to begin.

And that—more than anything—felt like a pleasant change.

SEVEN

> "I took a deep breath and
> listened to the old brag of my
> heart: I am, I am, I am." —
> Sylvia Plath

Saturday afternoon arrived with the kind of clear October weather that made the countryside outside Nashville feel almost impossibly calm.

Beau had sent directions earlier that morning, along with a brief message reminding me not to worry about bringing anything except an appetite. The drive itself took less than an hour, the city slowly giving way to rolling stretches of farmland and quiet country roads that wound through pockets of trees already beginning to turn faint shades of amber and gold.

By the time I turned onto the gravel drive Beau had described, the air carried that unmistakable scent of fall—dry leaves, distant wood smoke, and the faint earthy smell of fields preparing for the colder months ahead. The farm appeared gradually as the road curved around a small grove of oak trees.

It wasn't the kind of massive operation people sometimes imagined when they heard the word farm. Instead, it felt older, steadier—white fencing stretching across gently sloping pastureland, a red barn standing near the edge of the property, and a large farmhouse set back slightly from the road beneath the shade of several towering maples.

Several trucks and SUVs were already parked near the house. Children's voices carried across the yard, punctuated by bursts of laughter that drifted through the warm afternoon air. I stepped out of the car just as the front door opened and Beau appeared on the porch.

"There you are," he called, walking down the steps toward me.

"You sound relieved."

"I was starting to wonder if you'd gotten lost."

"I followed the directions," I replied.

"Oh yeah?" he said with a chuckle. "How many wrong turns?"

"I'm a historian, not an explorer."

He laughed softly before glancing toward the house.

"Come on," he said. "Everyone's out back."

As we walked across the yard the sounds of the gathering grew clearer. A long table had been set up beneath a row of trees near the edge of the property, covered with trays of food and a large birthday cake that appeared to be under heavy supervision from several adults attempting to keep small children from investigating it prematurely.

"Caleb!" Beau called.

A small boy darted across the yard immediately, skidding to a stop in front of him.

"Uncle Beau!"

Beau knelt to hug him. "Happy birthday, buddy."

Caleb pulled back with the seriousness of someone who had recently turned six and felt the weight of that seniority.

"I'm getting two pieces of cake," he said confidently.

"That seems ambitious."

"It's my birthday."

Beau let out a chuckle as he stood back up.

Caleb glanced at me. "Who's that?"

"This is Nate."

Caleb studied me carefully before nodding once, as if confirming something important.

"You can have cake too," he said.

"Well," I replied, "that's very generous."

Beau smiled. "Come meet everyone."

The introductions happened gradually. A tall man with weathered hands and an easy smile stepped forward first.

"You must be Nate," he said, extending his hand. "Thomas Hale."

"Nice to meet you."

"Beau tells us you're a professor."

"That's what they pay me to do," I said pleasantly.

"Well," Thomas said with a small grin, "you're welcome here as long as you don't start lecturing anyone about the Civil War."

"I'll do my best."

A woman approached a moment later, wiping her hands lightly on a dish towel.

"Nate," Beau said, "this is my mom."

"Margaret Hale," she said warmly, taking my hand with a firmness that carried the quiet authority of someone who had hosted many gatherings like this one.

"We're glad you came."

"Thank you for having me."

"Oh," she said, waving the comment away gently. "Anyone Beau brings out here is already welcome."

Nearby, another couple stood watching the exchange with mild amusement.

"My sister Emily," Beau said, gesturing toward the man beside the table, "and her husband Luke."

Luke lifted a hand in greeting.

"Nice to meet you."

"Same here."

"And you've already met Caleb," Emily added, nodding toward the boy who had now returned to circling the cake like a small, determined shark.

The easy warmth of the introductions surprised me slightly. No one seemed particularly interested in interrogating who I was or how long I had known Beau. Instead, the conversation flowed naturally, the kind of relaxed curiosity that accompanies family gatherings where new people occasionally appear. At some point Beau stepped away briefly to help his father move a cooler across the yard.

I watched the exchange quietly. Thomas handed him one side without a word, and the two of them carried it across the grass with the easy familiarity of people who had done similar things together for years. It was a small moment, but it revealed something about Beau I hadn't fully seen before: At the Bluebird he had been charismatic. At the Capitol he had been thoughtful and deliberate. Here, standing in the middle of a family gathering beneath an open sky, he looked completely at ease—like someone who belonged exactly where he was.

"You're Nate, right?"

The voice beside me carried a slightly different tone— confident, measured.

I turned to see a woman I hadn't noticed earlier. She appeared to be in her late fifties, her posture carrying the quiet composure of someone accustomed to being listened to in a room.

"Yes," I said.

She extended her hand.

"Debbie Frazier."

The name was immediately familiar.

"Senator Frazier," I said.

She smiled faintly. "Debbie is fine, dear." She gazed about the yard casually before turning back to me. "I knew Beau before he ever thought about politics—before he could even vote really" she added.

"That's probably handy context to have," I replied.

"It keeps him humble."

She glanced toward Beau, who had just returned to the table carrying a tray of drinks.

"You know," she added quietly, "your friend there has a habit of ending up in interesting places."

"I can't say that surprises me."

Debbie watched him for another moment before smiling slightly.

"He'll do something bigger eventually," she said. "Mark my words. He is always thinking about how to do more."

I followed her gaze across the yard. Beau was kneeling beside Caleb again, helping him tie a loose shoelace while several other children gathered around to inspect the birthday cake.

In that moment he didn't look like a rising political figure. He looked like a man who simply cared about the people in front of him. Beau moved easily through very different worlds: Music halls and political panels. Historic buildings and open farmland. Family gatherings and public conversations. Few people carried that kind of balance naturally—but Beau did. And watching him laugh as Caleb attempted to explain the complicated rules of six-year-old birthday parties, I found myself wondering what it might feel like to belong somewhere inside that world too.

The afternoon drifted forward in the easy, unstructured way family gatherings often do. Children ran through the yard in loose circles while several adults rearranged chairs near the long table beneath the trees. Someone turned on music from a small speaker sitting near the porch, and the faint sound of an old country song floated across the grass as the October sun began its slow descent toward the western edge of the property.

Beau had disappeared briefly to help his father check something near the barn, leaving me standing near the food table with a paper plate that had gradually filled with more than I had intended.

"You're doing well so far."

I turned to see Margaret standing beside me, her arms folded lightly as she surveyed the yard.

"With the food?" I asked.

"With the family," she said with a small smile.

"I appreciate the distinction."

She laughed softly. "We can be a lot for people who aren't used to us."

"I haven't noticed anything alarming yet."

"Oh," she said calmly, "give it time."

With amusement, we both watched the children racing across the grass. Caleb had now gathered a small group of cousins who appeared to be attempting to build something out of sticks near the edge of the yard. The project had the chaotic energy of an idea that would almost certainly collapse within minutes.

"Beau told us you teach at Vanderbilt," Margaret said.

"That's right."

"Political history?"

"Mostly American."

"Well," she said, nodding thoughtfully, "you're certainly in the right city for that."

"Yeah," I replied. "I jumped pretty quickly when I learned of the fellowship."

She leaned slightly against the edge of the table. "You're from Kentucky originally, Beau said?"

"Yes, ma'am," I replied as the two of us moved to sit down at a nearby picnic table.

"Oh goodness," she said gently, waving a hand. "Please don't call me that."

"Margaret then."

"That's much better."

The conversation settled briefly into silence. I had the hushed sense that Margaret was someone who preferred listening to speaking—the kind of person who took her time forming impressions of the people around her.

"Beau seems happy," she said.

The statement was simple, almost casual, but the way she said it carried the soft weight of something more deliberate.

"I'm glad," I said.

"So am I."

Her attention shifted across the yard, landing on Beau as he and his father made their way back from the barn. He stopped halfway to kneel beside Caleb again, listening with full attention as the boy attempted to explain something about the structure that had already collapsed once.

"You know," she continued, "Beau's life has been… busy for a long time."

"I imagine politics keeps him moving," I replied.

"It does." She paused briefly. "But even before that he always felt responsible for a lot of things—just always trying to 'fix' something," she added with an air-quote finger gesture.

I followed her gaze toward Beau.

Margaret smiled faintly. "He has a way of taking responsibility for things that don't always belong to him," she added. "If something feels unsettled—he wants to fix it. Make it right."

"I can see that," I replied.

"It's who he is." She paused, not searching for the next thought, but allowing it to arrive on its own. "And it's something I've always admired about him."

Another small pause.

"But it's also the thing I worry about."

I glanced toward her.

Margaret's expression hadn't changed, but there was something stilled beneath it now—something more deliberate.

"He takes care of people easily," she said. "Sometimes so easily that he doesn't notice what it costs him to keep doing it."

The words didn't land heavily. She didn't push them forward or underline them. She simply let them exist, as if trusting they would carry their own weight.

"And I think," she added after a moment, her voice softer now, "that kind of instinct can make it difficult to recognize when you're the one who needs looking after. All I've ever wanted for Beau," she said gently, "is for him to be truly happy."

I nodded. "That seems like a reasonable goal."

"It does," she said, though her tone suggested she understood how rarely things were that simple. Her gaze moved back across the yard once more. "And I haven't seen him this happy in a long time."

There was no question in it. No expectation of a response. Just a subtle acknowledgment of something she had already decided was true. The words landed with surprising warmth. I wasn't entirely sure how to respond. Part of me still struggled to believe that something between Beau and me had grown significant enough for someone else to notice. But standing there beside Margaret Hale beneath the serene shade of the trees, I realized she wasn't speaking with the curiosity of someone trying to understand a situation. She was simply sharing something she had already observed.

She smiled once more before heading back toward the table where several cousins had begun circling the cake again with renewed determination. I remained where I was, standing still, watching the scene unfold across the yard. The late afternoon light had softened across the fields beyond the house, turning the edges of the trees into faint shades of gold and copper. It was a gentle kind of moment. Unremarkable in almost every way.

But as I watched Beau there among his family—moving easily through the familiar rhythm of the place—I grasped something that hadn't been obvious to me until that afternoon. For so long, I had carefully avoided the kinds of situations that suggested permanence—family gatherings, shared holidays. Standing there on a sun-soaked farm, watching the easy warmth that surrounded Beau's world, I felt the smallest shift in my thinking: maybe belonging somewhere didn't have to feel like a risk.

By the time the cake had finally been cut and distributed— with Caleb successfully securing two full slices exactly as he had promised—the afternoon had begun its slow transition toward evening. The air carried a noticeable chill now, the kind that arrives in October just as the sun begins dipping lower across open fields. A few of the younger children had retreated toward the porch while several adults gathered near the long table beneath the trees, lingering over mild conversation.

I had just finished helping Luke fold up a few empty chairs when Beau appeared beside me.

"Come on," he said quietly.

"Where are we going?"

"I want to show you something."

"You and your surprise adventures," I replied.

"Relax," he said with a grin. "There aren't any stairs this time." He nodded toward the far side of the property where a small gravel path curved around the barn. "Trust me."

I followed him across the grass. Two ATVs sat parked beside the barn, their tires still dusted with dried mud from what appeared to be recent use.

"You're kidding," I said.

"Not at all," Beau replied with goofy confidence.

"I haven't driven one of these in years."

"Perfect," Beau replied. "Then it'll feel nostalgic."

"Or like a broken leg," I replied.

"Just follow me," he said as he tossed a helmet to me.

"And if I drive into a fence?"

"We've been meaning to put new fence panels up anyway," Beau laughed as he swung onto the first ATV and started the engine. The machine rumbled to life beneath him. "You'll be fine," he said over the noise.

With a small sigh I climbed onto the second one. The gravel path curved gently away from the house, carrying us past the barn and out toward the open fields that stretched along the edge of the property. The wind moved cool against my face as the ATV picked up speed, the late afternoon sun casting long golden streaks across the pastureland ahead of us.

Beau drove easily, clearly familiar with every turn in the narrow trail. We passed through a small stand of trees before the land opened into a wide clearing bordered by a low wooden fence. Beyond it, the countryside rolled outward in isolated layers of farmland and distant hills. After several minutes Beau slowed and turned down a smaller trail that dipped gradually toward a cluster of trees near the far edge of the property. When he finally stopped, the engine noise faded into a sudden hush that made the entire landscape feel still. I pulled up beside him.

"Alright," I said, removing the helmet. "That was actually fun."

"I told you." He nodded toward the trees ahead. "This way."

We walked the rest of the way on foot. A small pond appeared between the trees, its surface reflecting the fading colors of the sky as the sun lowered toward the horizon. The place carried the docile calm that often settles over water at the end of the day.

"You come out here a lot?" I asked.

"I used to."

"When you were younger?"

"Yeah."

Beau stepped closer to the edge of the pond and picked up a small flat stone from the ground.

"My grandfather built this pond before I was born," he said. "Said every farm needed at least one place where people could sit and think."

"That sounds wise."

"It usually worked."

He skipped the stone across the surface of the water. It bounced three times before disappearing.

We lingered in the stillness, neither of us feeling a need to speak. The sequestered nature of the place seemed to invite stillness rather than conversation. I stretched out on the grass near the edge of the pond, the cool ground pressing gently against my back as I looked up at the sky. The first faint colors of sunset had begun appearing above the distant tree line. Beau planted himself down beside me a moment later.

We simply watched the sky alter its colors, unhurried and gentle. The quiet rhythm of the farm felt different from the city. Even the passing of time seemed slower here, the fading light stretching gently across the landscape as the evening settled around us.

Historians spent most of their lives studying the memory of places—how landscapes carried the sober imprint of the people who had lived there before. Standing there beside the pond, it wasn't difficult to imagine the decades that had unfolded across the property before this afternoon—families gathering, children running across the same grass, unassuming conversations unfolding beneath the same sky.

"You fit here," I said after a moment.

Beau turned his head slightly.

"What do you mean?"

"With your family."

"How so?"

"Some people belong to one world very clearly," I said. "But they struggle when they step outside it."

"And you think I don't?"

"I think you move between them effortlessly."

Beau considered that.

"Music rooms," I added. "Political panels. Farms."

For a moment he watched the sky again before he smiled slightly. "I like that you notice things like that."

"Details matter," I replied.

The sun dipped lower behind the distant trees. The surface of the pond caught the last golden light, turning briefly into a sheet of tranquil color. And lying there beside Beau in the fading warmth of the day, I felt something settle gently into place inside me.

The sky moved through its familiar transformation—the pale gold of late afternoon deepening gradually into shades of amber and violet as the sun drifted toward the distant line of trees. The water caught each change in color like a mirror, the surface barely disturbed except for the occasional ripple of wind moving across it. Beau rested on one elbow beside me, lazily skipping another small stone across the pond.

"That one only got two," he said.

"Your technique is slipping," I jabbed.

"I'm out of practice," Beau replied.

The silence between us stayed easy, the kind that comes when people feel no need to fill every pause with conversation. Eventually Beau spoke again.

"I was in Baltimore not that long ago," he said, almost as if the thought had arrived without planning.

I turned my head slightly. "What for?"

"A friend's wedding," he said. "One of a few, actually. Feels like everyone I know is getting married lately."

"That sounds like a pattern."

"It is," he said. "Different cities, same conversation."

"What conversation?"

He smiled slightly. "The one where everyone pretends they're not thinking about what comes next."

I let that sit softly.

"Do you think they are?" I asked.

"Thinking about it?" he said. "Yeah."

"And you?"

Beau didn't answer right away. He watched the water instead, the last of the sunlight shifting across its surface.

"I think people like the idea of something lasting," he said finally. "Even if they don't always know what that looks like yet."

"That's optimistic."

"Maybe," he said. "Or maybe it's just practical."

I glanced back at the sky, where the color had deepened into something softer.

"For a long time," I said, "I trusted history more than anything that hadn't happened yet."

"That feels on-brand."

"It probably is."

"But lately," I continued, "I'm starting to think the future deserves a little more attention."

Beau turned his head slightly, studying me for a second before smiling.

"Well," he said, "that's encouraging."

We let that settle.

Then he shifted slightly onto one elbow, the movement small but intentional.

"Alright," he said. "Let me ask you something."

"That sounds like a setup."

"It's not."

"That's what people say before it is."

He laughed quietly. "It's hypothetical."

"That doesn't make it better."

"Just answer the question."

I hesitated, then nodded. "Alright."

"If you could get married anywhere," he said, "where would it be?"

I exhaled, looking back up at the sky.

"That's not a casual question."

"It's a simple one."

"It's not."

"Just answer it."

I let the silence stretch for a beat, letting the question settle instead of reacting to it.

Places surfaced almost immediately—old buildings, obscure courtyards, spaces where time seemed to layer over itself rather than pass cleanly through.

One of them stayed.

"The George Peabody Library," I said.

Beau glanced over. "At Johns Hopkins?"

"That's the one."

"With the atrium and the iron balconies?"

"Yes."

He leaned back slightly, considering it.

"That's a good one."

"It's one of the most beautiful spaces in the country."

"You've thought about this before."

"More than once."

The light had shifted almost completely now, the last line of sun slipping behind the trees.

"Why there?" he asked.

I took a moment before answering.

"Because it feels like the kind of place where history and possibility exist at the same time," I said. "Like neither one cancels out the other."

Beau watched me for a second, then smiled.

"Well," he said lightly, "I'll keep that in mind."

I turned toward him. "You're planning ahead?"

"Just gathering information."

"That seems premature."

"Maybe."

He shrugged, easy, unbothered.

"But it's good to know the options."

The sky had deepened fully into evening now, the first stars appearing faintly above the trees. We didn't say anything else—I didn't feel as though we needed to. The light over the pond faded gradually, the sky deepening into placid shades of blue as the first stars appeared above the trees. Moments like this—unremarkable while they're happening—rarely announce themselves for what they are. They settle into memory later, recognizable only once something else has shifted.

EIGHT

"I'm not fucked, not quite."
— Sufjan Stevens

November arrived almost without notice, and Nashville had begun its slow transition into late autumn. The air across Vanderbilt's campus carried a steady chill now, the kind that lingered just long enough to make walking between buildings feel brisk and deliberate. The tall oaks lining the walkways had already surrendered most of their leaves, leaving scattered patches of copper and gold across the sidewalks that crunched faintly beneath passing footsteps.

From my office window the campus looked quieter than it had a few weeks earlier. Midterms had come and gone, and students moved through the final stretch of the semester with the slightly more serious rhythm that always seemed to settle in once November arrived.

What I noticed most during those weeks wasn't the change in the weather or the academic calendar. It was the way Beau had quietly become part of my everyday life. Not through grand gestures or dramatic declarations. Nothing about the early weeks of whatever we were becoming had unfolded that way. Instead, it happened gradually—through small, unremarkable moments that began to appear in spaces that had once been defined almost entirely by routine.

Routine had been useful. After everything that had come before Nashville, it had been more than structure—it had been insulation. Predictable mornings, controlled schedules, evenings that unfolded the same way each night. There was a certain safety in repetition, in knowing exactly how a day would begin and end. Nothing unexpected meant nothing had the chance to shift— nothing had the chance to unravel.

For a long time, that had been enough. But over the course of those weeks, Beau began to occupy those carefully maintained spaces—not abruptly, not in a way that disrupted them, but gradually enough that I didn't recognize the change until it had already taken hold.

Coffee between meetings. Late-night movies at my apartment. Conversations that moved easily from politics to music to history without either of us noticing how much time had passed.

Looking back, the weeks after Caleb's birthday felt less like a sequence of days and more like a collection of moments— small, distinct, and vivid in a way that suggested they mattered more than I had allowed myself to realize at the time.

One of the first came on a cool Tuesday afternoon at Vanderbilt. Marcia Carrington had arrived in Nashville earlier that morning. She was in town for a conference at the university and had insisted on stopping by campus to see my office.

"So, this is where you've been hiding," she said, stepping inside and glancing around the room with the careful curiosity of someone evaluating a newly renovated apartment.

"It's mostly books," I replied.

"That's your aesthetic."

She walked slowly along the shelves, scanning the spines.

"American political development… Reconstruction policy… constitutional theory…" she read aloud. "You've made yourself very comfortable."

"That was the goal."

We settled into the chairs opposite my desk while she recounted the conference she had temporarily escaped from. Marcia had always possessed a talent for making academic politics sound far more dramatic than it was.

"I swear half the department chairs in the country are here," she said. "You would think we were drafting a new constitution."

"And you must be the new James Madison," I joked.

"Of course," she said. "But with better wigs."

A knock sounded at the door before I could respond.

"Come in," I called.

The door opened and Beau stepped inside carrying two paper coffee cups and a small brown bag. He paused slightly when he noticed Marcia.

"Oh," he said with an apologetic smile. "I didn't realize you had company."

"Perfect timing," I replied, standing. "Marcia, this is Beau Hale."

Recognition crossed her face almost immediately. "The Beau Hale who wrote the bill to end taxes on feminine hygiene?" she asked.

Beau looked surprised, but with humble amusement. "Yes," Beau replied. "I gave it a shot."

Marcia stood and extended her hand. "Marcia Carrington."

"Nice to meet you."

"I was passing across town and thought Nate might need caffeine."

"That's very thoughtful," Marcia said.

For the next fifteen minutes the three of us talked easily. Beau asked Marcia about Baltimore, she asked him about dynamics of the state legislature, and somewhere in the middle the conversation drifted toward the strange similarities between academic politics and actual politics.

"I'm convinced faculty meetings are worse after hearing the two of you," Beau said at one point.

Marcia nodded immediately. "That's because professors believe they're always right."

"Politicians don't?" I asked.

"Mostly just when the cameras are on," Beau replied.

Eventually he checked his watch. "I should probably get back downtown," he said. He looked at me briefly. "Dinner later?"

"Shawarma?" I asked.

He smiled. "I was hoping you'd say that."

Marcia watched the exchange with quiet interest.

"Enjoy the rest of your visit," Beau told her before heading toward the door.

"Nice meeting you," she replied.

Once the door closed behind him, Marcia leaned back slowly in her chair and studied me with the same expression she often used when evaluating a particularly interesting research argument.

"Well."

"That seems ominous," I replied.

"That man," she said, "is very clearly taken with you."

"I don't know about that," I replied, reaching for a pen I didn't need.

"Oh, you absolutely do," she said.

"I think you're projecting."

"I think," she said, leaning forward slightly, "he walked in here with coffee he didn't need to bring, forgot I existed after ten seconds, and asked you to dinner like it was already decided."

"That's an interpretation."

"It's an accurate one."

I shook my head slightly. "You've known him for five minutes."

"Five minutes is plenty."

She stood, gathering her bag.

"For what it's worth," she added, "I like him."

"That's reassuring."

She paused at the door, her tone softening just slightly. "You deserve someone who doesn't hesitate about you, Nathaniel." Marcia smiled, then disappeared down the hallway, leaving me alone in the office with two cups of coffee and the gentle realization that the last few weeks of my life were beginning to open into something new.

Not all of the moments from those weeks carried the same easy humor as Marcia's visit. Some were quieter—more private.

The first night Beau stayed at my apartment came without much ceremony. He had come over after a late committee meeting one evening in early November, arriving with a paper bag from a small Thai restaurant a few blocks from campus and an expression that suggested the day had required more patience than usual.

"You look exhausted," I said as he stepped inside.

"That's because I've been listening to three hours of debate about transportation funding."

"That sounds riveting."

"It was not," Beau replied with an exaggerated exhale.

We ate dinner on the small couch in my living room, the television playing quietly in the background while the conversation drifted lazily between the events of our day. Beau talked about the strange dynamics of legislative committees—the careful choreography of compromise and persuasion that unfolded behind the more visible parts of public debate. I told him about a student who had submitted a paper arguing that the Reconstruction Amendments had been secretly inspired by ancient Roman political philosophy.

"That sounds ambitious," Beau said.

"It was creative."

"Did you pass him?"

"I admired the effort."

At some point we started a movie neither of us seemed particularly invested in watching. The lights in the apartment were dim, the only real illumination coming from the soft glow of the television from across the room. Outside, the quiet hum of Nashville's late evening traffic drifted faintly through the windows.

By the time the credits rolled it was well past midnight. Beau stretched slightly on the couch beside me.

"I should probably head home," he said.

"You could stay."

The words left my mouth before I realized what I was saying. Beau looked at me carefully, perhaps studying the surprise I'd just stirred in myself with my own words.

"You sure?"

I hesitated only briefly. "Of course."

He nodded once. "Alright."

Despite the surprise, the moment felt comfortably simple. There were no dramatic declarations, no awkward uncertainty about what the decision meant —just the quiet understanding that neither of us felt particularly ready for the evening to end.

Later, lying in bed beside him, I noticed something that set my thoughts drifting. For the past few years, the idea of sharing a bed with someone had carried a quiet tension beneath it—a lingering sense that closeness might eventually give way to something less gentle. But that night, the feeling of uneasiness lying next to another never appeared. In its place, there was only the quiet rhythm of Beau's breathing as he fell asleep beside me, the soft warmth of another person occupying the same small space in a way that felt unexpectedly natural.

For so long, the insecurities of another had shaped the way I experienced closeness. Even the smallest gestures of intimacy carried the faint shadow of memories I had spent a long time trying to bury.

Lying there beside Beau, in the quiet darkness of my apartment, that shadow seemed noticeably lighter—not gone entirely, but loosened.

When morning arrived, sunlight spilled across the bedroom floor in long pale streaks. I opened my eyes just in time to see Beau studying the ceiling with the thoughtful expression he often wore when considering something carefully.

"Good morning," I said.

He turned slightly.

"Morning," he replied with a faint rasp still in his voice.

He smiled faintly. The quiet comfort of the moment settled easily between us.

Eventually Beau swung his legs over the side of the bed and stood.

"Coffee?" he asked.

"Please."

A few minutes later I found him standing in my kitchen wearing one of my old Hopkins sweatshirts, pouring two cups of coffee while sunlight filled the small apartment. The time we spent together continued to become more frequent, comfortable, and something I found myself looking forward to instead of shying away from.

One Saturday Beau convinced me to walk with him to Centennial Park.

"There's a craft festival," he said.

"That sounds like something made to sell expensive pottery."

"That's because it is," he replied.

"And you want to go anyway."

"Of course."

The park was already crowded when we arrived.

Rows of white tents stretched across the open lawn near the Parthenon replica, each one filled with artists displaying paintings, handmade jewelry, pottery, wood carvings, and an impressive number of scarves considering the temperature was still hovering somewhere near sixty degrees. Music drifted across the park from a small stage set up near the far walkway, and a line had formed beside a food truck selling funnel cakes that filled the air with the unmistakable scent of fried sugar.

We wandered slowly through the rows of tents, occasionally stopping to admire something that caught Beau's attention. At one booth an older man demonstrated how he carved small wooden birds from blocks of cedar, the delicate shape of the wings appearing gradually beneath his knife. Beau watched captivated with reticent fascination.

"That's impressive," he said.

"It is," I replied. "Certainly beyond my skillset."

A few tents later Beau stopped again, this time in front of a display of small metal sculptures shaped like trees. Each one was made from twisted strands of copper wire, the branches spreading outward in delicate patterns that caught the sunlight.

"That one's nice," he said, pointing.

"It's a tree."

"It's a sculpture."

"It's a metal tree."

He ignored the comment and spoke briefly with the artist before returning with the sculpture wrapped in brown paper.

"You bought it."

"I did."

"Where are you planning to put it?"

"No clue," he said amusingly. "Maybe I'll come back for more and have a metal forest."

We continued walking until the music from the small stage drew us toward a patch of grass where a crowd had gathered. A bluegrass band was playing, the quick rhythm of a fiddle carrying easily across the park while a few children attempted enthusiastic but largely uncoordinated dancing near the front of the stage. Beau and I settled onto the grass near the back of the crowd and for a while we simply sat there listening.

The afternoon sun had begun its slow descent behind the Parthenon replica, casting long shadows across the lawn while the music drifted through the warm autumn air.

"This is nice," Beau said after a moment.

"It is," I replied.

"You don't sound surprised."

"I'm not."

"You usually question my plans."

"That's because your plans often involve unknowns."

"I do love surprises," Beau replied. "Not everything needs to be clear before diving in, professor."

We watched the band finish their song while the crowd applauded politely. At some point Beau reached over and took my hand. The gesture was casual, almost absentminded, the kind that suggested he hadn't spent much time deciding whether to do it—the movement so natural I barely noticed at first.

Looking around at the families sitting on blankets, the artists still talking with visitors beneath the rows of tents, and the slow movement of people wandering through the park on a mild November afternoon, I realized something that hadn't fully occurred to me before.

For years my life had been structured carefully around work and solitude: teaching, research, long evenings spent alone with books and lecture notes.

But somewhere between quiet mornings in my apartment and crowded afternoons like the one at the park, Beau had begun to alter that rhythm. Without my noticing, this earnest politician had changed the chords of my life—and I did not mind to let the music continue to play.

One afternoon later that month, Beau texted me shortly after my last class ended.

You busy?

I was standing outside the lecture hall gathering my notes when the message appeared.

"Just finished last class," I replied.

*Come downtown. There's a floor vote this afternoon
and the gallery is pretty empty today.*

The Tennessee State Capitol had already begun to feel familiar to me by that point. The building carried a quiet kind of gravity even on ordinary days, the limestone walls and tall windows holding the accumulated weight of decades of political argument and compromise.

Beau met me just inside the entrance.

"You made it," he said.

"You sounded convincing."

"Good."

He led me through the hallways toward the chamber where the House met, nodding occasionally to staff members or other legislators passing in the corridor.

"Is this where the exciting part happens?" I asked quietly.

"That depends on your definition of exciting," he answered.

"Democracy is my Super Bowl," I replied.

Before entering the chamber Beau paused near the gallery staircase.

"You'll have to watch from up there," he said.

"I assumed I wasn't voting."

"Not yet," he smiled briefly before heading toward the chamber floor.

I climbed the stairs to the gallery and found a seat overlooking the room below. From above, the chamber looked almost theatrical. Rows of desks arranged carefully across the floor, microphones angled toward each seat, the quiet murmur of conversation rising and falling as legislators moved between discussions. A few minutes later Beau entered from the side of the room and took his place at his desk.

The transformation was subtle but unmistakable. The relaxed ease I had seen in him at the park or brewing coffee in my kitchen gave way to something slightly more focused. He listened carefully as another representative spoke, occasionally making notes or leaning toward a colleague seated nearby.

From the gallery I could hear fragments of the debate— discussion about transportation funding, questions about proposed amendments, the careful language legislators often used when disagreeing with one another within the confines of Roberts Rules of Order.

At one point Beau rose from his seat. He spoke for only a few minutes and I couldn't hear every word from where I sat, but the tone was clear—calm, measured, confident without becoming theatrical. It wasn't the performance of someone trying to win attention. It was the voice of someone explaining something he believed should make sense to the people listening.

When he finished, he returned to his seat and the debate moved forward. Eventually the vote was called. Electronic panels lit across the chamber as legislators cast their votes, small green and red lights appearing beside each name. I watched Beau lean back in his chair once the vote concluded, exchanging a brief word with the representative seated beside him before gathering his papers.

For the first time since we had met, I understood something about him that had only been partially visible before. At the Bluebird, Beau had been charming. At the farm, he had been grounded and easy with his family. But here—inside the quiet machinery of government—he looked entirely at home. Not because he enjoyed the performance of politics, but because he seemed genuinely interested in the work itself.

A few minutes later he appeared in the gallery beside me.

"So," he said quietly, sliding into the seat next to mine. "What did you think?"

"I think you enjoy that more than you admit."

He smiled as he turned to gaze down at the House floor where a few staffers stood conversing.

"No," he replied softly. "I'll admit it one hundred percent."

The way he said it was soft and unambiguous. Beau didn't just respect the work—he believed in it. To Beau, his public service was less of a career and more of a privilege. Watching him inside the Capitol that afternoon, I understood something I hadn't quite put into words before: Beau wasn't chasing politics. He believed in it. That belief, more than anything else, made it impossible not to admire him.

By the end of the month, that familiarity had deepened.

Beau arrived just after sunset one typical Tuesday evening, the cold air following him briefly through the door before the warmth of the apartment settled back in.

"You look like someone who's been grading papers all day," he said.

"That's because I have."

"Tragic."

"It's the job."

He glanced at the stack of essays on my desk. "How many left?"

"Too many."

Beau considered the pile, then pushed the top few pages aside with quiet finality.

"You're done for tonight."

"That's not how grading works."

"It is tonight."

There was something gently insistent about the way he said it—not controlling, not dismissive, just certain in a way that made resistance feel unnecessary.

Eventually, we moved to the couch, the television on more out of habit than interest. The conversation faded without either of us noticing exactly when, leaving only the quiet light of the screen and the low hum of the city beyond the windows.

Beau leaned back, one arm resting along the back of the couch behind me.

For a while, we didn't speak. The silence didn't ask anything of us. It had become something I recognized in our time together—the way quiet could exist without needing to be filled, without signaling distance.

After a moment, Beau reached over, brushing his hand lightly against mine. The gesture was small—almost absentminded. But when our fingers intertwined, the warmth of it settled in slowly, steady and unforced. I found myself paying attention to that. Not just the moment itself, but the ease of it. How little effort it required. How little anticipation. Beau shifted slightly, turning toward me.

"You're thinking," he said.

I exhaled quietly, not pulling my hand away.

"I used to do this differently," I said.

He didn't interrupt.

"I used to try to understand everything as it was happening," I continued. "What something meant. Where it was going. Whether it was… safe to let it keep going."

Beau's thumb moved slightly against mine—just enough to signal he was still there, still listening.

"And now?" he asked.

I glanced down briefly at our hands.

"Now I'm not trying to get ahead of it," I said. "I'm just here."

He studied me for a beat—not evaluating, just taking it in.

"That seems like progress," he said.

"It feels different."

"Different how?"

I considered that.

"Quieter," I said. "In a good way."

He nodded slightly, like that answer made sense to him.

For a spell, neither of us spoke. The quiet settled between us, not empty, but full in a way that felt almost deliberate—as if something had reached its natural edge and was waiting to be crossed.

I didn't think about it for long. I turned toward him, closing the distance slowly, giving him just enough time to meet me there. When I kissed him, it wasn't hesitant or searching. It felt certain in a way I hadn't allowed myself to feel in a long time—like something I didn't need to analyze before trusting.

The moment unfolded without urgency, steady and unforced, as if it had been building quietly over time and had finally been given permission to exist. There was no sense of stepping into something unknown, no instinct to pull back before it could change. Only the quiet recognition that whatever existed between us had already begun to take shape. When we finally pulled back, Beau rested his forehead lightly against mine. The room was still, the faint hum of traffic far below the windows the only reminder that anything else existed beyond it.

For years I had believed the past had permanently reshaped the way I experienced intimacy. I had learned to protect certain parts of myself carefully, keeping relationships at a safe distance from the memories that still lingered beneath the surface. Somewhere along the way—between quiet mornings in my kitchen, crowded afternoons in the park, and evenings like this one in the quiet warmth of my apartment—those defenses had begun to loosen—not because they disappeared, but because Beau had quietly stripped away their necessity.

Later that night we moved to the bedroom, the quiet closeness between us unfolding naturally in a way that felt less like a decision and more like the continuation of something that had already begun long before either of us had spoken about it. Afterward we lay beside one another in the soft darkness of the room, the faint glow of streetlights tracing pale patterns across the ceiling. Beau rested on his side; one arm draped lightly across my chest as the quiet rhythm of his breathing gradually slowed.

I stared up at the ceiling for a while, listening to the stillness. For years, sharing space with someone had felt like something to manage carefully—something that required distance, even in its closest moments. But lying there beside Beau, that instinct no longer held the same authority.

The defenses I had built hadn't disappeared all at once. They had simply begun to loosen—no longer fixed in place, no longer necessary to hold.

What remained felt steadier than the fear that had built them—and, for the first time in a long time, something that felt safe to trust.

NINE

> "What we call our destiny is truly our character." — Kazuo Ishiguro

It was one of those late-November Sundays where the air is was thin and clear it felt like you could hear for miles. The sky was an impossible, scrubbed-clean blue. Beau pulled into the church lot and cut the engine, letting the silence of the morning settle in around us.

"You're sure it's alright if I'm here?" he asked.

The question was casual, but I could hear the sincerity beneath it.

"Of course it is."

"I don't want to intrude," he replied.

"You're not," I said with a comforting smile.

Beau glanced toward the front of the building where several people were already gathering on the steps. Inside, the sanctuary carried the warm, familiar quiet that always seemed to settle over the room before a service began. Soft light filtered through the tall windows along the side walls, illuminating the rows of wooden pews while a small group of musicians arranged themselves near the front of the room.

The church's music director was arranging sheet music across several stands while members of the choir gathered in clusters of quiet conversation.

"It's beautiful in here," Beau said quietly beside me.

"Mostly original," I replied.

There was something about the space that felt immediately calming. The architecture was simple, unpretentious, the kind of place designed less for spectacle than for reflection.

For years, walking into a church felt like stepping into an argument I couldn't win. The sermons and the expectations of my youth didn't fit the life I was actually living or the man I'd become. I grew up with a faith that felt as natural as breathing, but somewhere along the way—somewhere between the pews and the scars, it felt like it had been taken from me. This place had slowly become something different—something safer.

We found seats about halfway back in the sanctuary just as the musicians began their warm-up. A violin carried the first notes of a familiar hymn across the room, the sound soft at first before gradually filling the space as the rest of the instruments joined in.

Beau leaned slightly closer.

"Do you come every week?" he asked quietly.

"Most."

"What do you like about it?"

I considered the question genuinely. "It feels honest."

"How so?" he asked.

"No one here pretends life is simpler than it is," I replied as I rested my hand over his.

The music began in earnest and the choir rose slowly from their seats and moved toward the front of the sanctuary while the congregation settled into attentive silence. That morning's performance was built around a series of traditional hymns arranged for choir and string quartet. The first piece began gently, the voices rising together in careful harmony that seemed to fill the entire room with sound.

The music continued, each piece building slightly in complexity before giving way to the next. The sound of the choir blended with the violin and cello in a way that made the sanctuary feel larger than it actually was.

About halfway through the program, my attention shifted. Beau was sitting with his eyes closed, tuned into the music rather than the room. He looked the way he did during our long talks— thoughtful, settled, and completely elsewhere. For a long minute, I forgot about the singers and just watched him.

The final hymn ended softly, the last note lingering briefly in the air before fading into silence. A gentle murmur of appreciation moved through the congregation. As people began standing and gathering their coats, Beau leaned toward me again.

"That was beautiful," he said.

"I thought you might like it," I said.

Beau glanced around the sanctuary once more. "Thank you for letting me tag along today," he replied

People stood slowly, gathering coats and greeting one another in the aisles. A few children darted past the pews toward the back of the building where coffee and pastries had already appeared on a folding table near the entrance. Beau stretched slightly as we stepped into the aisle. We moved with the slow flow of people toward the back of the sanctuary. A few members of the congregation nodded or stopped briefly to say hello; the casual familiarity of a place I had begun to feel return to each week.

Beau noticed.

"You know people here already," he said.

"A few."

"That didn't take long."

"I've been coming most Sundays since I found the place," I said. "Everybody has been pretty welcoming."

Just as we reached the back of the room, Daniel emerged from a side hallway carrying a binder full of sheet music. He spotted me almost immediately.

"Nate," he said, smiling as he crossed the room.

"Good to see you."

"You too."

Then his eyes shifted to Beau. "And who did you bring with you this morning?"

"Daniel, this is Beau."

Beau stepped forward and extended his hand. "Beau Hale," he said with the humble confidence I'd grown accustomed to.

Recognition flickered briefly across Daniel's face. "Ah," he said. "That Beau Hale."

Beau looked mildly amused. "Uh oh," he said with a chuckle.

Daniel laughed.

"Nashville is a small city when it comes to politics."

"Well, I hope the reputation's been kind."

"So far," Daniel said with a grin as they shook hands.

Beau gestured toward the sanctuary behind us. "That music program was beautiful, by the way."

Daniel glanced toward the choir members still gathering their coats. "I'll pass that along. Our music director takes it very seriously."

A familiar voice joined the conversation from behind Daniel.

"Are you going to keep people standing in the doorway all

morning?" Elijah asked as he appeared carrying two cups of coffee, one of which he handed to Daniel before looking toward us.

"Elijah," Daniel said, "this is Nate's friend Beau."

Elijah studied Beau for a brief second before breaking into a friendly smile. "Nice to meet you."

"You too," Beau replied.

The four of us stood there talking easily while the last few people drifted out of the sanctuary. At one point Daniel glanced toward me again, studying my face for a moment with the same quiet attentiveness I remembered from our first conversation weeks earlier.

"You seem well," he said simply.

The remark was casual, but there was something deliberate in the way he said it.

"I am," I replied.

He nodded once, satisfied with the answer.

Elijah took a sip of his coffee and looked between us. "Well," he said, "this has been a lovely morning, but I'm hungry."

"That's because you skipped breakfast again," Daniel replied.

"I had toast."

"That was six hours ago."

Elijah turned toward Beau and me. "What are you two doing for dinner tonight?"

The question caught me slightly off guard.

"Nothing planned," I said.

"Perfect," Elijah replied. "Come over to our house later for dinner."

"If you're free, you're both welcome," Daniel added.

Beau glanced toward me briefly before answering. "I'd like that."

"Wonderful," Elijah said. "Now we just have to make sure Daniel doesn't spend the entire evening talking about theology."

"That's unlikely," Daniel said.

"*Highly* unlikely," Elijah corrected.

Beau laughed softly beside me. As we stepped back outside into the cool November sunlight a few minutes later, Beau pulled his coat a little tighter around himself.

"I like them," he said.

"I figured you would," I said.

Daniel and Elijah lived in a small bungalow tucked into a quiet neighborhood about fifteen minutes from the church. By the time Beau and I arrived that evening the sky had already slipped fully into darkness, the streetlights casting soft yellow pools across the narrow road as we pulled into the driveway. The house itself looked exactly the way I had imagined it might. Warm light glowed from the windows, and the faint sound of music drifted out through the screen door as we walked up the short front path.

Beau glanced toward the porch.

"This feels welcoming already," he said.

"That's Elijah's influence."

Before I could knock, the door swung open.

"You're right on time," Elijah said, stepping aside to let us in.

Daniel appeared from the other side of the room carrying a bottle of wine and four glasses.

"Good to see you both again," he said.

"You too," Beau replied.

The kitchen opened into a small dining area where the table had already been set. Candles flickered softly in the center while a stack of plates sat waiting near the counter.

"This is a beautiful place," Beau said, glancing around.

"Thank you," Daniel replied. "It's old enough that the floors creak but not old enough to be historically preserved."

Elijah slid the lasagna from the oven and set it carefully on the stove.

"Alright," he said. "Give it a few minutes to cool unless you enjoy third-degree burns."

While Elijah finished setting the table, Daniel poured wine into the glasses and handed one to each of us.

"To new friends," he said simply.

We raised the glasses together. The conversation settled easily as we took our seats around the table. For a while the topics stayed light—stories about Nashville neighborhoods, Elijah recounting an incident earlier that week where Daniel had accidentally locked himself out of the church office, Beau describing the strange rhythm of legislative committee meetings.

At one point Elijah leaned back slightly in his chair and studied Beau with a curious expression.

"So, tell me," he said. "What's the most frustrating part of being a state representative?"

Beau laughed quietly. "Only one?"

"I'll allow a short list," Elijah replied with a dramatic hand gesture.

Beau thought about it briefly. "Honestly? The assumption that politics has to be cynical."

"That's a fair observation," Daniel replied with a nod.

"A lot of people believe public service is just another form of performance," Beau continued. "Like everyone involved is secretly playing a game they don't actually believe in."

"And you disagree?" Elijah asked.

"I do," Beau replied resting his hands loosely on the table. "I think most people who get into it start out because they believe the work matters. It's easy to forget that once you've been around the process long enough."

"That's an endearing perspective to hold onto," Daniel replied as he watched Beau softly.

Naturally, the conversation settled into a comfortable pause while Elijah refilled our glasses.

"You know," Daniel said after a moment, "there's a long tradition in Christian thought about public service."

Beau looked interested. "Oh?"

Daniel nodded. "Augustine wrote quite a bit about the idea that governing could be an act of stewardship if it was approached with humility."

"That's a lot of pressure to put on elected officials," Elijah said.

"It's really a reminder, I think," Daniel replied. "That power is meant to serve people rather than elevate the person holding it."

Beau considered that for a moment. "We could certainly benefit from more humility," he replied gently.

Elijah pointed his fork toward Daniel. "Careful," he said. "If you keep talking like that, Beau might recruit you for a campaign speech."

Daniel laughed softly. "I suspect I'd be terrible on a campaign stage."

"You'd be honest," Beau said.

"That's exactly why he'd be terrible," Elijah replied.

The table broke into quiet laughter. As the conversation drifted forward, the topics moved easily between philosophy, local politics, books, and music. Elijah told a long story about the first time Daniel had attempted to cook Thanksgiving dinner on his own, while Beau described a recent committee meeting that had stretched nearly six hours because two legislators refused to stop arguing about a budget amendment.

At some point I leaned back slightly in my chair, watching the three of them talk.

The scene unfolding across the table struck me with a quiet clarity.

For most of my adult life, evenings like this had been rare.

Not because I lacked friendships, but because the deeper parts of my life—faith, love, vulnerability—had often existed separately from one another like facets incompatible with coexisting. But here they were now sitting around the same table. Daniel and Elijah, whose quiet spiritual guidance had helped me begin confronting parts of my past I had once avoided. And Beau, who had entered my life unexpectedly and somehow managed to loosen the fears that had kept those walls standing for years.

At one point Daniel glanced toward me with a thoughtful expression while Elijah and Beau endeavored into a diatribe about local architecture.

"You look peaceful tonight," he said.

The comment was simple but it carried a deeper understanding.

I smiled slightly. "I think I am."

Daniel nodded once, as though that answer told him everything he needed to know. Outside the window, the November night had settled fully across the quiet neighborhood, the warm light from the kitchen spilling softly across the table as the conversation continued long after the plates were cleared.

TEN

"There is no charm equal to tenderness of heart." — Jane Austen

The weeks between Thanksgiving and Christmas slipped by almost without notice in Nashville—measured less by days than by deadlines, colder mornings, and the steady build toward winter break. At Vanderbilt the final stretch of the semester arrived the way it always did—all at once. Students hurried across campus carrying stacks of books while the library lights stayed on well past midnight. My own days filled with final lectures, grading, and the steady stream of office hours that always appeared once deadlines began looming.

In the middle of it all, Beau had begun appearing more and more often. One evening during finals week, I was halfway through a particularly ambitious paper on Reconstruction-era constitutional theory when a light knock sounded at my office door. Before I could answer, Beau stepped inside carrying a paper bag and two cups of coffee.

"How long have you been stuck on that page?" he asked.

I glanced up. "Long enough to know it's not getting any

better."

He set the bag down on the edge of my desk. "Then I brought a solution."

I looked inside, the smell hitting first.

"You brought hot chicken," I said, a grin breaking through before I could stop it.

"You mentioned once that grading makes you crave it."

I shook my head, still smiling. "I appreciate your attention to detail."

"I try," he replied confidently.

We ate across from one another while the hallway outside my office filled with the restless movement of students finishing their own long days of studying. At one point Beau reached toward the stack of papers beside me and picked up the one on top.

"What's this about?"

"Final paper," I said. "Enemies of Reconstruction."

He read the first line silently before setting it back down.

"I'm glad no one expects legislators to write like this."

Moments like that had begun appearing quietly throughout my weeks—Beau stopping by campus after meetings downtown, bringing dinner or coffee and settling into the easy rhythm of my workdays as if he had always been part of them.

Outside the university, Nashville had begun transforming for the holidays. Christmas lights appeared along the streets almost overnight. Storefront windows filled with garlands and wreaths while the air carried the faint scent of pine from trees stacked outside neighborhood markets. With a stack of papers stuffed in my bag to be graded back at home, Beau and I headed out of the now-empty lecture building. Instead of walking towards our cars, he grabbed my arm.

"There's something happening at the Capitol tonight," he

said.

"What kind of something?"

"Christmas tree lighting."

"That sounds festive."

"It's the fun part of the job," he admitted. "I thought you might want to tag along?"

"I think I can wait to grade these," I said as I followed him to his car.

The lawn in front of the Tennessee State Capitol was already crowded when we arrived. Families stood gathered along the walkways, children bundled in winter coats while a brass ensemble near the front steps played familiar Christmas carols beneath the glow of temporary stage lights. A tall evergreen stood at the center of the lawn; its branches wrapped carefully in strands of lights that had yet to be switched on.

"Do you come to this every year?" I asked.

"Most years," Beau said. "It's one of the quieter events."

"Quieter?" I asked glancing at the growing crowd.

As we moved through the gathering of people, several stopped Beau to greet him.

"Representative Hale," a woman said warmly, shaking his hand.

"Good to see you again."

Watching him navigate those small conversations reminded me of something I had noticed before. Beau carried himself in public the same way he did everywhere else—without the stiffness or self-importance that sometimes accompanied political life. To Beau, every conversation, handshake, and angry constituent email mattered equally.

At one point a familiar voice called from behind us.

"Well, I thought that was you."

We turned to see Senator Debbie Frazier approaching

through the crowd.

"Senator," Beau said.

"Good evening," Senator Frazier replied. "It's a chilly one." Her attention shifted toward me almost immediately. "And Professor Whitaker," she said with a knowing smile. "Good to see you again."

"It's nice to see you too," I said, extending my hand.

"I didn't realize you'd already been recruited for Capitol events," she added lightly.

Beau laughed. "I told him this one was harmless."

"Those are the most dangerous kinds," she replied.

For a few minutes the three of us stood together talking while the brass ensemble finished their final song. Then the governor stepped onto the small stage near the front of the lawn, drawing the attention of the crowd. A brief speech followed, the familiar cadence of holiday remarks drifting across the cold December air before someone began counting down from ten— the entire crowd joining in. When the final number echoed across the lawn, the lights along the tree suddenly flickered to life. Applause rippled through the crowd as the branches glowed softly against the dark evening sky.

For a moment the entire scene seemed suspended in that quiet brightness—the Capitol rising behind the illuminated tree, the crowd gathered beneath the winter air, the music beginning again somewhere near the steps. Standing beside Beau, I watched him look toward the glowing branches. There was something thoughtful in his expression, as though the moment carried a significance that went beyond the ceremony itself.

"Do you ever get tired of things like that?" I asked.

"Sometimes," Beau admitted.

"But events like that remind people the government belongs to them."

A few nights later Beau helped me load the last of my bags into the car. Final grades had been submitted, my office door locked for the break, and the muffled calm of winter settled over campus.

Beau leaned casually against the car while I closed the trunk.

"So," he said. "Ready for Kentucky?"

I looked down the quiet street before answering.

"Yeah," I said. Then I glanced back toward him. "I think I am."

The drive from Nashville into western Kentucky wasn't one I had made very often. Most of my trips home over the past several years had begun somewhere else entirely—Baltimore, usually. Airports and rental cars had replaced the familiar highways of my childhood, and visits to Kentucky had become shorter, squeezed between semesters or conferences.

But that afternoon, leaving Nashville for Christmas break, the journey felt different—closer, more immediate.

Beau drove while I watched the city gradually disappear behind us. Within half an hour the skyline had faded into open stretches of farmland and narrow clusters of trees standing bare against the winter sky.

"Hard to believe you've only been in Nashville a few months," Beau said.

"Sometimes it feels longer."

"Maybe that's a good sign," he replied.

"Of a busy semester," I said with a slight laugh.

He smiled faintly at that.

The landscape outside the window had settled into the muted stillness of late December. Fields stretched quietly on both sides of the highway, the pale winter light flattening the colors of everything it touched. An hour later we crossed the Kentucky state line.

Beau tapped the steering wheel lightly. "Welcome home."

"Thank you."

"You don't sound excited."

"It's not that," I said. I kept my eyes on the road ahead before continuing. "It just feels strange."

"How so?" Beau asked.

"I haven't come back like this in a long time."

Beau glanced over briefly before returning his attention to the road.

"You mean bringing someone with you."

"Something like that."

For most of my adult life, trips home had been solitary ones. A few quiet days with family before returning to whatever city I had been living in at the time. This felt different. Now, Beau sat beside me, guiding the car easily down a highway that slowly carried us closer to the place where my life had begun.

"You nervous?" he asked after a moment.

"A little."

"That's understandable."

"It's not that they won't like you," I said.

"That's reassuring."

"It's just… new."

Beau nodded. "Meeting family always is."

The road curved gently as we left the highway and moved onto smaller roads leading toward town. The houses grew more familiar with each passing mile—gas stations I remembered from high school, churches whose steeples had stood in the same place for decades.

Eventually a familiar water tower appeared in the distance above the trees.

"We're getting close," I said.

"To your mom's place?"

"About ten minutes."

Beau slowed slightly as we passed through the edge of town.

"This where you grew up?"

"Yeah."

"Small."

"Very."

He glanced out the window at the quiet streets. "I like it."

A few minutes later we turned onto the street where my mother's house sat near the end of the block. The porch light was already glowing softly against the winter dusk. As Beau pulled the car into the driveway, I noticed movement through the front window: my mother, waiting. The front door opened before we had even reached the porch.

"Nate!"

My mother stepped out into the cold evening air, pulling her sweater tighter around herself as she crossed the short distance between us.

"Mom," I said, laughing as she wrapped me in a quick hug.

"Look at you," she said, stepping back just long enough to study my face before pulling me into another embrace. Then her attention shifted to Beau. "And you must be Beau."

Beau stepped forward easily. "Yes ma'am."

"Oh, none of that," she said, waving him off. Then, after a brief glance between us, she added with a small, knowing smile, "I was wondering when I'd meet you."

"Are you going to leave them out there all night?" Colt asked as he appeared in the doorway, his expression breaking into a wide grin when he saw me. "There he is," he said.

I stepped forward and hugged him quickly. "Good to see you."

He stepped back and looked me over the same way my mother had.

"You look good," he said with a slight hint of sibling sarcasm. Then he turned toward Beau. "You must be the famous Beau."

"I'm not sure about famous," Beau said.

Colt shook his hand firmly. "Colt."

Just then another figure appeared behind Colt.

"Everyone standing in the doorway again?" she said.

Colt stepped aside and gestured toward her. "This is my wife, Hannah."

Hannah smiled warmly as she walked toward us, one hand resting lightly against the gentle curve of her stomach.

"You must be Beau," she said.

"That's me," Beau replied warmly.

By Christmas she was visibly pregnant now, her winter sweater stretched slightly across her growing belly.

"How are you feeling?" I asked.

"Like I'm carrying a bowling ball most days," she replied cheerfully.

The five of us let out echoes of laughter, still standing in the December chill. Hannah glanced toward Colt.

"He's already picking out 'baby's first football,'" she said

"Got to start them young," Colt said.

My mother shook her head. "Come inside before you all freeze."

The warmth of the house wrapped around us the moment we stepped through the door. The smell of something baking drifted from the kitchen while soft Christmas music played somewhere in the background. A tree stood in the corner of the living room, its lights glowing softly against the dim evening light. For a second, I simply stood there taking it all in—some things about home never really changed.

"This is a beautiful place," Beau said quietly.

"Oh," my mother said with slight excitement. "Thank you. It's been ours a long time." She took Beau's coat and hung it on the rack by the door before leading us toward the kitchen.

"Dinner's almost ready," she said. "But you two must be starving after that drive."

Colt leaned casually against the counter while Hannah settled carefully into one of the chairs at the kitchen table.

"So," Colt said, looking between us, "how long did it take for Nate to start lecturing you about the most surprising American election outcomes in the car?"

Beau considered the question thoughtfully.

"About twenty minutes."

"That might be a new record," Colt said.

"I was explaining something important," I replied.

"You always are," Beau said smiling at me.

Laughter moved easily through the room. I watched Beau as he spoke with my mother about the drive and answered Hannah's questions about Nashville. He moved through the conversation naturally, listening as much as he spoke, the same quiet attentiveness that had drawn me to him from the beginning.

At one point my mother caught my eye from across the room and flashed me a soft smile. Not the broad welcoming smile she had given us as we stepped out of the car—something smaller and knowing. It was as though she had already begun noticing something about the way the two of us stood beside one another. And for the first time since we had pulled away from my apartment, I realized the nervousness I had carried with me during the drive had quietly begun to fade.

Watching Beau laugh with my brother while Hannah described the baby's latest round of midnight gymnastics, I felt something settle quietly in my chest—the kind of calm certainty that only arrives when something you once believed impossible begins to feel real.

Christmas morning arrived with the kind of quiet brightness that only seemed possible in small towns and movies. Sunlight filtered through the thin curtains in the guest room where Beau and I had slept, casting pale lines across the wooden floor. Somewhere down the hallway I could hear the soft clatter of dishes and my mother moving around in the kitchen.

Beau stirred beside me.

"What time is it?" he asked, his voice still heavy with sleep.

"Too early," I said.

He rolled onto his back and stared up at the ceiling for a moment. "You know," he said, "your hometown is very quiet."

"That's because it's Christmas morning."

"I bet it's quiet all the time."

"That too," I replied.

A few minutes later we made our way down the hallway toward the kitchen. My mother was already standing at the stove with a skillet while Hannah sat at the table nursing a cup of coffee.

"Merry Christmas," my mother said when she saw us.

"Merry Christmas," Beau replied.

Colt appeared from the back door carrying a small armful of firewood.

"You two finally awake?"

"Barely," I said.

Breakfast unfolded in the easy rhythm that family mornings always seemed to find. Plates of eggs and toast appeared on the table while someone turned on the television in the living room where a quiet parade broadcast flickered across the screen.

Beau helped carry dishes to the table, listened patiently while my mother told a long story about a neighbor's Christmas decorations, and laughed with Colt about the increasingly complicated process of assembling a crib.

Later that afternoon, after presents had been opened and the dishes cleared away, the house settled into the slower rhythm that always follows a holiday meal. My mother and Hannah remained in the kitchen talking while Beau and Colt drifted outside toward the backyard.

I noticed when they left, but didn't think much about it. After a few minutes I found myself glancing toward the kitchen window. Through the glass I could see them standing near the edge of the yard. Colt had his hands tucked into the pockets of his jacket while Beau listened with the same quiet attentiveness he seemed to bring to almost every conversation. They weren't arguing, but the tone of their conversation looked serious in a way that made me pause for a moment longer than I expected.

"What are you staring at?" my mother asked from behind me.

"Nothing," I said.

Just then Colt laughed at something Beau said, the tension dissolving as easily as it had appeared. A moment later they turned and began walking back toward the house. By the time the door opened again the scene had returned to its earlier warmth.

Colt stepped inside first. "Cold out there," he said.

"Did you forget it was December?" Hannah asked.

"Just confirming."

Beau followed him inside, brushing the cold air from his jacket before glancing briefly toward me. His expression was calm and accompanied by a gentle, thoughtful small smile. There was something attentive in it—something that lingered just long enough to make me wonder what exactly he and my brother had been talking about out there in the winter air.

By late afternoon the house had settled into the slow quiet that always seemed to follow Christmas Day. The television hummed softly in the living room where Colt and Beau had migrated after lunch, the low sound of a football game drifting down the hallway while Hannah rested on the couch with a blanket pulled gently over her lap.

I found my mother standing alone in the kitchen rinsing the last of the dishes.

"You don't have to do that right now," I said, leaning against the counter.

"If I don't do it now, it'll still be here tomorrow," she replied.

She dried her hands on a towel and turned toward me. She didn't say anything at first. She just studied my face the way she had the night before when we arrived.

"What?" I asked finally.

"You look happy."

The remark was simple, but something about the way she said it carried a quiet certainty that made it difficult to brush aside.

"I am happy," I said.

She nodded slowly. "I can see that."

She glanced briefly toward the hallway where the faint sound of Beau and Colt's voices drifted from the living room.

"He seems like a good man," she stated.

"He is."

"You didn't always bring people home," she added.

The observation wasn't accusatory—simply factual.

"I know."

She leaned lightly against the counter beside me. "When you moved away for grad school," she said, "you changed a little."

"That's what usually happens when people grow up."

"Yes," she said gently. "But this was different."

I didn't respond right away. She wasn't wrong.

Over the years my visits home had become shorter, quieter, and less frequent. Something about that distance had felt necessary for a long time—at times, required.

"You carried something with you for a while," she continued. She didn't ask what it was. She didn't need to.

"That's part of life sometimes," I said carefully.

"Yes," she said. "But whatever it was… it seems lighter now."

The words hung quietly between us. She reached over and squeezed my hand.

"I haven't seen you this relaxed in years," she added.

I looked down at the kitchen floor before answering.

"I think Nashville has helped."

She smiled slightly. "And Beau?"

I felt my expression shift before I could stop it—a smile blossoming. "Yes," I said. "Beau has helped too."

She nodded once, as though that confirmed something she had already suspected. "Well," she said, pushing gently away from the counter, "that's all a mother really wants."

"What is?" I asked.

"To see her child find something that makes them feel like themselves again."

From the living room Colt's voice rose suddenly in laughter at something Beau had said. My mother glanced toward the sound and smiled.

"He seems to be holding his own with your brother," she said.

"That's not easy."

"No," she agreed. "It isn't." She picked up the dish towel again and turned back toward the sink.

Beau and I finished packing our things that evening to head back to Nashville the next morning. As I flung myself into bed in a grateful exhaustion, Beau crawled in next to me resting his head on my chest. The two of us stayed there for some time as his fingers gently caressed my chest.

"I've enjoyed meeting your family," Beau eventually said.

"I'm glad," I replied.

Another moment of quiet passed.

"Your brother seems like a great guy," he added.

"He's always been there for me."

"I can tell he really cares about you," he said before pausing a moment. "He cares if you're happy or not."

I didn't respond at first. It was clear to me that what Beau was saying was a reflection of whatever he and Colt had discussed outside earlier in the day. Although I didn't know for sure what the two of them had discussed, I had an idea.

"I am," I said finally. "Happy."

Beau didn't say anything else—I didn't need him to. He simply reached to turn the lamp next to the bed off before pulling my body close to his own. I stayed awake a while longer after his breathing began to slow, aware of the fixed weight of him beside me, the steady cadence of it. Whatever I had spent years holding in place no longer felt quite as immovable as it once had.

ELEVEN

"The deeper that sorrow carves into your being, the more joy you can contain." — Khalil Gibran

As the new year settled in, campus returned to motion almost overnight. Students moved quickly between buildings, their schedules still fresh, their expectations not yet worn down.

By mid-morning, I was back at the front of the lecture hall, flipping through notes I'd only slightly revised. The material was familiar—political realignment, shifting coalitions, the kind of changes most people only understood in hindsight.

A few students filtered in early while others lingered in the doorway, finishing conversations before class began. I set my notes on the podium and glanced out across the room. There was something steadying about this part of the job—the structure of it, the quiet agreement that, for the next hour, we would try to make sense of something larger than ourselves. A student in the second row looked up from his laptop.

"Professor?"

I paused. "Yes?"

"Did you hear about Senator Frazier?"

The question landed casually, as though it were no different from asking about the reading assignment.

"I can't say that I have," I replied.

"She announced this morning she's retiring."

A low murmur moved through the room. I considered that for a moment. Debbie Frazier had been a fixture in Tennessee politics for decades. Even before I had met her at the farm, her reputation had carried well beyond the state—first woman to serve as Senate Majority Leader, a figure whose career had shaped not only policy but the structure of leadership itself. Retirement wasn't surprising—but it was significant.

"Well," I said, resting my hands lightly against the edge of the podium, "that marks the end of a rather substantial chapter in this state's political history."

A few students nodded. Moments like this always presented an opportunity. History, after all, wasn't confined to textbooks—it was always happening in real time.

"That's usually where the real story is," I said. "Not in the stability, but in the transition. When someone with a legacy such as Frazier steps away, it doesn't just open a seat—it shifts the landscape around it."

The room quieted slightly.

"The next Senator from Tennessee," I added, almost as an aside, "will have a great deal to live up to."

I let that sit for a brief moment before shifting back toward my notes.

"Alright," I said. "Let's talk about political realignment."

The lecture moved forward easily after that.

By the time my last class ended that afternoon, the campus had settled into its usual weekday rhythm. Students moved quickly across the quad, the early January cold keeping most conversations brief as people hurried from one building to the next. I made my way back to my office, balancing a stack of papers beneath one arm while mentally sorting through the rest of the week's schedule.

Inside my office, I set the papers down on my desk and sank into the chair behind it, letting out a quiet breath. The room still carried that faint smell of books and paper that seemed to settle into the walls over time. I allowed myself to sit reflectively, letting the silence settle. Then my phone buzzed lightly against the desk—Beau. I smiled slightly before answering.

"Hey, there," I answered.

"Hey," he said. "You survive your first week back?"

"Barely."

"That bad?"

"Let's just say the students came back with opinions."

I could hear the faint background noise of his day on the other end of the line—voices, a door closing somewhere, the distant echo of movement that suggested he was in between meetings.

"I wanted to see if you were free for dinner tonight," he said.

"Dinner?" I leaned back slightly in my chair. "That's new," I replied.

"How so?"

"You usually just show up with takeout and interrupt my grading."

"I prefer to think of that as improving your evening."

"It does."

He laughed quietly.

"So, you're free?"

"I am," I said. "What did you have in mind?"

"I made a reservation."

That caught my attention.

"You made a reservation."

"I did."

"Somewhere I need to wear something nicer than this?" I asked, glancing down at the sweater I hadn't bothered to change out of since the morning.

"Wouldn't hurt."

I smiled to myself.

"Well now I'm intrigued."

"That was the goal," Beau replied. There was something in his tone I couldn't quite place—not serious, but more deliberate than usual.

"Everything alright?" I asked.

"Yeah," he said. "Everything's great."

Another brief pause.

"I just thought it'd be nice to do something a little different."

I considered that briefly.

"Alright," I said. "What time?"

"I'll pick you up at seven."

"I'll be ready," I replied. As I ended the call and set my phone back on the desk, the quiet of the office returned around me.

I sat there, staring absently at the stack of papers I had meant to start grading. Dinner reservations weren't unusual—but they weren't typical for us either. Most of our evenings had settled into something simpler over the past few weeks—takeout at my apartment, late conversations over half-finished meals, the quiet rhythm of two people growing comfortable in one another's presence.

By the time I made it back to my apartment, the early January light had already begun to fade. The city outside my window carried that quiet, in-between feeling that comes just after the holidays—decorations still lingering in storefronts, but the pace of everyday life steadily returning. I set my bag down by the door and stood there for a moment, letting the stillness of the apartment settle around me.

I moved toward the bedroom and changed into something a little more appropriate than what I had worn to campus that day. A dark jacket, a button-down shirt—nothing overly formal—just enough to match the tone Beau had hinted at.

As I adjusted my sleeves in the mirror, I caught myself pausing. There was a time not long ago when an evening like this might have come with a different kind of weight—uncertainty or hesitation. The instinct to overthink what something might mean before it had even begun. Now, standing there in the soft light of my apartment, that feeling was absent. In its place was something steadier—quiet intrigue and anticipation.

By the time Beau arrived, the streetlights had fully taken over from the fading daylight. He stepped out of the car as I locked the apartment door behind me.

"You clean up well, Professor," he said.

"I had proper motivation."

"I'm glad I could provide that."

We exchanged a brief, easy smile before he opened the passenger door for me.

The restaurant sat tucked along one of Nashville's quieter streets, the kind of place I had passed before but never had much reason to stop in. Soft lighting filtered through the windows, and the low hum of conversation met us as we stepped inside.

Beau gave his name to the host, who led us to a table near the back of the dining room.

"This is nice," I said as we sat down.

"I thought you'd like it."

For a while, the conversation stayed exactly where it

needed to—simple, familiar, grounded in the rhythm we had already built over the past few months.

"How was your day?" I asked as we looked over the menus.

"Busy," Beau said. "Met with a couple of advocacy groups this morning. Education funding, infrastructure—things that sound straightforward until you get into the details."

"That sounds like most things in government."

"That's accurate."

He set the menu down and leaned back slightly in his chair.

"What about you?"

"First week back," I said. "Students are still pretending they're going to stay on top of their reading."

"How long does that last?"

"Two weeks, maybe three if I'm lucky."

Beau smiled faintly.

At some point during the meal, somewhere between the first course and the quiet lull that followed, I found myself mentioning something Colt had sent earlier that afternoon.

"He texted me a picture today," I said.

"Of what?" Beau asked.

"It says 'I love my uncle' across the front," I replied.

Beau laughed softly. "That sounds perfect."

The conversation settled into a quiet pause before Beau reached for his glass, turning it slightly between his fingers.

"Did you hear about Senator Frazier?" I asked.

"I did," he said.

"When?"

"Late last night," he answered quickly. "She called."

That caught my attention.

"She called you?"

"We've known each other a long time," he said. "She wanted to let a few people know before the announcement this morning."

I thought back briefly to the classroom earlier that day. For Beau, it had arrived differently—more directly.

"What did she say?" I asked.

"That she was ready," he replied. "That it felt like the right time."

His tone had shifted—he sounded more focused. "I've been thinking about it too," he said. "About what comes next."

"For her seat?" I asked.

Beau nodded. "I talked to her about it. About what it would mean to step into that kind of role."

I watched him carefully. "And?" I asked.

Beau held my gaze. "I've decided I'm going to run."

The words landed calmly without dramatics—just clear and certain. Momentarily, the noise of the restaurant seemed to recede.

"That's… big," I said, the weight of it settling in. I leaned back slightly, letting it register. "You'd be good at it."

"I think I could be," Beau replied.

"That's not the same thing," I added.

"No," he admitted. "But it's a start."

"When would you announce?" I asked.

"Soon," he said. "There's a lot to put in place first." There was no hesitation in his voice—only clarity.

It was the recognition that this—whatever we had been building—was about to exist inside something much larger than the two of us. And as I sat there across from him, watching that certainty settle into place, the future I had only recently begun to imagine had just expanded in a way I hadn't fully anticipated— not out of reach, but no longer simple.

TWELVE

"The world as it is not the world as it should be." — Barack Obama

The shift happened faster than I expected. When Beau said he would be announcing soon, I had assumed he meant something more measured—weeks of quiet preparation, conversations behind closed doors, a gradual build toward whatever came next.

But within days, the pace had already changed. By the end of that first week, there were meetings I hadn't heard about, names I didn't recognize, and conversations that seemed to begin mid-sentence whenever Beau stepped out to take a call. Still, some things hadn't changed—at least not yet.

One evening, not long after the start of the semester, Beau sat beside me on the couch in my apartment, a blanket pulled loosely over both of us while a documentary played quietly on the television: The Legacy of the Tennessee Valley Authority.

Black-and-white footage flickered across the screen—men standing along riverbanks, early construction of dams rising slowly out of the landscape, narration describing a government project that had once reshaped entire regions of the South.

"Hard to imagine something like that getting approved today," Beau said.

"Not without a decade of debate," I replied.

On the screen, water moved steadily through the channels carved decades earlier, the narrator's voice describing the promise of electricity reaching rural communities for the first time. It was the kind of history I had always been drawn to because it was not just policy or theory. It was something tangible—something that changed the way people lived.

Beau shifted slightly beside me, his arm resting comfortably along the back of the couch.

"Your kind of documentary," he said.

"It is."

"I can tell."

For a while we sat there in easy silence, the low hum of the television filling the space between us. Then Beau's phone buzzed against the coffee table. He glanced at the screen, his expression shifting slightly—not tense, but focused in a way I had begun noticing more often over the past few days.

"I should take this," he said.

He stepped into the kitchen, his voice lowering as he answered. I didn't try to listen. Instead, I watched the screen as the documentary moved forward—footage of turbines spinning, power lines stretching across open land, entire towns gradually coming into light. It was the kind of history that didn't just sit in books. It changed landscapes, lives, and legacies.

A few minutes later Beau returned, slipping his phone back into his pocket as he sat down beside me again.

"That was Claire," he said.

Claire had been Beau's campaign manager for his previous state representative campaigns and was his first choice to oversee his run for the United States Senate.

I glanced toward him. "What did she say?"

"They sent over some branding mockups," he said. "Logos, color palettes… that kind of thing."

"That was quick," I replied.

He reached for his laptop on the coffee table and opened it, pulling up an email.

"Want to take a look?" he asked me.

I shifted slightly closer as he turned the screen toward us.

"I feel underqualified for this," I said.

"You're a historian," he replied with a smirk. "You understand symbolism better than most people."

The first design appeared on the screen. It was clean, traditional—deep navy lettering, a simple layout that leaned heavily on familiarity.

"Thoughts?" Beau asked.

"It feels… safe," I said after a moment.

"Safe?"

"In a good way," I added. "But maybe a little predictable."

He nodded. "That's what I thought."

He clicked to the next option. This one was sharper. Brighter colors, a more modern font that leaned toward something almost corporate.

"That one feels like it's trying too hard," I said.

Beau smiled slightly. "My thought, too."

A third design appeared. This one sat somewhere between the two—balanced, understated without being plain. The lettering was strong without feeling heavy, the colors familiar but softened just enough to feel intentional rather than traditional. I found myself looking at it a little longer.

"What about that one?" Beau asked.

I considered it thoroughly before answering.

"It feels like someone who knows where they come from,"

I said slowly, "and where they're heading."

Beau glanced at me.

"That's a very specific interpretation."

I gestured lightly toward the screen. "It doesn't feel like it's reaching for attention," I added. "It just… fits."

For a moment he didn't say anything. Then he smiled. "I think you're right, professor."

He clicked back to the email and typed a quick response, confirming the selection before closing the laptop.

"Look at that," I said. "I've officially contributed to a senate campaign."

"I'll make sure that's properly documented," Beau replied with a quiet chuckle.

He leaned over and pressed a brief, soft kiss against my temple before settling back into the couch.

"Alright," I said, reaching for the remote. "Back to federally funded infrastructure."

"As riveting as ever."

We resumed the documentary, the quiet rhythm of the evening slipping easily back into place. At some point, without either of us noticing exactly when, the conversation faded. The narrator's voice continued softly in the background as the screen shifted from one piece of history to another. Beau's hand found mine beneath the blanket, his fingers lacing loosely with mine as the warmth of the room settled around us. By the time the credits began to roll, we had both fallen asleep. The television cast a soft glow across the room, the final images of a project that had once reshaped the South flickering quietly in the background. And for a little while longer, before everything already set in motion gathered its full momentum, the world remained still.

***

In the weeks that followed, the pace Beau had warned me

about fully arrived. It wasn't sudden in the way a single moment might be. It was steady—relentless, even.

What had started as a handful of phone calls and late-night emails quickly expanded into something larger—something structured, coordinated, and increasingly difficult to contain within the quiet boundaries our lives had settled into over the past few months.

There were names now—people I hadn't met but heard referenced often: a finance director, field organizers, communications staff.

At some point, Beau's calendar stopped looking like his own. Evenings that had once belonged to takeout dinners and half-finished conversations were gradually replaced by strategy sessions and meetings that stretched later than expected.

Still, he made time. One night, he arrived at my apartment just after nine, his tie loosened slightly, the edge of exhaustion visible in the way he dropped his keys onto the counter.

"Long day?" I asked.

"That obvious?"

"You forgot to text me back."

"That's serious."

"It is," I said jovially.

He smiled faintly, crossing the room to press a quick kiss against my cheek.

"Sorry," he said. "It got away from me."

"That's going to happen sometimes," I said with gentle reassurance.

He didn't answer right away.

Even as the rhythm of our time together began to shift, the foundation of it still felt steady. If anything, the changes only made the moments we did have feel more deliberate and intentional.

A few days later I found myself standing in the back of a small event space downtown, watching Beau speak to a group of donors gathered beneath soft overhead lighting. It wasn't the formal launch—not yet—but it was close enough to feel like something real.

He moved through the room with the same ease I'd seen before—shaking hands, listening carefully, speaking with a quiet confidence that didn't demand attention so much as earn it. At one point he caught my eye from across the room for a brief moment—long enough to offer a small, familiar smile before turning back to the conversation in front of him. I'd grown accustomed to the ease with which Beau moved through environments such as that. Not as someone trying to prove himself, but with the natural grace of someone who already understood it.

Later that night, as we walked back toward the car, the air still cold from the lingering edge of winter, Beau slipped his hands into his coat pockets.

"It's moving faster than I expected," he said.

"You don't seem surprised."

"I'm not."

He glanced over at me.

"Are you?"

I considered that pensively.

"Yes," I said.

"But not in a bad way."

"That's good."

We walked the rest of the block in quiet. The city around us carried the low hum of a place that was always in motion, even late into the evening.

"Launch is in two weeks," Beau said finally.

I looked over at him. "Already?"

He nodded. "Union Station."

The name alone carried weight—historic, intentional, and very public.

"That's… a big stage," I said.

"It needs to be," he replied. "And you'll be there," he added.

I slowed slightly. "Beau—"

"I mean it," he said, stopping just enough to turn toward me. "I want you there."

"That's your moment," I said. "Your family should be up there with you."

"They will be," he said, holding my gaze. "So will you."

For a second I didn't respond. The idea of standing beside him in a setting like that felt different from anything we had done so far. It was more visible and more defined.

"I'm not family," I said quietly.

Beau shook his head. "That's not what I said."

I hesitated and he stepped slightly closer.

"I want the people who matter to me standing there," he said. "And I'm lucky enough to say that includes you."

That simplicity of it left very little room to argue—so I didn't. Instead, I nodded once.

"Alright," I replied gently as we resumed walking. I felt the weight of what he had asked settle quietly into place.

The next two weeks passed smoothly amid the new routine of campaign chaos the two of us had been adapting to. Beau stayed busy, but he still made time, intentionally, to spend with me or give me a call even if for only briefly. As the campaign launch event arrived, Beau had spent many nights lying across my lap, working through his announcement speech—intentional with each word, each line.

When the evening to announce came, I met Beau at Union

Station. It looked different at night. The building rose out of the street with a kind of quiet authority, its stone façade illuminated by warm light that softened the edges of its age without diminishing it. Arched windows stretched upward toward the vaulted ceiling inside, the structure carrying the weight of more than a century of movement—arrivals, departures, lives passing through on their way to somewhere else.

As Beau and I stepped inside, the space opened around us. The ceiling soared above the main hall, carved wood and stained glass catching the light in a way that made the entire room feel both grand and intimate at once. The echo of voices carried softly across the space, blending with the low hum of conversation and the occasional clink of glass from the reception area set along one side.

It was already full. Supporters, donors, staff—people who seemed to know exactly where to stand and who to speak to, moving through the room with a kind of practiced purpose. Near the front, a small stage had been set beneath the largest archway, framed by banners that bore Beau's name in the design we had chosen together just weeks earlier. Seeing it there—no longer on a laptop screen but stretched across fabric, lit and visible—shifted something slightly in my understanding of what this had become.

"You ready?" Beau asked beside me.

I glanced toward him. He looked composed—not performative, just focused in a way I had come to revere.

"As I'll ever be," I said.

He smiled briefly, then reached for my hand for just a moment before someone from his team approached, pulling him into a quick conversation about timing and order. The next several minutes moved quickly—introductions, handshakes and names I tried to remember but couldn't quite hold onto as the room filled further and the energy shifted from conversation to anticipation.

At some point, Beau's mother appeared at his side, followed closely by Colt and Hannah. Hannah moved carefully through the crowd, one hand resting instinctively against her stomach as she smiled at people who stopped to greet her.

Beau introduced me again to someone whose name I missed, then another. Each interaction was brief, polite, and efficient. And all the while, the room continued to fill. Eventually someone signaled from near the stage: It was time.

Beau turned toward me. "You good?" he asked quietly.

I nodded. He studied me for just a second longer, as if making sure. Then he gave a small, reassuring smile.

"Stay close," he added.

We moved toward the front together.

The stage felt slightly smaller up close, though the room itself seemed to expand as we stepped onto it. The lights were warmer there, directed just enough to separate the stage from the crowd without blinding us to the faces gathered below.

Beau's family and I stood to one side. I hesitated for the briefest moment at the edge of the stage. Not because I didn't want to be there, but because I was suddenly aware of how visible it all was. Beau noticed. He reached back slightly, his hand brushing mine in a small, grounding gesture.

The room quieted as Beau approached the podium. For a second, he didn't speak. He just looked out across the crowd.

Then—

"Thank you all for being here tonight."

His voice carried easily through the room, steady and measured in a way that didn't feel rehearsed so much as certain.

"It means more than I can say to stand here surrounded by so many people who care about this state the way I do."

A few nods from the crowd. A quiet murmur of

agreement.

"I want to start by saying something simple," he continued. "None of this happens without the people who came before us."

There was a subtle shift in the room—recognition.

"Senator Frazier has spent decades serving Tennessee with integrity and purpose," Beau said. "And because of that work, we're standing on a foundation with ample opportunity and reason for hope."

Applause rose briefly, then settled. Beau waited just long enough before continuing.

"She's shown what leadership can look like when it's rooted in service. And I'm grateful—not just for what she's done for this state, but for the example she's set for those of us who come after."

I watched him as he spoke—the way he held the room without forcing it. People leaned in, not because they were told to, but because they wanted to hear what came next.

"We have an opportunity now," he said, "to carry that work forward."

"To bring new energy to the same commitment. To build on what's been done and continue moving this state in the direction it deserves."

Another wave of applause—stronger this time. Around us, the room felt alive in a way that was difficult to describe. Beau spoke for several more minutes, his words moving between policy and principle, between vision and practicality. I didn't catch all of it—not in the way I might have in a classroom or reading a transcript later. Instead, I noticed the way the room responded. People listened and they believed him. And standing there beside him, I realized something with a kind of quiet clarity: This wasn't just ambition—it was momentum.

When he finished, the applause filled the room fully this time, echoing off the high ceilings and settling into something that felt larger than the space itself. Beau stepped back from the podium, shaking hands with those closest to the stage before turning briefly toward us—toward me. For a second, the moment narrowed. The room, the crowd—all of it fading into the background. And there, in the middle of everything that had just begun, he smiled.

The applause didn't end all at once. It softened gradually, giving way to movement as people stepped forward, conversations picking up where they had left off before the speech. The room shifted back into motion—supporters approaching the stage, hands extended, voices rising slightly as the formality of the moment dissolved into something more immediate.

Beau was pulled into it almost instantly. Someone reached him first—a donor, then a staff member, then another introduction that led to another conversation. The space around him filled quickly, the same steady energy from earlier now directed entirely toward him.

I stepped back slightly, giving him room. From the edge of the stage, I watched as he moved through the crowd—listening, responding, shaking hands, each interaction brief but attentive. It was seamless.

For a while, I remained where I was, letting the moment settle. People moved around me in small clusters, conversations overlapping in quiet fragments—policy, strategy, timelines, names I didn't recognize but would likely hear again.

At some point, one of Beau's staff members approached me.

"You're Nate, right?" she asked.

"I am."

"I've heard about you," she said with a polite smile. "I'm Claire."

We shook hands briefly.

"Congratulations," I said. "It looks like things are moving quickly."

"They are," she replied. "He's been ready for this for a while."

Her tone carried a kind of calm confidence, the kind that comes from knowing exactly how the next several weeks would unfold.

"Well," I said, glancing back toward Beau, "it shows."

She followed my gaze intently before nodding once. With that, she was pulled away into another conversation, leaving me once again at the edge of the room.

Eventually, Beau glanced toward me. I made my way over as one of his staff members stepped aside.

"That was incredible," I said.

"Yeah?"

"Absolutely."

He smiled, though there was already a shift in his focus—his attention pulled in multiple directions at once.

"I'm glad you were here," he said.

"Me too."

Behind him, someone called his name. Another question. Another conversation waiting.

He turned slightly, then looked back at me.

"I've got to head out soon," he said. "We're leaving tonight."

"Tonight?"

He nodded. "East Tennessee first. Then we'll work our way back across the state."

"For how long?"

"Couple of weeks," he said. "At least."

I let that settle gradually.

"That's… a lot," I said.

"It is."

Another voice called for him, closer this time. He glanced over his shoulder, then back at me. "I'll call you," he said.

"I know," I replied softly, the applause still echoing around us.

Beau stepped closer and pressed a quick kiss against my cheek. "I'll talk to you soon."

"Safe travels," I replied

He smiled once more, then turned—already being pulled back into motion before he had fully taken a step away. I stood there for a moment longer, watching as he disappeared into the cluster of people moving toward the exit.

Within minutes, the room began to thin.

Conversations wrapped, staff members moved with quiet efficiency, and the energy of the evening settled into something softer—less about possibility now, more about execution. I made my way outside.

The air had turned sharply cold, the kind that settles in after the last of the evening's movement begins to fade. The city stretched out in front of me, lights reflecting off the pavement as traffic moved steadily through the night. Behind me, Union Station stood illuminated against the dark sky, unchanged and steady.

The city moved around me the way it always did—steady, indifferent, unchanged. For a long time, I had been careful about love. Careful in a way that had once felt necessary. But somewhere along the way, without fully noticing when it happened, that distance had begun to give way to something else.

And as the night settled in and the momentum of

everything Beau had just stepped into carried him further away, I found myself surprised by something simple.

Not fear.

Just the quiet recognition that I cared—and that I didn't have to be afraid of that anymore.

THIRTEEN

"The loneliest moment in someone's life is when they are watching their whole world fall apart." — F. Scott Fitzgerald

The weeks after Beau left Nashville settled into something that felt both structured and slightly off-balance. I kept to my routine in the ways that mattered. Classes filled my weekdays, the cadence of lectures grounding me more than I expected. Sundays meant church. Saturdays, more often than not, meant a call with Colt—updates on Hannah, on the baby, on a life that felt, in contrast, remarkably certain.

In the space between all of that, I worked. The fellowship had reached its midpoint, and with it came the expectation of something tangible. A paper. Something publishable. Something that contributed—however modestly—to the field I had spent years trying to understand.

Lately, I'd been focusing on political realignment—periods where power didn't collapse all at once, but shifted beneath the surface. Coalitions that held for decades beginning to fracture. Alliances reforming into something new before most people recognized the change.

It was the kind of transformation that, in hindsight, seemed obvious. While it was happening, it was almost imperceptible. Beau and I talked when we could—which was not as often as either of us would have preferred. There were calls I made that went unanswered, followed hours later by a text apologizing for the schedule, the travel, the pace of it all. There were calls he made that I missed—caught in a lecture, a meeting, a moment I couldn't step away from. It wasn't intentional. That was what made it harder to define. Nothing was wrong. And yet, something felt different.

I was halfway through a chapter of a book I had already read once before when my phone lit up on the coffee table— Beau.

For a moment, I just looked at it—not because I didn't want to answer, but because earlier that day, I had called him twice. Both times, it had gone to voicemail. The night before, he had called while I was in a faculty meeting that I couldn't leave. By the time I returned the call, hours later, he was already somewhere else, already moving on to the next thing. It had been like that lately.

The phone buzzed again and I reached for it.
"Hello."

"Hey," Beau said, his voice coming through slightly distorted before the video connected.

The image steadied after a second. He was standing in what looked like a dressing room—bright lights, a mirror behind him, the edge of a suit jacket hanging just out of frame.

"Where are you?" I asked.

"Knoxville," he said. "Got an event in about ten minutes."

"That explains the lighting."

"Do I look that good?" Beau replied with that humble

confidence I'd grown to enjoy.

"How's your day been?" I asked.

"Busy," he said. "Long. I could use one of your shoulder massages right about now."

"All yours," I replied. "As soon as you get back." I studied him briefly. He looked tired—not in a concerning way, but a bit worn at the edges.

"I saw you on the talk show this morning," I said.

"Oh yeah?" he added. "You were up early then."

"You did well," I replied. "Your tie was wrong, though."

He frowned slightly. "What?"

"Pinstripes don't translate well on camera. Too much movement. It's distracting."

Beau looked down at himself, adjusting the tie instinctively. "That would have been good to know earlier."

"You're welcome," I grinned.

He shook his head, smiling. "I'll run all outfits by you going forward."

"You should."

"I'll be back in Nashville this weekend," he said. "Fundraiser in Belle Meade."

I felt it before I had time to think—relief, sharper than I expected.

"That's good," I said.

"You should come."

"I'd like that," I replied.

Someone knocked lightly in the background.

"Two minutes," a voice called.

Beau glanced over his shoulder, then back at me.

"I've got to go."

"I figured."

"I'll see you this weekend?"

"Yes," I answered. "You will."

Beau hesitated for just a second. "I miss you," he said.

I felt that land more fully than anything else in the conversation. "I miss you too."

And then the call ended.

***

Belle Meade carried a kind of quiet wealth that didn't need to announce itself. The house sat back from the road, framed by trees that had likely been there longer than most of the people moving through its front doors that evening. Warm light spilled from the windows, and the low hum of conversation drifted out across the driveway as I stepped inside.

The space was already full. Not crowded in a way that felt chaotic—but dense with presence. Conversations layered over one another, glasses in hand, voices low but constant. I paused just inside the entrance, taking it in. For a moment, I wasn't entirely sure where to go. Someone approached me almost immediately.

"Can you grab another round from the kitchen?" they asked, handing me an empty glass without really looking at me.

I hesitated for half a second.

"I—" I started, then stopped.

"It's down the hall," they added quickly, already turning back toward their conversation.

"Actually," I said, more gently than I expected, "I'm not—"

The person looked back, registering me properly for the first time. "Oh—sorry," they said quickly. "I thought you were with—"

"No, it's alright."

They nodded once, already moving on. The moment passed as quickly as it had arrived. I set the glass down on a nearby table and moved further into the room. It didn't take long to find Beau.

He stood near the center of the space, mid-conversation, his attention focused entirely on the person in front of him. Even from across the room, I could see the ease with which he carried it—the balance of listening and speaking, the quiet confidence that seemed to draw people toward him rather than push outward.

He looked up at some point and caught sight of me—and for just a second, everything else seemed to fall away.

He excused himself quickly and crossed the room.

"It's so good to see you," he said.

"Right back at you," I said.

The hug that followed came easily, and Beau's embrace brought a familiar comfort. I didn't realize how much I had needed it until it happened.

"Glad you made it," he said. He kept a hand lightly at my back as he turned, already guiding me into the rhythm of the room. "Come on," he said. "I want you to meet some people."

For a while, we moved through the evening together—introductions, handshakes, names I really didn't try to remember. It was easy enough to just follow his lead—to step into the conversations, to listen, to offer something when it felt appropriate. Though, even as we stood side by side, there were moments when I could feel the distance—not physical, not even intentional. Just the quiet recognition that his attention no longer belonged solely to the space we occupied together.

At one point, I found myself standing just slightly behind him as another conversation took shape in front of us.

By the time we left Belle Meade, the night had settled into something quieter. The conversations, the movement, the constant rhythm of introductions and expectations—all of it seemed to fade as we stepped out into the cool air and made our way back toward my car.

Beau exhaled as soon as the door closed behind him like he'd been holding in place for the past several hours.

"That was a lot," he said.

"It looked like it."

He leaned his head back against the seat with a hushed exhale, eyes closed.

"Give me five minutes," he added. "I'll be a real person again."

I smiled faintly, starting the car. For a few minutes, we drove in silence—Beau gazed out the window, seeming to find ease in the reprieve away from people and staffers. The kind of quiet that felt earned.

When we reached my apartment, Beau followed me inside without saying much, setting his keys down on the counter before loosening his tie with one hand. By the time I turned around, he had already shrugged out of his jacket, draping it over the back of the chair as he moved toward the couch.

He sat, then leaned back, stretching out with a quiet exhale.

"I'm not moving for a while," he said.

"You'll hear no complaint from me," I replied.

I crossed the room slowly, stopping just long enough to take in the way he looked—tie loosened, shirt partially unbuttoned, the edges of exhaustion no longer hidden behind practiced composure. For the first time that evening, he looked like himself again—or at least, the version of himself that existed outside of everything else.

I sat beside him, then shifted, easing myself closer until I could lean into him fully. He didn't say anything, just adjusted slightly to make space, one arm coming around me without thought. I let my head rest against him, the quiet of the apartment settling around us. For a beat neither of us spoke—together, alone, was enough.

"Do I need to carry you to bed, Senator?" I said eventually, my voice low.

He let out a quiet breath that might have been a laugh.

"I think I'll manage," he said. "Don't jinx it, Professor."

We stayed like that a little longer than I first realized. Or maybe exactly as long as we needed. Eventually, Beau shifted, pushing himself upright with a soft groan.

"Alright," he said. "Before I fall asleep right here."

He reached for my hand as he stood, pulling me up with him, and together we moved down the short hallway toward the bedroom. The room felt warmer than the rest of the apartment, the soft light from the bedside lamp casting a kind of quiet calm over everything.

There was nothing rushed about what followed—no urgency, no performance. Just the slow, familiar rhythm of being close to someone you hadn't realized you had been missing until they were there again. At some point, Beau's hand found mine, his fingers tightening just slightly as if grounding himself in the moment.

I felt it then—not in any single movement, but in the space between them—a kind of steadiness I hadn't known I had been yearning for. And for a moment—just a moment—I allowed myself to stay there, without questioning what it meant or how long it might last.

Sometime later, the room had gone still again. Beau lay beside me, already asleep, his breathing slow and even in a way that suggested a kind of exhaustion deeper than anything he would have admitted out loud. I turned slightly, watching him for a moment. In sleep, there was no campaign and no expectations—no movement pulling him in a dozen different directions at once. I reached out, almost without thinking, letting my hand rest lightly against his arm.

The next morning came earlier than I expected. When I opened my eyes, the light had already begun to filter through the window, soft and quiet against the walls of the room. Beau was gone. For a brief second, something in my chest tightened. Then I heard movement in the kitchen. I pushed myself up, running a hand through my hair as I stepped out into the hallway.

He stood at the counter, fully dressed again, a cup of coffee in one hand as he glanced down at his phone.

"Morning," he said, looking up.

"Good morning," I replied.

"You sleep alright?"

"Very well," I said. "You?"

"Best I've had in a while," he said. There was a small pause.

"How long have you been up?" I asked.

"Not long."

"You didn't wake me."

"You looked like you needed it."

I nodded slightly, moving toward the counter. We stood there idly together in the quiet. Then Beau set his coffee down.

"I've got to head out," he said.

"I know," I said softly.

He reached for his jacket, slipping it on with practiced ease.

"I've got two stops before noon, then heading west this afternoon," he said stepping closer to me, his hand finding mine briefly before he leaned in, pressing a soft kiss against my lips.

"I'll call you later," he said.

"I know."

I hesitated, just slightly.

"When will I see you again?" I asked. The question came out more naturally than I expected. Beau paused—not long, just enough to consider it.

"I'll be back through Nashville next week," he said. "Or the week after. I'll figure it out."

I nodded.

"Okay."

It wasn't an answer. Not really. But it was the one he had. He kissed me once more—quick, familiar—before stepping back.

"I've got to go," he said.

"Drive safe."

"I will."

And then he was gone.

The door closed behind him with a quiet finality that lingered longer than it should have. The apartment was quiet again. I stood there for a second, the weight of the morning settling in more slowly than I expected.

Eventually, I moved back toward the living room, the remnants of the night before still scattered in small, ordinary ways—his jacket no longer on the chair, the faint impression of where we had sat still visible in the cushions.

My thoughts shifted, almost without warning—back to something I hadn't been thinking about, or maybe something I had been avoiding. My Vanderbilt fellowship. It would end at the close of the semester—a fact I had known from the beginning. The timeline that had always been there, and yet, somewhere along the way, I had stopped thinking about what came after.

Before Beau, the plan had been simple—return to Boston and pick up where things had left off at Hopkins. Now—I wasn't so sure.

I leaned against the edge of the kitchen counter, staring

absently at nothing in particular. *Should I talk to him about it?* The question surfaced before I could dismiss it. The answer didn't. *Did it matter if I did? Did it matter if I didn't?*

The future no longer felt like something I could keep at a distance. And for reasons I wasn't entirely ready to name, that realization sat heavier than I expected. The apartment remained quiet—still. And as the morning settled in around me, I found myself standing there a little longer than necessary, caught somewhere between what had been and what might come next. Not afraid. Not uncertain, exactly. Just aware that something had shifted—and that I couldn't quite make sense of it yet.

FOURTEEN

"A single person is missing
for you, and the whole world
is empty." — Joan Didion

By Sunday morning, a stillness had already begun to take shape.

It wasn't tied to any single moment—no argument, no shift I could point to with certainty. Just a gradual thinning. Conversations that ended a little sooner. Calls that came at the wrong times, or not at all. Nothing that, on its own, meant very much. But enough, taken together, to notice.

I turned my head slightly, looking toward the window. Nashville was already moving. A car passed slowly along the street below. Somewhere nearby, a screen door shut with a soft but distinct rhythm. The kind of ordinary sounds that usually faded into the background—but this morning, they felt sharper. More defined.

I glanced at my phone on the counter—no new messages. That, too, wasn't unusual. Beau had mentioned the schedule ahead of him—early meetings, travel, the steady pace of a campaign beginning to take shape. It made sense. There was nothing about it that required interpretation. Still, I found myself looking at the screen as if waiting for to speak to me.

I moved through the morning without much urgency—coffee, a brief attempt at reading that didn't hold, the familiar routine unfolding in a way that felt intact on the surface. By the time I stepped outside, the air had warmed just enough to carry the beginning of spring. Nashville in the morning had a different rhythm than it did at night. Less noise. More intention. People moving with purpose rather than leisure.

The walk to church had become familiar without my realizing when that happened. Same streets. Same turns. The same stretch of sidewalk where the city seemed to quiet just slightly before opening up again closer to campus. There was comfort in that familiarity. Not in any profound sense—just enough to keep things steady. I wasn't sure when I had started needing that.

The sanctuary was already filling by the time I stepped inside. Sunlight moved through the tall windows in long, diffused lines, settling across the pews in a way that made the space feel warmer than it actually was. Conversations lingered in low tones—never quite rising above a murmur, as if everyone present had agreed, without saying it, to keep the morning gentle.

I slipped into a seat near the center aisle, letting my hands rest loosely together as I looked toward the front. For a moment, I tried to focus on nothing at all—something that had become more difficult lately.

If something had been clearly wrong—an argument, a shift I could point to, a moment that marked a change—I would have known what to do with it. Historians are trained to identify turning points. To isolate cause and effect. To trace a line from one moment to the next and explain how things changed—but this wasn't that.

Pastor Daniel stepped forward as the room settled, his presence grounding the space almost immediately.

"There are seasons in life," he said, "when we're asked to wait without clarity."

I kept my gaze forward, but the words pulled my attention in more fully than I expected.

"Not waiting with a clear outcome," he continued, "and not waiting with the assurance that what we hope for will arrive. Just… waiting."

I felt something in my chest shift slightly. Daniel paused before continuing, his tone steady but deliberate.

"In the book of Proverbs, we're told, 'Hope deferred makes the heart sick, but a longing fulfilled is a tree of life.'"

The verse settled into the room with a quiet kind of weight.

"It's a simple line," he said. "But it acknowledges something we don't always like to admit. Waiting—especially when it involves the heart—can wear on you. Not all at once. Not in ways that are obvious. But slowly."

I let out a breath I hadn't realized I was holding. There had been a time—not long ago—when things with Beau hadn't felt like something I needed to examine. It had existed without analysis. Without the need to define it in precise terms. The kind of connection that felt steady simply because it existed. Now, I found myself noticing the edges of it. Places where certainty used to sit without question.

Daniel's voice softened slightly.

"We tend to think of waiting as passive," he said. "As something we endure. But more often than not, waiting reveals something to us."

I shifted slightly in my seat, my hands tightening together. I wasn't sure I wanted anything revealed—not yet.

"Sometimes," he continued, "we're not waiting for something to begin." There was a brief pause. "We're waiting to understand whether something is meant to continue."

That was the moment that stayed with me. It didn't feel dramatic. It didn't feel like revelation. It felt precise—like a question that had already been forming somewhere beneath the surface—quiet enough that I hadn't been forced to acknowledge it directly.

The service moved forward around me—music rising softly through the room, voices joining together in practiced harmony—but my attention remained fixed on that single idea.

By the time the service ended, the morning had fully settled into place. People moved slowly through the aisles, stopping to talk in small clusters, lingering in a way that suggested no one was in much of a hurry to return to the rest of their week. I remained seated a moment longer than usual, letting the space empty around me before finally standing.

Outside, the air had warmed. The kind of gradual shift that happens without much notice—cool at the start of the morning, softer now, the edges of winter giving way to something less defined. Spring in Nashville never arrived all at once. It unfolded slowly, in increments you only recognized if you were paying attention. I had always been good at noticing small changes. That was, more or less, the foundation of my profession.

The walk back to my apartment felt shorter than it had earlier. Or maybe I was just less aware of it. My mind had settled into a quieter rhythm—not resolved, not even particularly focused, but occupied in a way that made everything else feel slightly distant.

When I stepped inside, my apartment felt exactly as I had left it—still, ordered, unchanged. I set my keys on the counter and glanced, almost instinctively, toward my phone. Nothing. I told myself, again, that it didn't mean anything. Beau had said he'd be traveling most of the week. Fundraisers, meetings, early mornings that turned into late nights. The kind of schedule that didn't leave much room for anything else.

I moved through the rest of the morning the way I usually did—coffee, a brief attempt at reading that didn't quite hold my attention, notes for the week ahead spread across the small table near the window.

Monday morning arrived with the familiar rhythm of campus already in motion by the time I crossed through it. Students moved in clusters between buildings, coffee cups in hand, conversations overlapping in the easy way they tend to when the semester is fully underway.

By the time I reached my classroom, the room was already beginning to fill. I set my notes down on the podium, glancing briefly at the clock before looking out across the seats. A few students were mid-conversation. Others scrolled through their laptops, half-engaged in whatever had their attention before class began.

"Alright," I said, stepping forward as the clock turned. "Let's pick up where we left off."

The lecture moved easily. Reconstruction policy. Federal overreach. The balance between progress and resistance. Familiar material, delivered in a way that required just enough engagement to keep the room attentive without pushing too far into abstraction.

At one point, a student raised a question about political momentum—how quickly it could build, and how quickly it could disappear. I paused for a moment before answering.

"Momentum," I said, "is often mistaken for permanence."

A few students glanced up from their notes.

"It feels stable while you're inside it," I continued. "But history tends to show us that most movements—political or otherwise—are more fragile than they appear in real time."

I let that sit observantly before moving on. It wasn't until later, walking back to my office, that I realized I hadn't been talking only about Reconstruction.

The rest of the day passed in pieces. Office hours. Emails. A late afternoon meeting that ran longer than it needed to. By the time I finally sat down at my desk, the campus had begun to quiet again, the steady pace of the day giving way to something slower.

I reached for my phone—still nothing. I hesitated, then typed out a message: How's Knoxville?

I stared at it for a moment before pressing send. The response came about twenty minutes later.

"Good. Busy. Wish you were here," Beau replied.

I read it twice. It was the kind of message that, a few weeks ago, would have felt easy. Reassuring. Familiar. Now, I found myself noticing what wasn't there. No follow-up. No question in return. It didn't mean anything—or at least, not necessarily.

By Wednesday, the pattern had settled more clearly into place. Messages came, just not always when I expected them. Calls happened, just not always when I was available—or when I had expected them to. Twice, I noticed missed calls from Beau during faculty meetings. Once, I stepped out of a lecture break to call him back, only for it to go unanswered. Later, a text would come through: sorry—got pulled into something. Call you later? Sometimes he did. Sometimes he didn't. None of it felt intentional—there was no moment I could point to. No clear shift in tone. No argument or misunderstanding that explained the change.

That evening settled into a quiet I hadn't planned on. I had intended to work—at least for a few hours—but the paper in front of me had stopped holding my attention somewhere around the second paragraph. The words blurred together in a way that suggested I was reading more out of habit than focus. Eventually, I closed the laptop and leaned back against the couch, letting the silence fill the apartment again.

At some point, without fully deciding to, I drifted—not fully asleep, but that in-between space where thoughts lose structure and time passes without much awareness. The sound of my phone cut through it. I reached for it without checking the screen.

"Hello?" My voice came out slower than I intended.

There was a pause on the other end.

"...Did I wake you up?" Beau asked.

I let out a quiet breath, blinking once as I sat up a little straighter. "Maybe."

He laughed softly. "That sounds like a yes."

"I was resting my eyes," I quipped. I rubbed a hand across my face, trying to shake off the last bit of sleep. "What time is it?"

"Late enough that I should probably apologize for calling."

"You don't have to apologize," I said. And I meant it.

There was a brief silence—comfortable, but not entirely settled.

"I've been meaning to call you all day," he said. "It just... got away from me." He exhaled lightly. "This week's been more than I expected."

"Busy?" I asked.

"Busier than that," he said. "I thought I had a handle on it, but..." He trailed off slightly. "Turns out I didn't."

I shifted, resting my elbow against the back of the couch. "You don't sound surprised."

"I'm not," he admitted. "Just... adjusting."

There was something in his tone that felt more honest than it had earlier in the week. Less divided. Like he'd finally stepped out of the noise, even if only briefly.

"I'm sorry," he added. "For being harder to reach."

The apology caught me slightly off guard. Not because it wasn't warranted, but because he said it directly.

"You don't have to be sorry," I said.

"I do, a little."

I hesitated, then let it go. "It's okay."

Another small pause.

Then—

"I'll be in Nashville this weekend," he said. "Friday and Saturday."

That pulled me a little more fully into the moment.

"Yeah?"

"Yeah," he said. "No travel. No overnight events."

I nodded to myself, even though he couldn't see it.

"That's good."

"It is," he agreed. Then, a little lighter, "And I was hoping you might make some plans for us."

I smiled faintly, the idea settling easily. "What kind of plans?"

"Whatever you want," he said. "Something that doesn't involve a microphone or a donor list."

"That narrows it down," I said before pausing. "Alright, I can manage that."

"I had a feeling you could, Professor."

The nickname landed the way it always did—familiar, grounding.

For a moment, neither of us spoke. The quiet felt full in a way that mimicked a gentle embrace.

"I've missed you," he said. The words were softer this time—less automatic.

"I've missed you too," I replied.

And I had.

That part didn't require analysis.

"I wish it was longer than a couple days," he added.

"Me too."

Another pause.

There was a shift on his end—subtle, but familiar. The kind that suggested the rest of his world was beginning to pull back in.

"I should probably let you get back to sleep," he said.

"I wasn't asleep," I replied.

"Alright," he said, amused. "I believe you."

I leaned my head back against the couch. "Drive safe this week."

"I will."

Another beat.

"Goodnight, Nate."

"Goodnight."

The line clicked softly, and the apartment fell quiet again. For a moment, I stayed where I was, the phone still resting loosely in my hand before setting it down on the table beside me and leaning back, staring at the ceiling. I was looking forward to seeing him—that much was clear. The thought of two uninterrupted days—of time that felt like it belonged to us again—settled into something close to relief.

Still, as the feeling lingered, something else surfaced alongside it: I wished it were longer—not because two days wasn't enough, but because it felt like the kind of time you spend trying to hold onto something rather than simply existing inside it.

My thoughts drifted, almost naturally, toward something I had been avoiding more directly: The fellowship.

It was nearly March, which meant May wasn't far behind. For most of the year, that timeline had existed in the background—something I was aware of, but not actively planning around. The assumption had always been simple enough. Return to Baltimore. Resume the work I had stepped away from. Continue along the path I had already set. But now, the thought didn't land as cleanly as it once had. Not with Beau in Nashville. Not with whatever it was we were still… becoming. I shifted slightly on the couch, my gaze still fixed upward.

Maybe this weekend was the right time to bring it up—not as a decision, just a conversation. The kind that required more than a phone call squeezed between obligations. I closed my eyes again, not fully asleep, but not entirely awake either.

Friday arrived with a steadier sense of anticipation than I had expected. The week had carried its usual rhythm—classes, grading, scattered attempts at writing—but my attention had drifted more than once toward the weekend ahead. Not in a way that disrupted anything. Just enough to notice.

By early afternoon, I had finalized the plans. A private backstage tour of the Grand Ole Opry House at six-thirty. Dinner afterward, somewhere quieter, removed from the noise that tended to follow Beau wherever he went in public. I had chosen the Opry without much hesitation. It wasn't the most obvious choice, but it felt appropriate in a way I didn't need to over-explain. Places like that had a way of holding onto time—I had always understood that.

By the time I arrived that evening, the sun had begun to lower, casting a softer light across the wide expanse of the Opry complex. The building itself stood with a kind of quiet confidence—unassuming at first glance, but carrying a weight that didn't need to be announced.

I stepped up to the entrance and checked my watch: 6:14—early.

I leaned lightly against the railing near the door, watching as a handful of visitors moved in and out of the building. Conversations carried across the open space in fragments— laughter, directions, the low hum of people passing through a place they recognized as significant, even if they couldn't fully articulate why.

I checked my phone—no messages. That didn't concern me. Not yet.

6:21.

I shifted slightly, glancing toward the parking lot before returning my attention to the entrance. A couple walked past me, speaking quietly, their pace unhurried. Somewhere in the distance, a car door shut, followed by the faint echo of footsteps moving across pavement.

6:26.

Close enough now to notice the time with more intention. I reached for my phone, hesitated, then slipped it back into my pocket. Traffic. A delayed exit. Any number of reasonable explanations.

I had learned, over time, that not every delay required interpretation or expanded thought.

Still—

6:30.

I exhaled slowly and pulled my phone out again, pressing his name before I could reconsider.

He answered quickly.

"Hey," he said.

"Hey," I replied. "You close?"

"Yeah," he said. "I'm—" A brief pause. "I'm running a few minutes behind."

"That's fine."

"I'm almost there," he added. "Five, maybe. I'm sorry."

"You're good."

Another small pause.

"I'll be there," he said again.

"I know."

The call ended. I slipped the phone back into my pocket and looked out toward the road again, my attention catching on each set of headlights before moving on.

Five minutes wasn't anything, but I was aware of it—not in a way that felt like frustration. More like adjustment. There had been a time when I wouldn't have checked the time at all.

6:34.

Then—

"Nate."

I turned at the sound of my name. Beau was walking toward me from the far end of the lot, his pace quick enough to suggest he'd made an effort, though not quite rushed. His jacket was unbuttoned, his tie loosened slightly, as if the day hadn't fully let go of him yet.

"Hey," he said, reaching me with a familiar ease.

"Hey," I said, shooting a smile his direction.

He stepped in without hesitation, pulling me into a brief embrace. I felt the warmth of him, the faint scent of whatever cologne he had worn earlier in the day, something steady beneath the lingering edge of movement.

"I'm sorry," he said quietly. "I got held up leaving."

"It's okay," I replied.

He stepped back, his eyes searching my face for a moment, as if measuring whether I meant it.

"You've been waiting long?"

"Not long."

He nodded, though I could tell he was calculating it anyway. Then, as quickly as it had surfaced, the moment passed.

His hand brushed lightly against my arm as he glanced

toward the building. "So," he said, a faint smile returning, "the Opry."

"You sound surprised."

"I am," he admitted. "Didn't expect this to be your pick."

I gestured lightly toward the entrance. "You shouldn't be."

"No?"

"This place is part of the story," I said. "Not just the music. Everything around it."

He studied me for a second, something quieter settling into his expression.

"That sounds about right," he said. "You picking a place because of its historical significance."

"I have a brand to maintain."

He laughed softly. "Of course you do."

Inside, the building carried a different kind of presence. The backstage corridors were narrower than I expected, the walls lined with photographs that stretched across decades—faces captured in moments that had once felt immediate, now preserved as part of something larger. The lighting was warm, almost subdued, giving the space a sense of continuity rather than contrast.

Our guide—a middle-aged man with the practiced cadence of someone who had told these stories many times—walked us through it at an unhurried pace.

"Not a bad choice for date night," he said at one point, glancing between us with a knowing smile.

Beau chuckled. "I'll give him the credit."

"You should," I said.

The guide nodded approvingly. "History is built into this place. You don't get that everywhere."

"That's why we're here," I replied.

We moved through dressing rooms, past small plaques

marking where performers had once stood, waited, prepared. The details were subtle, but they accumulated.

By the time we stepped onto the stage, the space opened in a way that shifted everything. The auditorium stretched out in front of us, row after row of empty seats rising into shadow. Without a crowd, the room felt larger—less contained by energy, more defined by its structure. At the center of the stage sat the circle. A worn piece of wood carried over from the Ryman, embedded into the newer stage as a reminder of where it had all begun. I stepped into it without thinking. Beau followed, glancing down briefly before lifting his gaze toward the empty room.

"You can feel it," he said.

I nodded. "You can."

The guide lingered a few steps back, then spoke.

"Representative Hale," he said, his tone carrying a hint of familiarity, "I've heard from a friend over at the Bluebird that you've got a bit of talent yourself."

Beau shook his head immediately. "I think that's been exaggerated."

"Has it?" the guide replied, already gesturing toward a guitar resting off to the side. "We keep one nearby in case someone wants to test that theory."

Beau glanced at me.

I met his look, a small smile forming. "Your audience is waiting."

He exhaled through a quiet laugh, already stepping toward the guitar. "You're enjoying this."

"Immensely."

I moved down to the front row, taking a seat as he adjusted the strap over his shoulder. For a moment, he stood there, looking out across the empty auditorium. Then he settled his hand along the strings and played the first chord.

It was familiar almost immediately.

"Take Me Home, Country Roads."

He didn't announce it. He didn't need to.

The melody carried easily through the room, the acoustics catching it and holding it in a way that felt fuller than the space suggested.

He started to sing, his voice steady, unforced.

Almost heaven, West Virginia

Blue Ridge Mountains, Shenandoah River

The sound filled the auditorium without strain, each line settling into the quiet like it belonged there. I leaned back slightly in my seat, watching him.

He wasn't performing—not in the way he did at the Bluebird. There was no audience to win over, no expectation beyond the moment itself.

Country roads, take me home

To the place I belong

The lyrics carried something else with them now. Not just nostalgia—something about direction. Belonging. I found myself focusing on that word more than the others: Home.

I hear her voice in the mornin' hour, she calls me

The radio reminds me of my home far away

There was a quiet irony in it I couldn't ignore.

The idea of home had always been simple for me.

Baltimore. Hopkins. The life I had built there with a kind of certainty that didn't require much questioning. I shifted slightly in my seat, my attention returning to him.

Country roads, take me home

To the place I belong

The last line lingered a second longer before the sound settled back into the room. Beau looked out across the auditorium for a moment, then down at the guitar before handing it back to the guide with a small, self-aware smile.

"Well," he said, stepping down from the stage, "that might be a little too on the nose."

I smiled faintly. "You picked it."

"I didn't think it through," he replied.

He glanced at me, something in his expression shifting—amusement, maybe, but quieter than before.

"Don't get used to it."

We stepped back out into the Nashville evening a few minutes later, the air cooler now, the city beginning to lean fully into the night. For a moment, walking side by side toward the car, it felt easy again—familiar.

Dinner was quieter than the rest of the evening had been. The restaurant sat a few blocks removed from the main stretch of downtown—far enough that the noise of Broadway faded into something distant, more suggestion than presence. Inside, the lighting was low and deliberate, the kind that made conversations feel contained. Tables spaced just enough to allow privacy without isolation.

Beau had been there before. I could tell by the way he moved through the space without hesitation, offering a quick greeting to the host before leading us toward a table near the back. It wasn't secluded, but it was positioned in a way that felt intentional—slightly removed from the flow of traffic, angled just enough that we weren't directly in view of the entrance.

"This is nice," I said, settling into the chair across from him.

"It's one of my favorites," he replied. "Or at least it used to be before people started recognizing me more often."

I smiled faintly as a waiter approached, offering menus and a brief introduction before stepping away again. For a few minutes, everything felt familiar. We talked easily—about the

Opry, about the tour, about the small details that had stood out to each of us in ways that didn't require much explanation. Beau recounted a story from earlier in the week about a town hall that had run longer than expected, a voter who had insisted on explaining local zoning policy in unnecessary detail, the kind of moment that was equal parts frustrating and absurd.

I found myself laughing more than I had in days. It felt like us—uncomplicated.

The waiter returned, took our order, and left again. Beau leaned back slightly in his chair, his attention fully on me now in a way that hadn't been consistent all week.

"I missed this," he said.

"So did I."

He nodded once, like that confirmed something he already knew.

"I keep thinking things will slow down," he said. "Then something else gets added."

"That sounds like momentum," I replied.

He smiled faintly. "That sounds like something you'd say in a lecture."

"It probably is."

He studied me for a moment, the look softer now. "You're doing okay with it?"

"With what?"

He gestured vaguely, as if the word itself was too broad to define. "All of this."

I considered the question briefly. "I think so," I said.

That was the honest answer—or at least, the version of it I was willing to offer.

Before he could respond, a voice approached from just behind his shoulder.

"Representative Hale."

Beau turned instinctively, the shift immediate.

A man in his late fifties stood beside the table, well-dressed in the way that suggested both habit and expectation. Another man lingered just behind him, along with a woman who looked between them with polite familiarity.

"Didn't expect to see you here tonight," the first man continued, extending his hand.

Beau stood to meet it without hesitation. "Good to see you," he said easily. "How have you been?"

"Busy," the man replied. "But that's a good thing these days."

They exchanged a few more words—brief, efficient, the kind of conversation that existed more as acknowledgment than substance. The second man nodded along, adding a comment here and there, while the woman offered a polite smile in my direction before returning her attention to Beau.

Then Beau glanced toward me. "This is Nate," he said. "He's teaching at Vanderbilt this year."

The first man turned, his attention shifting with practiced ease. "Professor," he said, extending his hand. "Pleasure."

I stood, returning the gesture. "Likewise."

"Vanderbilt's lucky to have you," he added, the tone carrying the kind of polite enthusiasm that didn't require follow-up.

"Thank you."

He nodded once, then glanced back at Beau.

"Well," he said, "we won't keep you. Just wanted to say we're looking forward to what's ahead."

"Appreciate that," Beau replied.

The man smiled, then added, almost as an afterthought—

"Enjoy the quiet while you've got it."

There was a brief pause.

"It's going to get a lot busier from here."

Beau let out a short, knowing laugh. "That seems to be the theme."

"It is," the man said. "And you're right in the middle of it."

Another round of polite nods followed before the group moved on, their presence dissolving back into the rest of the restaurant as quickly as it had arrived.

Beau sat back down, exhaling lightly.

"Sorry about that," he said.

"It's fine."

He studied my expression briefly, as if trying to read something I hadn't said. I smiled faintly, though something about the interaction lingered. Not the interruption itself—that had been expected. It was the phrasing: Enjoy this quiet while you've got it.

The food arrived a few minutes later, shifting the focus back to the table. For a while, the conversation found its rhythm again. Beau told another story—this one about a donor event that had gone unexpectedly well, followed by a moment where someone had asked him a question he hadn't anticipated. He mimicked the exchange with enough detail that I could picture it clearly, his tone balancing humor with a kind of practiced ease.

I offered updates of my own. The paper. The direction it had taken. A brief anecdote about a student who had attempted to connect Reconstruction policy to modern campaign strategy in a way that was more creative than accurate.

"And how'd you handle that?" Beau asked.

"Carefully," I said. "Encouraged the effort. Corrected the conclusion."

"That sounds diplomatic."

"I'm learning."

He smiled, something lighter returning to his expression. For a moment, it felt steady again. Then the restaurant began to thin. Tables cleared gradually. Conversations softened. The space shifted from full to partial in a way that made everything feel more contained. I took a sip of my drink, setting the glass back down as I glanced toward him.

"There's something I've been meaning to talk to you about," I said.

He looked up immediately, attentive.

"Yeah?"

"It's not—" I paused briefly, recalibrating. "It's nothing urgent. I just—"

His phone vibrated against the table. The sound was small, but it carried. He glanced down instinctively, the shift immediate and automatic.

"I'm sorry," he said, already reaching for it. "I need to take this."

"It's okay."

"I'll be right back."

He stood, stepping away from the table as he answered, his voice lowering as he moved toward the entrance. I watched him go for a moment before looking back down at the table.

The waiter appeared quietly at my side.

"Another bourbon?" he asked.

I hesitated for half a second.

"Yeah," I said. "Please."

He nodded and stepped away. I leaned back slightly in my chair, my gaze drifting toward the window, where the movement of the street outside continued uninterrupted. People passed. Cars moved slowly through the intersection. Beau stood just outside the door now, one hand pressed lightly against his ear, his posture angled in a way that suggested focus.

"I'm sorry," Beau said, sliding back into his seat. "That ran longer than I expected."

"It's alright."

He reached for his drink, taking a quick sip. For a moment, I thought about picking the conversation back up—starting where I had left off. But before I could—

"I need to knock something out tonight," he said. "Campaign stuff."

I paused. "Okay."

"It won't take long," he added quickly. "Just a few videos for donors. Thank-you messages."

I nodded slowly.

"We can head back to your place," he continued. "Finish our drinks there. I can get it done, and then we'll have the rest of the night."

"Yeah," I said. "That works."

"Good," he replied, relief flickering briefly across his expression.

He signaled for the check, the motion efficient, practiced. A few minutes later, we were back outside. The drive back was quieter, though not silent. Music played low through the speakers—something from the radio that neither of us commented on. The city moved around us in the familiar chaos of a Friday night, headlights stretching across the pavement, clusters of people spilling out onto sidewalks near Broadway. Beau sat in the passenger seat, his phone in hand.

I could hear him working through something quietly—notes, phrasing, the occasional line spoken under his breath as he refined it.

"Appreciate your support—" he muttered once, then stopped. "No, that sounds too—"

He typed something, paused, then tried again.

I kept my eyes on the road. The noise of the city filled the space between us, layered over the sound of his voice as he worked. At a stoplight, I glanced briefly in his direction. His focus was elsewhere—not intentionally, just directed.

By the time we reached my apartment, the music had faded into the background entirely. The apartment felt different when we stepped inside. Not physically—the same walls, the same arrangement, the same quiet that had greeted me every night since I moved in. But with Beau there—moving through the space, setting his phone and jacket down on the table—it shifted into something more contained. More aware of itself.

"I'll knock these out quick," he said, already loosening his tie as he moved toward the living room.

"Take your time," I replied.

I stepped into the kitchen, reaching for a glass and the bottle of bourbon I kept near the back of the cabinet. The familiar weight of it in my hand gave me something to focus on. Ice. Pour. The sound settled into the space in a way that felt steadier than my thoughts.

From the living room, Beau's voice carried clearly.

"Hey, this is Beau—wanted to take a second to say thank you for your support. It means a lot to me and to this campaign…"

I leaned against the counter, listening as he recorded another.

"And I'm grateful to have you with us as we build something that matters—" He paused. "No, that sounds—" I heard him exhale, then start again.

I poured the second glass and picked both up, the condensation already forming against my fingers as I stepped back into the living room. Beau had shifted slightly, his phone angled toward him as he adjusted his posture.

"…as we build something that lasts," he finished, nodding once before lowering the phone.

"That one sounded good," I said, setting the glass down beside him.

He glanced up, a quick smile breaking through the focus. "You think so?"

"I'd donate."

"That's reassuring."

I handed him the drink, and he took it with a quiet thanks before leaning back into the couch. For a moment, neither of us spoke. The room settled and the noise of the city outside filtered faintly through the window—distant, but present enough to remind us it was still there.

Beau took a sip, then set the glass down on the table. "Oh—" he said, turning slightly toward me. "You were about to say something earlier. At the restaurant."

I nodded.

"Yeah."

He shifted his attention fully to me now, the phone forgotten for the moment.

"What was it?"

I sat down across from him, resting my forearms lightly against my knees. "My fellowship," I said. "It ends in May."

He nodded once. "Right."

"I hadn't really thought about it much," I continued. "Not in a serious way. I knew it was coming, but it felt… further out than it actually is."

"I always assumed I'd go back to Baltimore," I said. "Back to Hopkins. Pick up where I left off."

Beau watched me carefully, not interrupting.

"But now," I added, "I don't know."

The words sat between us.

"What are you thinking?" he asked.

I hesitated—that was the question I myself had been struggling with lately.

"I don't have a clear answer," I said. "I know I need to decide something. I'm not good at leaving things open-ended."

He smiled faintly. "No, you're not."

"I've had a plan for a long time," I continued. "This is the first time I'm not entirely sure what it is."

Beau leaned back slightly, considering that.

"You've got options," he said. "You could stay here if you wanted to. Vanderbilt would be lucky to keep you."

I let out a quiet breath. "That's part of it," I said. "But it's not the whole thing."

He tilted his head slightly. "What do you mean?"

I looked down at my hands for a moment before answering. "I don't know what I'd be staying for."

The sentence landed softly. Beau didn't respond right away.

"For your work," he said after a moment. "For the department. For everything you've built here this year."

I nodded slowly. "That's part of it."

He studied me more closely now, something in his expression sharpening with attention. "What else?"

I met his eyes. "You." The word hung there. Clear. Uncomplicated.

Beau's expression shifted, not away, but inward. Like he was adjusting to the direction of the conversation.

"Nate—"

"I don't know where I fit in this anymore," I said.

He leaned forward slightly, his tone steady.

"That's not true."

"I'm not saying it as a conclusion," I replied. "I'm saying it because I don't know the answer."

He exhaled, running a hand briefly along the back of his neck. "You fit," he said. "You know you do."

I shook my head faintly. "I fit when we're here," I said. "When it's this. When it's the Bluebird, or tonight, or—" I paused. "When it feels like something we're both in."

"And you think that's changed?"

"I think it's harder now," I said.

He didn't argue that. That, more than anything, confirmed it. I leaned back slightly, letting the words come without forcing them.

"That guy at the restaurant," I said. "What he said."

Beau's expression tightened a fraction. "You mean about things getting busier?"

"Yeah."

He nodded once. "He's not wrong."

"I know." Silence settled between us. "I don't think I'm built for that world," I added.

He looked at me immediately. "What does that mean?"

"I mean this," I said, gesturing lightly between us. "The version of your life that exists outside of this room. The constant movement. The attention. The expectations that come with it."

"That's part of the job," he said.

"I know it is," I replied gently.

"Then what are you saying?"

I held his gaze. "I don't know if I'm someone who fits into that," I said. "Or someone you need there." That landed differently—more directly.

Beau sat back, the weight of it settling in. "That's not what I need," he said.

"I'm not saying it is," I replied. "I'm saying I don't know if

I can be that."

"You don't have to be anything different," he said.

"Don't I?"

He hesitated. That was the moment everything became clearer. Not because he didn't care, but because he didn't have an answer that resolved it—and perhaps neither of us understood what needed to be resolved. The silence that followed wasn't uncomfortable, but it carried weight.

"I don't want to lose this," he said quietly.

"Neither do I." The truth of it sat between us, unguarded. "But I don't know how this works right now," I added. "Or that it can keep working like it is."

He nodded slowly. "I guess I don't either."

Another pause—longer this time.

"Maybe we need some time," he said.

The words came carefully. I considered them—time, not an ending. Not a solution either.

"Maybe we do," I said.

Neither of us moved for a moment. Then Beau stood, crossing the space between us in a few steps. His hand found the side of my face, steady, familiar. The kiss that followed wasn't rushed. It wasn't driven by urgency. It carried something quieter—recognition. I let myself lean into it, my hand resting against his chest, feeling the steady rhythm beneath it. For a moment, everything else receded. No conversation. No questions. Only closeness. We moved toward the bedroom without speaking.

The familiarity of it felt unchanged. The way he touched me. The way I responded. The ease that existed between us when words weren't required. But beneath it—there was awareness. I found myself paying attention to small things: the way his hand lingered longer than usual, the way he exhaled my name like he was trying to hold onto something. I closed my eyes, letting the moment settle around me.

For a long time, I had believed this was something I wouldn't have again. Not like this. Not with someone who made it feel steady—safe. I had found that with him. And now—the thought surfaced before I could stop it. I didn't know if this was something we were holding onto, or something we were already beginning to lose.

Morning came quietly. I woke to the soft movement of Beau getting dressed, the light filtering through the window in pale lines across the floor. I stayed where I was for a moment, watching him. He moved carefully, deliberately, like he didn't want to disturb anything more than necessary.

When he turned, he saw me awake.

"Hey," he said softly.

"Hey."

He stepped closer, leaning down to press a kiss against my forehead. "Take care of yourself, Professor." The words landed gently.

I nodded, my voice slower than usual. "You too."

He lingered for a moment, his hand resting briefly against my arm. Then he stepped back. A few seconds later, the door closed. The apartment fell quiet again.

I stared at the ceiling, the weight of the night settling into something harder to define. The apartment had returned to its familiar stillness, the kind that settled in completely once the door closed behind him. It wasn't unfamiliar. I had lived in it for months. But it felt different now—more defined, somehow. Like the space had been briefly altered and then restored, leaving behind the awareness that something had changed.

I turned my head slightly, looking toward the edge of the bed where he had been standing only minutes before. It would have been easy to assign meaning to the moment—to call it an ending, or the beginning of one. But it didn't feel that clean. If anything, it felt unfinished. Like something that had been paused mid-sentence before deciding how it was supposed to end.

I sat up slowly, resting my hands against the mattress as I let my thoughts settle into place. The question from Sunday morning returned without effort: not whether something had begun—whether it was meant to continue.

I had spent most of my life believing that answers revealed themselves through time—that if you studied something long enough, traced its patterns carefully enough, the outcome would eventually make sense. History worked that way. Causes led to consequences. Movements rose and fell with some degree of explanation, even if it took years to fully understand.

This didn't feel like that. There was no clear turning point to mark. No single moment I could point to and say this is where it changed. Only a series of small shifts. And now—space.

I stood, moving slowly through the apartment, stopping briefly at the window. Nashville was already in motion again. Cars passing. People moving through the morning with purpose. The city continuing forward without pause, as it always did.

I rested my hand lightly against the glass, watching it for a moment. There was a version of my life that still existed somewhere beyond this. Baltimore. Johns Hopkins. A path that had once felt certain enough that I never questioned it. And there was this—something less defined, less structured, but no less real.

I thought about the conversation from the night before— about time, about distance, about the quiet recognition that neither of us had an answer we could hold onto with certainty. Maybe that was what this was. Not an ending. Not even a beginning. A moment in between. Whatever came next, I wasn't sure yet what it would look like.

FIFTEEN

"Loss is not the opposite of love. It is a part of it." — Teju Cole

The last few weeks of March took on a pattern I hadn't planned, but didn't resist. Time moved differently without anything marking it. Days carried forward in sequence—lectures, office hours, reading, writing—each one distinct in structure but similar in feeling. There was a steadiness to it I recognized, even if I hadn't fully returned to it yet.

By the time I noticed the shift, it had already taken hold. My classes continued without interruption. Midterm discussions gave way to broader conversations, students more willing to push ideas than repeat them. I found myself leaning into it more than I had earlier in the semester, letting discussions stretch longer, allowing space for disagreement in a way that felt productive rather than controlled.

It was easier to stay there—in that space. Defined expectations. Clear outcomes. History, at least in the classroom, behaved the way it was supposed to. Outside of it, my time filled in around the edges. I spent more evenings at my desk than I had intended, working through drafts of the paper that had begun to take shape in a way I hadn't anticipated. The argument had shifted somewhere along the way. What started as a study of political momentum had narrowed into something more specific—realignment not as a singular event, but as a process that unfolded gradually, often without recognition from the people living through it.

I wrote most of the sections out of order—a habit formed during my undergraduate studies. The introduction, as usual, remained untouched. There was a kind of clarity required for that part that I hadn't reached yet.

One afternoon, I met with the department chair, Professor Reynolds, to discuss the fellowship. His office overlooked a stretch of campus that was beginning to show signs of early spring—trees just starting to turn, the campus shifting almost imperceptibly from winter into something softer.

"I've read through your latest draft," he said, tapping a printed copy of my paper resting on his desk. "You've refined the argument considerably."

"I've tried to," I replied.

"The distinction you're making—between momentum and realignment—it's a strong one," he continued. "Most people collapse those ideas into the same thing."

"They often look the same while they're happening," I said. "It's easier to identify the difference after the fact."

He nodded, considering that. "Well," he said, "you're asking the right questions. That's usually a good sign."

"I hope so."

He leaned back slightly, folding his hands together. "How's the rest of the fellowship been for you?"

"It's been good," I said. "The department's been welcoming. The students are engaged."

"They are," he agreed. "And they've responded well to you."

I inclined my head slightly. "I've enjoyed the work."

The conversation stayed there. Focused. Professional. Contained within the bounds it was meant to occupy.

When I stepped back outside, the air had warmed enough that I left my jacket unbuttoned as I crossed through campus. Students moved past in small groups, conversations overlapping, the kind of energy that suggested the semester was beginning to narrow toward its final stretch.

I walked a little slower than I needed to. Not for any particular reason. Just to be outside of something structured for a few minutes longer.

One evening, I found myself down by the river. There had been a small acoustic set scheduled—nothing formal, nothing widely advertised. A few local artists, a temporary stage set up near the water, the kind of event that existed more for the people who happened to be there than for anyone who planned around it.

I hadn't intended to stay long. I stood near the edge of the crowd at first, hands in my pockets, listening without fully committing to it. The music carried easily across the water, stripped down in a way that made it feel closer than it was.

At some point, I stopped checking the time. The set shifted between performers, each one bringing something slightly different—some more polished, others less so. It didn't seem to matter. The crowd responded the same way, quiet in the moments that called for it, attentive without being demanding. I stayed through most of it. Not because I was waiting for anything—because I wasn't.

When it ended, people dispersed gradually, conversations picking up again as the music faded out. I remained where I was for a moment longer, looking out across the river as the last of the sound settled into the distance.

There was something uncomplicated about it. No expectation. No interruption. Nothing that required anything from me beyond being there.

As the last week of March settled in, Colt called me from a hospital back in Kentucky. I answered on the first ring.

"Hey—" I started, then stopped.

There was noise behind him—movement, voices, something metallic in the background that echoed slightly. His breathing came through uneven at first, like he had moved quickly to step away from it.

"He's here," Colt said.

For a second, I didn't respond. Then— "Yeah?"

"Yeah," he repeated, and I could hear the shift in his voice now. Not rushed. Not overwhelmed. Something steadier than that. "He's here."

I sat up a little straighter, my hand tightening slightly around the phone. "How's Emily?"

"She's good," he said. "Tired. But good."

"And—" I hesitated. "And him?"

Colt let out a short breath that almost sounded like a laugh.

"He's... small," he said. "I don't know how else to say it."

I smiled faintly. There was a pause, and then—

"You want to see him?"

"Yeah," I said, before he finished the sentence.

The screen shifted as the call moved to video. For a moment, the image blurred, the camera adjusting before it settled.

Colt's face came into view first, closer than usual, his expression different in a way I couldn't immediately name. Then the angle tilted, and I saw Emily in the hospital bed, her hair

pulled back loosely, her expression tired but calm. And then—
The baby. Wrapped tightly, barely moving, his face turned slightly toward the light.

I leaned forward without thinking. "Hey," I said quietly, as if the volume mattered.

Colt adjusted his hold slightly, careful in a way that was almost unfamiliar to watch.

"He's been sleeping," he said. "Mostly."

Emily smiled faintly. "He's already got better timing than his father."

I let out a quiet laugh; my attention still fixed on the small shape in his arms. There was something about it that didn't require interpretation. No complexity. No uncertainty. Only presence.

"What's his name?" I asked.

Colt glanced toward Emily before answering.

"James," he said.

I nodded once. "That's a good name."

For a moment, none of us spoke. The camera shifted again as Colt adjusted his grip, the baby's hand briefly visible against the blanket—small, loosely curled, unmoving.

"You coming down soon?" Colt asked.

I hesitated. "Yeah," I said. "I will." It wasn't a plan yet, but it felt like one.

"Good," he replied. "He should meet his uncle."

I smiled. "I think that's a solid idea."

We stayed on the call a few minutes longer—long enough for the moment to settle into something more than an announcement. When it ended, the screen went dark again, and the apartment returned to its usual quiet.

I set my phone down on the table beside me and leaned back against the couch. For a while, I didn't move. The feeling didn't come all at once. It unfolded gradually, the way most things seemed to lately—without urgency, without demand. It wasn't tied to anything uncertain or unresolved. It didn't ask for clarity or direction. It simply existed.

I thought about Colt—about the way his voice had changed, even in a short conversation. About Emily, steady in a way that didn't require explanation. About the child they had just brought into something that, for them, seemed unquestioned.

Sunday morning arrived with a kind of springtime earnestness. I had set an alarm, though I woke a few minutes before it went off. The light through the window had shifted—softer than it had been a few weeks ago, the kind that suggested the season was changing even if the days themselves hadn't fully caught up to it yet.

Daniel had invited me over before service. Breakfast, he'd said. Nothing formal. Elijah had added that I should come hungry, which I took more seriously.

Their home just a few blocks from the church, tucked into a quieter street that felt removed from the rest of the city without being distant from it. When I knocked, Elijah answered almost immediately.

"Hey—you made it," he said, stepping back.

"I did," I said. "Good to see you."

The kitchen carried the kind of warmth that suggested it had been in use for a while—coffee already made, something on the stove, the low rhythm of a morning that had started before mine.

Daniel looked up from the counter. "Nate."

"Morning."

"Coffee's there," Elijah said, nodding toward the counter. "Food's almost ready."

I poured a cup and took a seat at the small table near the

window. The conversation at first stayed where it was meant to—easy, familiar. Elijah asked about my classes. Daniel mentioned something about the week ahead at the church. I answered, listened, let the rhythm of it settle in. It felt balanced.

A few minutes later, Elijah set a plate down in front of me.

"You'll want to eat before Daniel turns this into a conversation," he said.

"I heard that," Daniel replied.

"That was the intention."

I smiled faintly, picking up my fork. For a while, conversation was light and general. And then—

"How's Beau's campaign going?" Daniel asked. The question landed cleanly.

I set my fork down, my attention settling a little more fully.

"It's going well," I said. "From what I can tell."

Daniel nodded once, waiting.

I exhaled lightly. "We're not… talking right now," I added.

Elijah's expression didn't change, but his posture shifted slightly, his attention sharpening.

"Not talking," he repeated. "Or taking space?"

"Taking space," I said. "Mutually."

Daniel remained quiet, his gaze steady.

"The schedule was getting difficult," I continued. "The campaign, travel, everything that comes with it. It wasn't leaving much room for anything else."

"That sounds right," Elijah said. "That kind of pace doesn't leave much untouched."

"It doesn't," I agreed.

Elijah leaned back slightly in his chair, studying me. "Those are real pressures," he said. "But they're not unusual ones."

I glanced up at him. "What do you mean?"

"I mean," he said, "those are things people work through all the time. Distance. Time. Competing priorities." He paused. "They're difficult," he added. "But they're not necessarily deciding."

I held his gaze for a moment. "I told him I don't think I'm what his life requires," I said.

The words came out more easily than I expected—not rehearsed, not forced, simply whole and honest. Elijah and Daniel exchanged a brief look—not of concern, rather recognition.

Elijah smiled slightly, kindly. "Do you know how Daniel and I met?" he asked.

I shook my head. "Not in detail."

"Most people assume it was something simple," he said. "Same circles. Same expectations. Something that made sense on paper." He glanced toward Daniel, who didn't interrupt. "It wasn't," Elijah continued. "Not even close."

I leaned back slightly, listening.

"I wasn't living the kind of life that aligned neatly with his," he said. "Different priorities. Different pace. Different ideas about what things were supposed to look like."

Daniel smiled faintly. "That's one way to put it."

Elijah returned it briefly before looking back at me.

"I spent a lot of time thinking I wasn't someone he should choose," he said. "Not because of anything he said. Because of what I assumed."

I didn't respond.

"I had a very clear idea of what someone in his position should want," Elijah continued. "And I didn't match it."

"And you decided that for me," Daniel added, his tone calm.

Elijah nodded. "I did."

Daniel leaned forward slightly, resting his forearms on the

table. "It wasn't the reality of how I felt," he said. "It was the reality Elijah had constructed for me."

The room quieted. I looked down briefly at the table, then back up. "It's not the same," I said.

"No?" Elijah asked.

I shook my head slightly. "What Beau is building—it's bigger than that. The expectations. The visibility. It's not—" I paused, searching for the right phrasing. "It's not a life that leaves much room for uncertainty."

"And you see yourself as uncertainty?" Daniel asked with air quotes.

The question landed more directly than I expected. I hesitated. "I don't know if I fit into it," I said.

"That's not what I asked."

I met his eyes.

"No," I said.

"Then what are you saying?" Elijah asked.

I exhaled slowly. "I think I spent a lot of time trying to figure out where I belonged in it," I said. "And the more I tried to define that, the less certain it felt."

Daniel nodded once, like that confirmed something.

"You're trying to map something while you're still inside it," he said.

The phrasing caught my attention.

"What do you mean?"

"You've already told me your work is about realignment," he said. "About how things shift gradually, without people recognizing it at the time."

I held his gaze.

"This isn't different," he continued. "You're expecting clarity from something that hasn't settled yet."

"That doesn't mean it works," I said.

"No," he agreed. "But it does mean you might be asking the wrong question."

Silence followed. Then Elijah spoke again, quieter now. "Can I ask you something?" he said.

I nodded.

"When you told him that—about not being what his life requires—did you believe it?"

I didn't answer immediately. "Yes," I said.

Elijah tilted his head slightly. "Or did you expect it?"

The distinction landed. I looked down briefly, my hand resting against the edge of the table. "I don't know," I said.

Daniel leaned back slightly, his voice calmer now. "When you first came to the church," he said, "we talked about fear."

I looked up at him. "You mentioned something like that before," I said. "In a sermon."

He nodded. "I did." A brief pause. "You weren't in the same place then," he added.

I didn't respond.

"Fear has a way of presenting itself as clarity," he said. "It tells you something is inevitable, even when it isn't."

Elijah picked up his coffee, glancing between us.

"It's efficient," he said. "Saves you from having to find out the hard way."

I let out a quiet breath. "That doesn't mean it's wrong," I said.

"No," Daniel agreed. "But it doesn't mean it's right either." He paused for a sip of coffee. "There's a passage I come back to," he said. "Not because it's easy to accept, but because it challenges that instinct."

I knew what was coming before he said it.

"There is no fear in love," he said. "Perfect love drives out fear."

The words landed differently this time—not unfamiliar, but not abstract either. Daniel didn't continue immediately. He let it sit.

"Fear doesn't always look like avoidance," he added. "Sometimes it looks like certainty. Like deciding something won't work before it has the chance to."

Elijah stood, gathering a few plates from the table.

"For what it's worth," he said, glancing back toward me, "Daniel was wrong about a lot of things when we met."

Daniel raised an eyebrow. "That feels unnecessary."

"It's accurate," Elijah replied. "And I was wrong about most of them, too." He carried the plates toward the sink. "We didn't figure it out all at once," he added. "We stopped trying to decide the outcome before we understood what we were actually building."

The room settled again, and no one rushed to fill it. After a moment, Daniel stood as well.

"We should head to service," he said.

I nodded, though I didn't move immediately. The conversation hadn't resolved anything. It hadn't needed to, but it had shifted something. Not the outcome—the way I understood it.

The apartment was quiet when I got back. I set my keys down and moved toward my desk, the familiar spread of books and marked drafts waiting where I had left them. Red ink in the margins. Sections rewritten more than once without quite settling.

The introduction was still blank. It always was. Beginnings required a kind of clarity I rarely had at the start. It came later— after the argument had taken shape, after something I hadn't understood at first finally revealed itself.

I sat down, pulling the draft closer, but instead of typing, I reached for one of the books beside me. Early maps of the

American West. I flipped determinedly to a marked page. The outlines were confident, even where the knowledge wasn't. Rivers assumed to connect. Distances never measured. Entire regions shaped more by expectation than observation. I rested my hand lightly against the page. It wasn't ignorance—it was assumption. A belief that the terrain would behave the way it was supposed to.

Lewis and Clark had carried maps like these. They had relied on them, at least at first. But what they found didn't follow those lines. Rivers didn't connect. Routes that seemed straightforward required detours, recalculations—adjustments that couldn't be anticipated from a distance. Progress didn't stop—it changed.

I leaned back slightly, my gaze drifting from the page to the blank document in front of me. Political realignment was often understood the same way—as a moment, something visible and defined. But it didn't work like that. Not in real time. Change moved differently. Gradual. Uneven. People didn't decide all at once—they shifted, incrementally, until the pattern only became clear after it had already taken shape.

I tapped my pen lightly against the desk, the sound steady in the quiet. That was the problem with studying something while you were inside it—there was no distance, no clean interpretation. Only fragments.

Old maps, I had written in the margin: useful—until they weren't. I let out a slow breath, my eyes settling again on the blank space at the top of the page. For most of my life, I had trusted patterns. That if something had happened once, it would happen again. That understanding the conditions meant you could anticipate the outcome. It had always made sense to me and it still did. But it wasn't complete.

The maps hadn't been wrong. They had just been incomplete. I looked back at the screen. The cursor blinked once.

Then again. Waiting. The terrain had not changed in a way I could point to—not clearly, not definitively—but I had.

I exhaled slowly, leaning forward as I placed my hands on the keyboard. For a moment, I let them rest there without moving. Then, carefully, I began to type.

> *Political realignment is rarely recognized in the moment it occurs.*

I paused, reading the line once before continuing.

> *It does not begin with a single event, nor does it announce itself with clarity. More often, it unfolds gradually—through small, unremarkable shifts in behavior that, over time, alter the structure beneath them.*

I stopped again. For a moment, I sat back, my eyes moving from the screen to the scattered notes across the desk. Lewis and Clark. Movement before recognition. Understanding after the fact. I leaned back slightly in my chair, letting the connection settle without forcing it further. There were still parts of it I didn't understand. Still questions that didn't have clear answers— that hadn't changed, but something about the way I was looking at it had. Less urgency. Less need to define it before it had taken shape.

I reached for my phone without thinking, unlocking the screen as my thumb moved instinctively to his name. It hovered there for a moment—close enough to act, close enough to undo the space we had both agreed to. I stared at it longer than I meant to. Part of me expected something else to be there. A message I hadn't seen. A missed call. Something that suggested the distance between us had already begun to close on its own. There was nothing.

I let out a slow breath, my thumb resting lightly against the screen. It would have been easy to change that—to call, to check in, to turn the quiet into something more immediate. But I didn't—not because I didn't want to. Because I understood what it meant that he hadn't. He was holding the line we had drawn. Not out of distance—but out of respect. That mattered more than I had expected it to. I lowered the phone back onto the desk, my attention returning to the screen in front of me. Some things needed time before they could be named—before they could be understood.

The introduction remained unfinished, but it had begun. And for now—that was enough.

SIXTEEN

"He began to feel something he had not felt before: the absence of something he had not known he needed." — Sally Rooney

April arrived without much announcement, the edges of spring beginning to take hold. I had fallen back into a rhythm that held without much effort: mornings beginning the same way, evenings ending without much variation. That morning, I let the television run in the background while I moved through the apartment, gathering what I needed for the day. Coffee. Notes. A stack of papers I had told myself I would finish reviewing before my afternoon class.

The news cycled through its usual sequence—local updates, weather, a brief segment on something that sounded more urgent than it was. I wasn't paying close attention, only catching pieces of it as I moved between rooms.

My phone rang just as I reached for my keys. I glanced at the screen.

Marcia.

I answered on the second ring.

"Good morning," I said.

"Well," she replied, "you sound awake."

"I've had coffee."

"That explains it."

I leaned lightly against the counter. "What's going on?"

There was a brief pause on her end, the kind that suggested she already knew the direction of the conversation before she started it.

"Nathaniel," she said, "at some point, I'm going to need to know whether I should be hiring someone."

I exhaled quietly. "I figured this call was coming."

"I've been patient," she said. "More patient than I usually am."

"That's true."

"And I'd like to continue being patient," she added. "But the department has timelines, whether I like them or not."

I nodded, even though she couldn't see it.

"I understand."

Another pause.

"Where are you with it?" she asked.

I glanced toward the television without really seeing it.

"I'm still thinking," I said. "About what makes the most sense."

"For your work," she said.

"Yes."

She let that sit for a moment.

"And?" she added.

I didn't answer immediately. "Can I give you something by the end of the week?" I asked.

There was a quiet exhale on her end.

"Yes," she said. "You can give me something by the end of the week."

"That's fair."

"It is," she replied. "And for what it's worth—"

She stopped.

"What?" I asked.

"I'd like you back," she said, her tone softer now. "But I'd like you to make the right decision more."

I smiled faintly. "I appreciate that."

"I mean it."

"I know."

The television shifted behind me, the tone of the broadcast changing slightly as the segment turned.

"In state politics this morning," the anchor said, "a debate has been scheduled between Republican Senate candidate Montana Jones and Democratic candidate State Representative Beau Hale—"

I stopped moving.

"—set for next Monday at six p.m. Central, right here in Nashville."

The words flooded into the room—grabbing at my attention.

"Next week?" Marcia asked.

I realized she had said something I hadn't fully heard.

"Sorry," I said, my eyes still on the screen. "What was that?"

"I said," she repeated, "end of the week."

"Right."

"You're distracted."

"Just the news," I said.

"Mhm."

I turned slightly, resting my hand against the edge of the counter as the segment continued in the background. A clip of Beau appeared briefly on the screen—mid-sentence, measured, composed in a way that felt both familiar and distant at the same time.

"I'll call you before Friday," I said.

"You'd better," she replied.

"I will."

A pause.

"Take care of yourself," she added.

"You too."

The line went quiet. I didn't move right away. The segment continued for another few seconds before shifting to something else, the image replaced, the tone changing as if nothing of consequence had just passed through it. I reached for the remote and muted the television. I watched the screen a moment longer, the image no longer holding my attention the way it had a few seconds before—the debate. Next week. Here.

Picking up my keys, I turned them once in my hand before slipping them into my pocket. My phone followed, the screen lighting briefly before going dark again. There was no message waiting. I hadn't expected one. It didn't stop the brief pause that followed. Then I exhaled, stepping toward the door. The week had already begun to take shape.

I got to campus earlier than I needed to. The building was quieter at that hour, the usual movement not yet fully underway. A few students moved through the hallways with purpose, but the pace hadn't picked up. It gave the space a kind of stillness I didn't often see during the day.

My classroom was empty when I stepped inside. I set my bag down on the desk, pulling out my notes as I moved toward the board. The outline for the lecture had already taken shape in my head, but writing it out helped settle it—key points, names, dates, the structure I planned to follow once the room filled.

Reconstruction had given way to broader discussions of

political shifts. Realignment—the timing wasn't lost on me. I picked up a marker and began writing across the board, the sound steady in the otherwise quiet room.

A knock came at the door a few minutes later. I turned slightly. Professor Reynolds stepped in, offering a brief nod as he closed the door behind him.

"Hope I'm not interrupting," he said.

"Not at all," I replied. "I've got a few minutes."

He glanced toward the board, then back at me. "I won't take much of your time."

I set the marker down, giving him my full attention.

"I wanted to follow up on our conversation last week," he said. "About your work here."

I nodded once.

"You've made an impression," he continued. "Students have responded well. Faculty too."

"I've appreciated the opportunity," I said.

"And we've appreciated having you," he replied. There was a brief pause, then— "We'd like to offer you a position," he said. "Associate professor. Tenure track."

The words landed cleanly—not unexpected, but not automatic either. I didn't answer right away. He seemed to expect that.

"I know your fellowship runs through May," he added. "There's time. But I wanted you to hear it directly."

I nodded slowly, letting the weight of it settle into something I could actually consider. "I appreciate that," I said.

"Of course."

Another pause.

"I don't need an answer today," he continued. "But I'd like to know where you're leaning."

"I'm thinking seriously about it," I said.

He studied my expression briefly, then nodded.

"That's all I can ask."

He stepped back toward the door, pausing once more before opening it. "For what it's worth," he added, "I think you'd do very well here."

"Thank you."

The door closed quietly behind him. Students began to filter in a few minutes later, the room filling gradually with conversation that softened as they took their seats. Laptops opened. Notebooks came out. The rhythm of the class settling into place before it had even started.

I moved back toward the board, picking up the marker again as the clock edged closer to the hour.

"Alright," I said, turning slightly toward the room. "Let's get started."

The lecture moved easily enough. The material had settled into something I didn't have to think about too deliberately anymore—Reconstruction giving way to broader shifts in political identity, the gradual reorganization of alliances that reshaped the landscape over time. I turned back to the board, writing out a sequence of dates before pausing.

"So," I said, without turning around, "what's the most common mistake people make when they try to identify a realignment as it's happening?"

There was a brief pause. Then—

"They assume it's already finished."

The voice carried easily. Measured, familiar. I knew it before I turned around. A few students shifted in their seats, glancing toward the back of the room. I turned. Beau sat near the center row, one arm resting casually against the back of the chair beside him, his attention fixed forward like he had been there the entire time.

There was the faintest hint of a smile at the edge of his expression. I let the moment settle for half a second.

"Well," I said, setting the marker down on the ledge, "Representative Hale."

A few students turned more fully now, recognition moving through the room in quiet waves.

"That's one way to look at it," I continued.

Beau leaned forward slightly, his tone even. "It's the most common way."

I tilted my head, considering that.

"Or," I replied, "it's the most convenient."

A few students let out a quiet laugh. Beau's expression shifted slightly, more engaged now.

"Convenient how?" he asked.

"It allows people to define it in hindsight," I said. "To assign meaning after the fact instead of recognizing uncertainty while they're inside it."

He nodded once, like he had expected that.

"Which is harder to do," he said.

"Considerably."

The exchange settled into something that felt almost familiar—measured, intentional, controlled. I glanced briefly at the rest of the room.

"Let's not let Representative Hale do all the work for us," I said. "Anyone else?"

The lecture moved forward and I didn't look at him again. At least, not directly—but I was aware of him. The same way I had been the first time.

By the time the class ended, the room emptied quickly. Students gathered their things, conversations picking back up as they filtered out into the hallway. A few lingered to ask questions, then moved on as well. I packed my notes slowly, stacking papers into something resembling order before placing them into my bag.

When I looked up again, he was still there. Seated along the side wall now, his phone in his hand, scrolling through something with the kind of focus that suggested he had been waiting without needing to make it obvious. I zipped my bag and slung it over my shoulder. He looked up. For a moment, neither of us said anything. Then he stood, crossing the room in a few easy steps.

"Professor," he said, a small smile settling in. "That was a solid lecture."

"Thank you," I replied. "I had a strong contributor."

"I try to stay engaged."

"I noticed."

A brief pause.

"I thought you'd be busy," I added. "Debate prep."

"I am," he said. "I will be." He exhaled lightly, his tone shifting just enough to matter. "I thought about calling," he said. "Didn't want to cross the line."

I nodded once. "That idea crossed my mind too."

"I'm in Nashville through next week," he said. "Working out of the district office, getting ready for the debate."

I listened, not interrupting.

"There's a concert down by the river Thursday," he added. "Nothing formal."

I glanced at him.

"I'm familiar."

He nodded once. "Would you want to go?" he asked. "We could get food after. Or before. Or not at all."

I let out a quiet breath, the corner of my mouth lifting slightly despite myself. There was a moment—brief, but noticeable—where I considered it. Not the logistics, rather what it meant. Then—

"I think I'd like that," I said.

Something in Beau's expression settled. "Good," he said. Another pause. "I'll text you," he added.

"I'll be there."

He nodded once, like that was enough. Then he stepped back slightly, giving the space room again.

"I'll let you get to your next class," he said.

"Try not to disrupt too many lectures on your way out," I replied.

"No promises."

I watched him go as the door closed softly behind him a few seconds later. For a moment, I stayed where I was. Then I exhaled, adjusting the strap of my bag before turning toward the hallway.

By the time Thursday evening settled in, the city had shifted into something more open. Spring in Nashville didn't arrive all at once. It moved in gradually—longer evenings, warmer air, the kind of energy that pulled people outside without much effort. Riverfront Park had filled in the way it tended to on nights like that. Music carried easily across the space, blending with conversation, movement, the low hum of a crowd that wasn't in a hurry to be anywhere else.

I changed before heading down. Nothing formal. Something that felt more like myself than anything I might have worn earlier in the week. The walk from where I parked took me along First Avenue, the noise building gradually as I got closer. Food trucks lined one side of the street, lights strung overhead, the smell of something fried mixing with the sharper scent of citrus and ice.

My phone buzzed as I crossed the street.

I'm in line for whiskey lemonades.

I smiled faintly. "Crossing First Ave now," I typed back.

By the time I reached the row of trucks, the line had already formed into something loosely structured. I stepped off to the side, leaning lightly against a metal barrier, scanning the crowd without trying to make it obvious.

He found me before I had the chance to find him.

"Nate."

I turned. Beau stepped out of the line, two plastic cups in hand, condensation already forming along the sides.

"Figured you might need one too," he said, handing one to me.

"I appreciate the assumption." I took a sip, the taste sharper than I expected. "That's strong."

"They don't do subtle here."

For a moment, we stood there, the space between us occupied by the noise of the crowd and the music drifting from the stage.

Then he nodded toward the open area near the side. "Come on," he said. "There's a table over there."

We moved through the crowd without much effort, settling at a picnic table partially shaded by a large umbrella. The band on stage was already midway through their set—something upbeat, easy to listen to without demanding attention.

I leaned back slightly, resting my arm against the table as I looked toward the stage.

"This is a good setup," I said.

"It is," he replied. "Low expectations."

"I tend to prefer those."

"I've noticed."

There was a quiet rhythm to the conversation at first— nothing heavy. Observations about the crowd, the music, the way the city seemed to open up once the weather shifted. Beau mentioned something about the debate prep—longer days, more structure than he preferred. I told him about my classes, the way the semester was starting to narrow toward the end. It felt easy, not forced. The way it had before.

The band shifted into their last song, the tempo slowing slightly as the light began to change overhead. The sky had softened into something quieter, the edges of the day fading without drawing attention to it. When the music ended, the applause came and went quickly, the crowd settling back into conversation almost immediately.

For a moment, neither of us spoke. Then—

"It's good to see you," he said.

I nodded once. "Likewise."

The words didn't need anything added to them. Beau looked down briefly at his drink, then back up.

"You know," he said, "you were wrong."

I tilted my head slightly. "That's a strong way to open."

"I've been thinking about it for a few weeks," he replied.

"That's reassuring."

He exhaled a quiet laugh, then shook his head slightly. "I didn't feel like anything was missing," he said. "Not at first."

I didn't interrupt.

"Things were moving," he continued. "Fast. The campaign, travel, everything stacking on top of itself. It filled the space." He paused. "But when it slowed down—when there was room to actually notice it—" He stopped there for a moment, searching for the right way to finish the thought. "I noticed you weren't there," he said.

I held his gaze, letting it settle before responding. "I thought I was making it easier," I said.

"For who?"

"For you," I replied. "For what you're building."

He shook his head almost immediately. "I never asked you to do that."

"I know."

"Then why did you?"

I looked down briefly at the table, tracing the edge of the cup with my thumb. "I think I let fear do more talking than it should have," I said. The words came more easily than they would have a few weeks ago.

"Fear of what?" he asked.

"That it wouldn't hold," I said. "That at some point, something would shift and I wouldn't fit into it anymore."

He leaned back slightly, studying me. "And you decided that ahead of time."

I nodded once. "Yeah."

He let out a slow breath, his expression steady. "That's not how I see it," he said.

"I know."

"I don't need you to change anything about who you are," he continued. "I don't want that."

I met his eyes. "I need you to be where you are," he added. "With me. Not trying to figure out how you fit into something that's still moving."

The phrasing caught slightly, echoing something I had heard before: mapping something while you're still inside it.

I let out a quiet breath. "I think I understand that better now," I said.

He nodded, like that was enough. "And for what it's worth," he added, a faint smile returning, "you fit just fine."

I shook my head slightly. "I've been wrong before."

"That's one way to put it."

We both smiled at that. The tension that had been there—subtle, but present—began to ease into something steadier.

"So," he said after a moment, shifting slightly in his seat, "are we…?" He didn't finish the sentence—he didn't need to.

I considered it for a moment. "I think we are," I said.

He nodded once, the movement small but certain. "Good."

A new band began setting up on stage, the sound of equipment shifting in the background as the space adjusted around us again. We sat there for a moment, neither of us in a hurry to fill the space. The crowd had settled into something steady—conversation, movement, the low rhythm of the night continuing without much direction.

Beau glanced out toward the stage, then back at me. "I was thinking about that night on the farm," he said. He smiled faintly. "The one by the pond."

I let out a quiet breath, the memory settling in easily.

"Yeah," I said. "I remember."

He nodded once, like he expected that.

"You said something that stuck with me," he added.

"That's concerning."

"It wasn't," he said. "You just didn't think I'd remember it."

I watched him for a moment, mentally replaying Caleb's birthday on the farm trying to remember what I might have said that Beau had held on to.

"I didn't forget about the Peabody."

I looked down briefly at my drink, a small smile pulling at the corner of my mouth before I looked back up at him.

"That was a very specific question," I said.

"You gave a very specific answer."

"I didn't think you were keeping track."

"I was," he said. There was no emphasis behind it—no attempt to make it more than it was. Which, somehow, made it more.

I shook my head slightly. "You said you were planning ahead."

"I was," he said.

I shook my head. "That's a bold assumption."

He smiled faintly. "Maybe," he said. "But the way I see it… what we're doing now—" Beau paused, like he was trying to find the words. "—it doesn't stay in the present very long."

I watched him.

"Give it enough time," he added, "and it turns into something you remember." He paused, focusing his attention on me now. "Something that ends up shaping what comes next."

By the time we made it back to my apartment, the night had settled into something quieter. The noise of the city didn't follow us inside. It lingered somewhere beyond the walls— distant, softened into something that no longer demanded attention.

I set my keys down near the door, glancing back as Beau stepped in behind me. I smiled faintly, moving toward the kitchen. "You want anything?"

"I'm good," he said. "Still working through this lemonade."

I nodded once, pulling a glass from the cabinet before deciding against it and setting it back down again. When I turned back, he had settled onto the couch, one arm resting along the back, his attention moving across the room in a way that felt familiar—observing, taking in details without needing to comment on them.

I moved to sit beside him, close enough that the space between us didn't feel intentional. For a while, neither of us spoke. The television filled the silence—some late-night program I hadn't paid attention to since turning it on, the sound low, more background than content.

Beau shifted slightly, his arm brushing against mine. Not accidental. Not deliberate enough to call attention to. I let my head rest back against the couch, my gaze drifting toward the screen before settling somewhere just beyond it. After a while, he turned slightly toward me.

"You alright?" he asked.

"Yeah," I said. "I am."

He studied me for a second, like he was deciding whether to ask something else—then he didn't. Instead, he reached for my hand, his fingers settling into mine with an ease that felt unchanged.

I looked down briefly, then back up.

"I forgot to mention something earlier," I said.

He glanced at me. "That sounds serious."

"It's not," I replied. "Or maybe it is."

"That's reassuring."

"Vanderbilt offered me a position."

He sat up a little straighter now, the shift immediate. "Yeah?"

"Tenure track," I said.

His expression changed—something like excitement breaking through before he tried to pull it back.

"That's—" He stopped himself, then shook his head slightly. "That's great, Nate. Congrats."

"It is."

"What did you say?" he asked.

"I told them I'd think about it."

"That sounds like you."

I smiled faintly. "I've had some practice."

He nodded, waiting.

"I have thought about it," I added.

He didn't interrupt. Beau simply looked at me, waiting for words to come out of my mouth, but I knew I didn't need to say anything. I just shot a soft smile at him, to which he shot one right back. Beau leaned back into the couch, his arm shifting slightly behind me as I moved closer without thinking. The television continued in the background, the sound blending into the quiet again. After a while, he pressed a light kiss against my temple. I closed my eyes briefly, letting the moment settle the way it was meant to. Morning came slowly.

I woke to the quiet movement of Beau getting ready, the light through the window softer than it had been the night before. The apartment felt still again, but not in the same way it had after he left the last time. There was no absence in it—only space for light to fill.

He stood near the door, adjusting his jacket as I sat up slightly on the couch.

"You heading out?" I asked.

"Yeah," he said. "Debate prep."

"That sounds important."

"That's what they tell me."

I smiled faintly.

He stepped closer, leaning down to press a kiss against my forehead.

"I'll call you later," he said.

"Okay."

He lingered for a second, like he might say something else. He smiled softly instead. The door closed behind him a moment later. I stayed where I was for a few minutes after he left, the quiet of the apartment settling around me again before reaching for my phone.

Marcia's name was still near the top of my recent calls. I pressed it before I could reconsider.

She answered on the third ring.

"That was fast," she said.

"I said I'd call before the end of the week."

"I expected midnight Saturday down to the minute."

"I didn't want to push it."

"That's new."

"I'm evolving."

She let out a quiet laugh. "I'll believe that when I see it."

I leaned back against the couch, my gaze drifting toward the window.

"I've made a decision," I said.

"I assumed you had."

"I'm going to stay," I said. "Vanderbilt."

There was a brief pause on the other end. Then—

"I thought you might," she said.

"You did?"

"I know you," she replied. "At least a little."

I smiled faintly. "I think it's the right move," I said.

"I do too."

Another pause.

"I'm happy for you, Nathaniel," she added. "Even if it means I have to interview PhD students for the next two months."

"I appreciate the sacrifice."

"It's a burden I'll carry."

I let out a quiet breath.

"And for what it's worth," she added, her tone shifting slightly, "I wouldn't want to leave that handsome southern gentleman either."

I shook my head, the smile coming easier now.

"That's not the only reason."

"I didn't say it was. But it's a factor," she added.

We both let that sit for a moment.

"I'll send over the formal details," she said. "Just in case you change your mind."

"I won't."

"I know."

The line went quiet and I set the phone down beside me, leaning back as the morning light filled the room a little more fully. Nothing felt uncertain. There were still things ahead that hadn't taken shape yet. Still moments that would require adjustment, patience, understanding—that hadn't changed. But for the first time in a while, I wasn't trying to resolve them before they arrived. I let the quiet settle around me, the outline of the day beginning to take shape without needing to be forced. And this time—I didn't question where I was.

SEVENTEEN

Beau's campaign office didn't look like the version of politics most people imagined. There were no cameras, no speeches, no polished lines delivered beneath bright lights. Just a long conference table, a scattering of laptops, and the low, steady hum of people trying to decide what could be said—and what couldn't be.

By the time I stepped through the glass doors, the conversation was already underway.

"…I'm not saying we avoid it entirely," a man near the end of the table was saying, his voice measured but firm. "I'm saying we don't anchor ourselves to it. Not like that."

Beau stood at the opposite side of the room, sleeves rolled, one hand resting against the back of a chair. He didn't look angry. If anything, he looked focused in a way I had come to recognize—quietly set in whatever position he had already decided was right.

"If they ask the question," he said, "I'm going to answer it."

A woman seated near the center of the table—Claire, I remembered—exhaled slowly and leaned back in her chair. "No one's saying you shouldn't answer it," she said. "We're saying you need to be careful how you answer it."

Beau's expression didn't change. "Careful usually means vague."

"It means electable," someone else added.

The word hung in the room for a moment.

I paused just inside the doorway, unsure whether to announce myself or slip quietly into the background. It didn't matter. Beau glanced up, noticed me immediately, and the tension in his posture softened.

"Hey," he said.

A few heads turned in my direction. Claire followed his gaze and offered a quick, polite smile.

"Professor," she said. "Good timing."

"I can come back," I replied.

"No," Beau said, almost too quickly. Then, more evenly, "You're fine. We're just… working through something."

"That's one way to put it," Claire muttered.

I stepped further into the room, taking an empty chair along the wall. From there, it was easier to see the shape of the conversation—notes scattered across the table, polling summaries open on multiple screens, a whiteboard covered in phrases that looked like they had been written, erased, and rewritten several times over.

Claire turned back toward Beau. "Let's just walk through it again," she said. "If they ask about wage enforcement and the penalties you've proposed, you pivot to economic growth. You talk about opportunity. You keep it broad."

"And if they ask me directly?" Beau said.

"They will," someone replied.

"Then I answer directly."

Claire pressed her lips together, patient but clearly reaching the edge of it. "Beau, the issue isn't whether you believe it. The issue is how it plays."

"How it plays," he repeated.

"Yes. Because when you start talking about penalties and enforcement, what people hear is regulation. What they hear is risk. Jobs leaving. Businesses shutting down. That's what your opponent is going to lean into."

Beau nodded once, like he understood the argument. "And what do they hear if I don't say anything clearly?" he asked.

"That you're reasonable," the man at the end of the table said. "That you're not trying to upend the entire system."

Beau let out a quiet breath, something just short of a laugh. "I'm not trying to upend anything," he said. "I'm trying to make it work the way people think it already does."

There was a brief pause.

Claire leaned forward, resting her forearms against the table. "And I don't disagree with you," she said. "But there's a difference between what's true and what wins."

The sentence landed heavier than the others.

I felt it before I fully understood why.

Across the room, Beau's gaze shifted—just slightly— before settling on me.

"Alright," he said. "Let me ask you something."

Every head at the table turned again.

I resisted the immediate instinct to deflect. "That feels like a setup," I said.

"Probably is," he replied. "But you're here."

A few people smiled faintly.

Beau gestured lightly toward the table. "You spend your life studying how this stuff plays out over time," he said. "So, tell me—what happens to the people who don't say what they mean when it matters?"

The room went quiet in a different way this time.

Not tense. Not argumentative. Just… waiting.

I leaned back slightly in the chair, considering the question more carefully than I probably needed to. It would have been easy to give him something simple. Something reassuring. Something that fit neatly into the shape of the room.

But that didn't feel like what he was asking for.

"History doesn't tend to remember careful answers," I said finally.

No one interrupted.

"It remembers clarity," I continued. "Not because it's always rewarded in the moment, but because it makes things easier to understand later. You can see what someone stood for. Whether it worked or not is a different question."

Claire tilted her head slightly. "That's a very academic way of saying it doesn't always end well."

"That's fair," I said.

Beau's expression hadn't changed, but I could see the way he was listening now—fully, not just waiting for his turn to speak.

"There are plenty of examples where clarity cost people something," I added. "Elections. Careers. Sometimes more than that."

The room stayed still.

"But," I said, glancing briefly at the whiteboard before looking back at him, "those aren't usually the people we forget."

Silence settled over the table again, but it felt different now. Less like disagreement. More like something shifting into place.

Claire exhaled slowly. "That's not exactly comforting," she said.

"No," I agreed. "It's not."

Beau let out a quiet breath and straightened slightly, his hand still resting against the back of the chair.

"Alright," he said.

It wasn't loud. It wasn't dramatic. But it carried the kind of finality that made it clear the conversation, at least for him, was over.

"If they ask," he said, "I'll answer."

Claire studied him for a moment, weighing whether to push further. Then she shook her head lightly, a small, resigned smile pulling at the corner of her mouth.

"Okay," she said. "Then we make sure you're ready for the fallout."

A few people around the table shifted, already moving on to the next set of notes, the next possible question, the next calculation of risk and response.

But Beau didn't move right away.

For a brief moment, his eyes met mine again.

There was no question in it this time.

Just certainty.

The drive back from the campaign office was quieter than I expected.

Not uncomfortable. Just… settled. The kind of quiet that follows a conversation that hasn't fully finished yet, even if no one says anything more out loud. Nashville moved around us in its usual rhythm—traffic lights changing, headlights stretching across the pavement, the low hum of a city that rarely seemed to pause long enough to notice itself.

Beau rested one hand lightly against the center console, the other on the wheel, his focus somewhere just ahead of us. He didn't turn on the radio. Didn't fill the space with conversation for the sake of it.

I didn't either.

By the time we pulled into the parking lot outside my apartment, the night had settled into something cooler, the early edges of spring softening the air. Beau cut the engine but didn't move right away. For a moment, we both just sat there.

"That was fun," I said finally.

He let out a quiet breath that almost passed for a laugh. "That's one word for it."

"You handled it well."

"I didn't do anything yet."

"No," I said. "But you already decided what you're going to do."

That earned a glance out of him. Brief, but knowing.

"Yeah," he said. "I guess I did."

Inside, the apartment felt the way it always did at the end of a long day—quiet, familiar, just dim enough that it took a second for your eyes to adjust. I dropped my keys onto the counter and shrugged off my jacket while Beau moved toward the kitchen like he'd been there enough times now to know the layout without thinking about it.

"You still have those beers from last week?" he asked, opening the fridge.

"Top shelf."

He grabbed two and set one on the counter in front of me before leaning back against it, twisting the cap off his own.

For a few minutes, neither of us said anything. We didn't need to. The quiet wasn't empty—it carried the weight of everything that had been said earlier, still settling into place.

Beau took a sip before glancing over at me. "You meant what you said in there?" he asked.

I frowned slightly. "About history?"

"About clarity."

I considered the question, turning the bottle slowly between my hands. "Yeah," I said after a moment. "I did."

He nodded once, like that confirmed something he had already suspected.

"Doesn't make it easier," he said.

"No," I agreed. "It doesn't."

Another pause settled between us. Beau set his bottle down on the counter and crossed his arms loosely, his gaze drifting toward the window before returning to me.

"So, what would you do?" he asked.

The question was more direct this time. Not theoretical. Not academic.

I leaned back slightly against the edge of the counter. "That's not really a fair question," I said.

"Why not?"

"Because I don't have to live with the consequences of it."

"You do if I get it wrong."

There wasn't any accusation in it. Just a simple statement of fact.

I let out a quiet breath. "That's not what I meant."

"I know," he said. "But I'm still asking."

For a moment, I thought about giving him something careful. Something balanced. The kind of answer that acknowledged both sides of the argument without committing too strongly to either of them.

But he hadn't asked Claire.

He'd asked me.

"I think…" I started, then stopped, searching for the right way to say it without sounding like I was delivering a lecture. "I think there's a difference between being strategic and being unclear."

He watched me closely now.

"You can choose your words carefully," I continued, "without avoiding what you actually believe. Those aren't the same thing."

Beau tilted his head slightly. "Claire would argue they are."

"Claire's job is to win an election."

"And yours?"

I smiled faintly. "To explain what happens after."

That earned a small laugh out of him, but it didn't break the focus of the moment.

I set my bottle down beside his. "Look," I said, a little more quietly. "If you answer that question honestly, some people aren't going to like it. You already know that."

"Yeah."

"But the people who do hear it—who actually hear it—they'll know exactly where you stand. And that matters more than people think it does."

He didn't respond right away.

The room was still. The kind of still that made even small movements feel noticeable—the shift of his weight against the counter, the faint sound of a car passing outside, the quiet hum of the refrigerator in the corner.

"What if it costs me?" he asked.

The question landed softly, but it carried more weight than anything else he'd said.

I didn't answer immediately.

Because the truth was, it probably would.

"Then it costs you," I said finally.

He held my gaze, searching my expression for hesitation, doubt—maybe a reason to push back.

He didn't find it.

"And you're okay with that?" he asked.

I thought about that for a moment longer than I expected to.

About the campaign. About what it meant. About everything that came with it—visibility, expectation, pressure. The way it had already begun to pull at the edges of our time together.

"I think," I said slowly, "if you start making decisions based on what won't cost you anything, you're probably not making the right ones."

He exhaled through his nose, a quiet, thoughtful sound.

"That's not exactly comforting either," he said.

"No," I said. "It's not supposed to be."

For a moment, neither of us moved.

Then Beau pushed himself off the counter and took a step closer, closing the small space between us in a way that felt instinctive now. Familiar.

"You know," he said, his voice softer, "most people in that room were trying to tell me how to answer the question."

"And I wasn't?"

"You were," he said. "You just didn't sound like you were trying to."

I huffed a quiet laugh. "That's because I don't have to stand on a stage tomorrow night."

"Still," he said, his eyes steady on mine. "It matters."

The words settled somewhere deeper than I expected them to.

For a second, I didn't trust myself to respond without overthinking it. So, I didn't. I just let the moment sit there between us, uncomplicated and clear in a way that felt... rare.

Beau reached past me to grab his bottle again, but his shoulder brushed lightly against mine as he did, the contact brief and casual and somehow more grounding than anything we'd said.

"We should probably get some sleep," he said after a moment. "Big night tomorrow."

"Yeah," I said. "Big night."

He nodded once, but didn't move away right away.

Neither did I.

And for the first time since leaving the campaign office, the tension that had followed us home seemed to settle into something steadier—not gone, not resolved, but understood.

Tomorrow would come whether we were ready for it or not.

At least now, he knew what he was going to say.

The building was louder than I expected.

Not chaotic—controlled—but alive in a way that felt different from anything I'd seen on campus or at the Capitol. Voices layered over one another in low conversations, staffers moving quickly through narrow hallways, the occasional burst of laughter that never quite reached the main room where the debate would take place.

Backstage, everything felt tighter.

More deliberate.

Beau stood near a long folding table, jacket back on now, sleeves no longer rolled. Someone had handed him a stack of notes he clearly hadn't looked at yet. He wasn't pacing. Wasn't rehearsing. Just standing there, one hand resting lightly against the edge of the table, like he was waiting for something to settle.

Or maybe deciding not to.

Claire hovered a few feet away, speaking quietly with another member of the campaign team. I caught fragments of it as I stepped closer—timing, order of questions, a reminder about staying on message. The same conversation from earlier, just…

sharpened.

Beau glanced up when he saw me.

"Hey," he said.

"Hey."

"You made it."

"I said I would."

He smiled faintly, then looked past me toward the curtain that separated us from the stage. The muffled sound of the audience drifted through—hundreds of voices settling into their seats, the low hum of anticipation that builds before something begins.

"You nervous?" I asked.

He shook his head once. "Not really."

"Confident?"

He considered that for a second. "Clear," he said.

That felt more accurate.

A stagehand passed by, offering a quick nod. "Five minutes," she said.

Claire stepped in then, her tone calm but direct. "Last thing," she said, looking between us before settling on Beau. "If it comes up, answer the question—but don't let them box you in. You don't have to carry the whole policy on your back in thirty seconds."

Beau nodded. "I know."

"I'm serious," she added. "You can believe something without overcommitting to specifics on a debate stage."

"I hear you."

She studied him for a moment, like she was trying to decide whether that meant agreement or acknowledgment.

"Alright," she said finally. "Just... be smart."

Beau smiled slightly. "I'll do my best."

Claire exhaled, something between resignation and trust,

then stepped back.

The room quieted a little as someone adjusted the curtain. A thin line of light spilled through the opening, cutting across the floor between us.

"Two minutes."

Beau rolled his shoulders once, then looked back at me.

"This is the part where you give me some last-minute historical wisdom," he said.

I smiled. "I think you've had enough of that for one day."

"Probably."

There was a pause. Not long, but just enough to feel the weight of what was about to happen.

"You'll be fine," I said.

He nodded once. "I know."

And the way he said it didn't sound arrogant.

Just certain.

A staffer stepped forward, gesturing toward the stage. "We're ready."

Beau took a breath, then moved toward the curtain. For a second, he hesitated—just long enough to glance back at me.

"Hey," he said quietly.

"Yeah?"

"If this goes sideways—"

"It won't."

He smiled faintly. "Still."

I held his gaze. "Then at least it'll be honest."

That seemed to settle something in him.

"Yeah," he said. "Yeah, it will."

And then he stepped through the curtain.

From backstage, the debate felt different than it did on television.

Closer. Less polished. You could hear the shift in the room

when someone landed a point—or didn't. The audience wasn't loud, but it wasn't silent either. There were small reactions, subtle movements, the kind of feedback that never quite makes it through a broadcast but changes the way a moment feels in real time.

I stood just off to the side, close enough to see Beau at his podium without being seen myself.

He looked exactly like he always did when he spoke in public—steady, composed, entirely at ease in a way that didn't feel rehearsed. If anything, he seemed more relaxed than he had backstage.

Or maybe just more himself.

The early questions moved predictably.

Economic growth. Infrastructure. Education.

Beau answered the way I expected him to—clear, measured, occasionally pushing back just enough to remind people he wasn't interested in playing entirely safe. His opponent—sharp, practiced—leaned into contrast wherever possible, framing answers in a way that sounded efficient, controlled.

Electable.

For a while, the rhythm held.

Then it shifted.

The moderator glanced down at her notes, then back up at the candidates.

"Representative Hale," she said, "you've proposed stronger enforcement measures for wage and labor standards, including penalties for companies that fail to meet those requirements. Critics argue that approach could drive businesses out of Tennessee and result in job losses. Are you willing to risk economic stability to pursue that agenda?"

There it was.

Even from backstage, I could feel the change in the room.

Not dramatic. Just… sharper. Like everyone leaned in a little without realizing it.

Beau didn't answer right away.

He rested his hands lightly against the sides of the podium, his gaze steady on the moderator for a brief moment before shifting out toward the audience.

And for just a second, I saw it—the choice.

Not whether to answer.

But how.

He glanced down once, briefly, like he was considering the version of the response that had been discussed earlier that day. The safer version. The one that softened the edges.

Then he looked back up.

"I think," he said, his voice even, "we've gotten used to measuring economic success in a way that doesn't actually reflect how people are living."

The room stayed quiet.

"When we talk about growth," he continued, "we talk about numbers. We talk about development. We talk about how many jobs are being created."

He paused, just slightly.

"But we don't always talk about whether those jobs are enough to build a life."

A few heads in the audience shifted. Subtle. But noticeable.

"I've met people across this state who are working full-time," he said, "doing everything they've been told they're supposed to do—and they're still struggling to afford rent, to keep up with bills, to plan for anything beyond the next month."

His voice didn't rise.

It didn't need to.

"So, when you ask if I'm willing to risk economic stability," he went on, "I think the better question is—stable for who?"

The words settled into the room, quiet but firm.

"Because if the system we're protecting only works for some people, then it's not really stable. It's just comfortable for the people it's already working for."

There was a faint murmur now. Not disruptive. Just present.

Beau rested his hands more firmly against the podium.

"I'm not interested in punishing businesses," he said. "I'm interested in making sure that work means something again. That if you show up every day, put in the hours, do what's asked of you—you can actually build a life with it."

He glanced briefly toward his opponent, then back to the audience.

"And if that means we have to rethink what we're calling 'success,' then yeah—I'm willing to have that conversation."

He paused.

Not for effect. Just long enough to let the words land where they would.

"Because people shouldn't have to choose between working hard and getting by," he finished. "That's not the kind of economy we should be defending."

For half a breath, the room held still.

Then the applause began.

It wasn't explosive at first—just a scattered burst from somewhere near the middle rows, as if a few people had decided before anyone else that the answer deserved a response. But it spread quickly after that, rolling outward in a wave of clapping that filled the auditorium with a warmth the earlier questions hadn't managed to stir. A few people even rose halfway from their seats before thinking better of it, smiling as they kept applauding.

From backstage, I felt my own mouth pull into the faintest smile.

Not because I was surprised by what he had said. I wasn't.

But because he had said it exactly the way he needed to.

Grounded. Certain. Without making himself larger than the people he was talking about.

Still, even as the applause carried on, I noticed the places where it didn't reach.

A man near the aisle in the front section sat rigid and unsmiling, his arms folded tightly across his chest. Two rows behind him, a woman leaned toward the person beside her and said something short into his ear without taking her eyes off Beau. Near the back, a few people remained still, their expressions unreadable in the dim light, but their silence felt heavier now against the sound of everyone else.

Support, I was learning, had a sound—so did resentment.

The moderator thanked the audience and guided the room forward, but the energy had shifted in a way that couldn't quite be called back. Beau stood steady behind the podium, one hand resting lightly against its edge, as if he hadn't just altered the temperature of the room. Maybe he hadn't. Maybe he had only named what had already been there. The moment the debate ended, the room seemed to exhale all at once.

From backstage, it was less dramatic than it looked from the audience. No sweeping music, no cinematic finality. Just a shift—chairs scraping lightly against the floor, conversations picking back up in low, immediate bursts, staffers already moving with purpose before the candidates had even stepped away from their podiums.

Beau disappeared from view for a few seconds as the

moderators wrapped, then reemerged through the curtain a moment later.

Claire was already waiting.

"You were clear," she said, handing him a bottle of water before he could even fully step offstage.

"That's one way to put it," Beau replied, twisting the cap.

"It landed," she added quickly. "You could feel it."

"I could."

There was a brief pause. Not tense, exactly. But not entirely settled either.

Claire crossed her arms, glancing past him toward the stage, where the audience was still filtering out in clusters. "We're going to get some pushback on that," she said. "Probably sooner rather than later."

Beau nodded once. "Yeah."

"But," she added, her tone softening just slightly, "you didn't stumble. You didn't hedge. That matters."

He gave her a small smile. "That sounds like a compliment."

"It is," she said. Then, after a beat, "With a warning attached."

A couple of other staffers stepped in then—quick words, a few handshakes, someone already talking about post-debate coverage and morning headlines. The conversation shifted around him, faster now, more logistical, but Beau didn't fully engage with it. Not right away.

Instead, his eyes moved across the room until they found me. I hadn't realized I'd stepped forward until I was already there.

For a second, everything else fell slightly out of focus. The noise, the movement, the quiet urgency of the campaign orbiting around him—it all blurred just enough to feel distant.

"You meant it," I said.

It wasn't a question.

Beau's expression softened, just slightly. "Yeah," he said. "I did."

I nodded once. "It showed."

That earned the faintest hint of a smile.

"Good," he said.

Behind him, Claire was already fielding another question from someone on the team, her voice steady but quick, moving them all forward whether they were ready or not.

Beau glanced back briefly, then returned his attention to me.

"How'd it sound out there?" he asked.

"Like you," I said.

He held my gaze for a second longer than necessary, like he was deciding whether that answer meant what he thought it did.

Then he nodded.

"I'll take that."

A staffer approached, leaning in just enough to be heard without interrupting the moment entirely. "We've got press waiting in the side room," he said. "And Claire wants to regroup in ten."

Beau exhaled quietly. "Of course she does."

"Welcome to the next twelve hours," the staffer replied with a sympathetic grin.

Beau shook his head once, then looked back at me.

"I'll be in and out for a bit," he said. "Don't disappear."

"I won't."

He nodded, then turned, slipping back into the current of people moving around him—questions, cameras, conversations already pulling at his time.

I stepped back toward the edge of the room, watching as

he moved through it.

Confident. Steady. The same quiet certainty he had carried onto the stage still visible in the way he spoke, the way he listened, the way people leaned in when he answered them.

It would have been easy to think the night had gone exactly the way it should have.

In a lot of ways, it had.

Still, as the crowd thinned and the noise shifted from anticipation to reaction, I caught pieces of conversation that didn't carry the same warmth as the applause had.

"…too much, too fast…"

"…easy to say that when you're not the one signing paychecks…"

"…he's going to have a target on his back with that kind of talk…"

The words weren't loud. Most of them weren't even directed at anyone in particular. Just fragments, drifting through the space between people as they made their way out.

But they lingered longer than they should have.

Near the far end of the hallway, a man stood still while others moved around him, his gaze fixed in Beau's direction. Not curious. Not impressed.

Something harder than that.

I looked away after a moment, not wanting to assign meaning where there might not have been any.

Campaigns, I reminded myself, brought out strong opinions. That was the nature of it. Disagreement wasn't unusual.

It was expected.

Across the room, Beau laughed at something one of the reporters said, the sound easy and unguarded, like none of it had touched him at all. Maybe it hadn't—or maybe he had already decided it didn't matter. I watched him for a moment longer, the noise of the room settling into something more distant. Some people had heard what he said and leaned in. Others had heard the same thing and pulled back. And standing there, it was clear that both reactions were going to matter.

EIGHTEEN

"You can't go back and change the beginning, but you can start where you are and change the ending." — C.S. Lewis

The apartment felt different the morning after the debate, though nothing in it had changed. The same light filtered through the blinds. The same low hum of traffic drifted in from the street below. The same stack of papers still sat untouched on the corner of the desk where I'd left them. But the stillness didn't land the same way.

I stood in the kitchen for a moment longer than necessary, coffee cooling slightly in my hand as I stared out the window without really seeing anything in particular. The night before replayed itself in fragments—the stage lights, the question, the brief pause before Beau answered. *Clear.* That was the word he had used—and it had been right.

My phone buzzed lightly against the counter, pulling me out of the thought. A message from Beau:

Headed east this afternoon. Couple stops, then laying

low for a day or two before next swing.

I read it once, then again. A few weeks ago, I would have thought about it differently. Logistics. Timing. Whether it made sense. Whether it fit into the version of my life that existed neatly on paper—lectures, office hours, research deadlines, the quiet predictability I had spent years building for myself. Now, standing there with the morning still settling in around me, none of that felt particularly urgent.

Another message came through before I could respond.

You should come.

I set the phone down on the counter and took a sip of coffee, letting the warmth settle before it faded. Outside, a car rolled slowly past the building, music faintly audible through an open window. Somewhere down the block, a door closed. The city moving, as it always did, without asking if anyone was ready for it.

I glanced back at my phone. There was a version of me— the one that had spent years learning how to avoid uncertainty— that would have typed out a measured response. Something about my schedule. My responsibilities. A promise to try and make it work another time.

Instead, I picked up the phone and typed:

Give me an hour.

The reply came almost immediately:

I'll be ready.

I smiled before I could stop myself. It wasn't a dramatic decision. It didn't feel like one. Just a small instinct. A step slightly outside the pattern I had grown used to following. The kind of choice that, on its own, didn't seem to carry much weight.

The drive east unfolded at an unhurried pace, the kind that makes distance feel less like something to cover and more like something to move through. Nashville receded gradually in the rearview mirror, replaced first by stretches of open highway and then by the soft, rising contours of the landscape as the terrain began to shift. Early spring had started to take hold in the trees lining the road, a thin wash of green spreading through branches that still held traces of winter.

The farther I drove, the less the week seemed to follow me. Emails, lectures, the steady cadence of academic routine—all of it remained where I had left it, suspended without consequence. The air itself felt different as the miles passed, cooler and clearer, carrying a quiet that did not exist in the city.

Beau's message had been brief. An address outside a small town I recognized only vaguely, followed by a single line: Last stop before I disappear for a day. Come find me.

The event was already underway when I arrived. It lacked the scale and polish of the debate the night before, but it carried a different kind of presence—something more grounded, more immediate. A modest crowd gathered outside a community center, campaign signs planted unevenly in the grass, volunteers moving through the space with an ease that suggested familiarity rather than coordination. Conversations overlapped without urgency. People lingered.

Beau stood near the edge of the crowd, sleeves rolled, tie gone, speaking with an older man who gestured broadly as he talked. Beau listened without interruption; his attention fixed in a way that made the exchange feel unhurried despite the movement around them. It was a quieter version of the work he did on stage, stripped of performance, but no less deliberate.

I remained where I was for a moment, watching. This was the part that never made it into headlines or speeches—the steady accumulation of small conversations, each one carrying its own weight, its own expectation of being heard.

Beau's gaze lifted as if he sensed it. When he saw me, the

shift in his expression was immediate, though subtle enough that no one else would have noticed. He said something to the man in front of him, shook his hand, and stepped away.

"Well," he said as he approached, "you made it."

"I said I would."

He smiled, the expression easier now than it had been the night before, and pulled me into a brief embrace. The gesture was natural, unremarkable in a way that no longer needed explanation.

"You didn't rush," he said.

"No."

"Good," he replied. "This part of the state doesn't respond well to that."

I glanced around again, taking in the pace of it—the absence of urgency, the way people seemed content to let conversations unfold without pressing them forward.

"I can see that."

Beau followed my gaze for a moment before nodding toward the building behind him. "Give me a few minutes," he said. "Then we're done here."

"And after that?"

There was a brief pause, the hint of a smile returning.

"After that," he said, "we get to be somewhere no one's asking me questions."

The road narrowed as we left the town behind, winding upward in long, gradual curves that followed the shape of the mountains rather than cutting through them. Houses thinned out, then disappeared entirely, replaced by dense stretches of trees that rose on either side of the road. By the time Beau turned onto a gravel drive that veered off without much warning, the rest of the world felt distant enough to be irrelevant.

The cabin sat back from the road, partially hidden by the trees, its structure simple against the slope of the land. It wasn't large, and it wasn't trying to be. A narrow porch stretched across the front, two worn wooden chairs positioned side by side, angled toward a view that opened out beyond the tree line.

Beau cut the engine and stepped out, the quiet settling in almost immediately once the door closed. There were no passing cars, no voices carrying from nearby buildings, no background noise competing for attention. Only the low movement of wind through the trees and the faint crunch of gravel underfoot.

"It's not much," he said, pulling a small bag from the backseat.

"It doesn't need to be," I replied.

He glanced at me for a moment, then nodded, like that answer confirmed something he hadn't said out loud.

Inside, the cabin was exactly what it appeared to be from the outside—functional, quiet, and removed from anything unnecessary. A small kitchen opened into a living space with a single couch and a stone fireplace. The windows were wide enough to let in the late afternoon light, framing the trees instead of competing with them. There was nothing about it that asked for attention, and because of that, everything felt settled.

Beau set his bag near the door. "Campaign perk," he said. "Donor owns it. Let's us use it when we're out this way."

"I can see why."

I moved further into the room, running my hand lightly along the back of the couch before stopping near the window. The stillness wasn't empty—it felt intentional, like the space had been built to hold quiet rather than fill it.

Beau crossed into the kitchen and opened a cabinet without hesitation. "I think there's something to drink in here," he said. "Or at least something that used to be."

"That's a risk I'm willing to take."

He glanced over his shoulder with a faint smile before

pulling out two glasses and a bottle that looked like it had been left behind by someone more prepared than either of us. He poured without measuring and set one of the glasses on the counter.

I stepped closer, taking it, leaning back lightly against the edge of the counter. The conversation came easily after that, but without urgency—small observations, passing thoughts, nothing that needed to be carried further than the moment it belonged to.

Outside, the light began to shift, the sun lowering behind the ridge and stretching shadows through the trees. Beau nodded toward the door. "Come on," he said. "You should see it before it gets dark."

The porch faced west, opening out toward a view that extended farther than I expected. The mountains layered into one another in muted blues and grays, their edges softened by distance in a way that made them feel almost unreal.

I rested my arms against the railing, letting my gaze follow the horizon as the light changed.

"It's different up here," I said.

Beau stepped beside me, close enough that our shoulders brushed without either of us moving away. "Yeah," he said. "It is."

We stood there without speaking for a while, watching as the last of the daylight settled into the landscape. There wasn't anything to add to it, and neither of us tried.

At some point, I became aware of how quiet my own thoughts were. Not absent—only settled. I wasn't trying to anticipate anything. Not the next week, not the campaign, not where any of this was supposed to lead. The moment didn't feel like something that needed to be understood to be held.

It was enough to be in it.

Beau shifted beside me, turning slightly. When I looked at him, he was already watching me.

"You're quiet," he said.

"I don't think this is something that needs commentary," I replied, nodding toward the horizon.

He followed my gaze for a moment, then nodded once. "Fair."

When he reached for me, it wasn't hesitant. His hand found mine first, an easy point of contact that lingered for a moment before closing the space between us. The kiss that followed was unhurried, shaped more by familiarity than discovery, the kind of closeness that comes from knowing rather than searching.

There was nothing to question in it. No need to define it or hold it up against anything outside of itself. The light faded gradually behind us, the mountains slipping into shadow as the evening settled in around the cabin.

By the time we stepped back inside, the last of the light had settled behind the ridge, leaving the cabin in a softer, more contained quiet. Beau moved ahead of me, switching on a single lamp near the couch. The room filled with a warm, low glow that didn't reach every corner, but didn't need to.

He paused near the fireplace, glancing at the stacked wood beside it. "You want a fire?" he asked.

"Feels like the kind of place that expects one," I said.

"That's what I was thinking."

He knelt briefly, setting a few logs in place with the ease of someone who had done it enough times not to think about it. It took a minute, maybe two, before the flame caught and settled into a steady burn. The sound of it filled the space in a way that felt immediate but not intrusive, something steady to sit alongside rather than compete with.

I took a seat on the couch, watching as Beau stood and brushed his hands together before crossing the room. He dropped down beside me, close enough that the space between us felt unnecessary.

For a while, neither of us spoke. The quiet budged again, not the open stillness from outside, but something more contained. The kind that comes at the end of a long day, when there's nothing left to prove or explain.

Beau leaned forward slightly, elbows resting on his knees, his gaze fixed on the fire.

"You know," he said after a moment, "Claire's probably rewriting half of what I said by now."

"That assumes she thinks it needs rewriting."

He glanced at me. "You don't?"

"I think she knows exactly what you said," I replied. "Whether she likes it is a different question."

He let out a quiet breath that passed for a laugh. "Yeah. That sounds right."

The fire shifted, a small crack running through one of the logs as it settled further into the flame.

"I meant it," he said after a moment.

I didn't need to ask what he was referring to. "I know."

"It's easy to say things like that in a room full of people," he continued, his voice steady but lower now. "It's different when you start thinking about what comes after."

"That doesn't make it less true."

"No," he said. "It just makes it heavier."

I watched him for a moment, the way his attention stayed fixed forward even as he spoke, like he was still working through the edges of it.

"You don't seem surprised by that," he added.

"I'm not," I said. "You knew that before you walked out

there."

He turned then, resting his arm along the back of the couch behind me. "Knowing something and feeling it aren't always the same thing."

"That's fair."

The conversation settled there, not unresolved, but complete in a way that didn't require anything further. Beau leaned back, his shoulder pressing lightly against mine, and for a while we let the quiet return without interrupting it.

At some point, the distance between us disappeared without either of us acknowledging when it happened. His hand found mine first, then my shoulder, then closer still, the movement unhurried and familiar. When he kissed me, it carried none of the urgency from earlier in the day, only a steady kind of certainty that didn't need to prove itself.

Time moved differently after that.

Slower. Less defined.

The fire burned lower as the night deepened, the room growing warmer, quieter, until the only sound left was the faint shifting of the logs and the occasional movement against the floorboards. At some point, we moved from the couch without much thought, the transition from one space to another as natural as everything else.

Later, lying beside him, the room dim except for what remained of the fire, I found myself watching the way the light settled across the ceiling, shifting slightly with each movement of the flame.

Beau's hand rested loosely against my side, his breathing steady, even.

"You're thinking again," he said, not opening his eyes.

I let out a muted laugh. "Is it that obvious?"

"Only when you're quiet like this."

I turned slightly, resting my head back against the pillow. "It's not anything complicated."

"That sounds like a lie."

"It's not," I said. "It's… simpler than that."

He opened his eyes then, looking at me without moving.

"I'm not trying to figure anything out," I said. "Not tonight."

That seemed to settle something in him.

"Good," he said.

There was no follow-up question. No push for more explanation. He didn't ask what that meant for tomorrow, or the next week, or anything beyond the space we were in.

He didn't need to.

Neither did I.

The fire burned down to embers sometime after that, the last of the light fading gradually until the room slipped into darkness. The quiet remained, steady and uninterrupted, holding its place as the night settled fully around us.

I woke before he did.

The room had cooled overnight, the last of the fire reduced to ash in the hearth, a faint trace of smoke lingering in the air. Early light filtered through the window in thin, pale lines that stretched across the floor and up the opposite wall. I stayed where I was for a moment, watching the way it settled into the room, slow and unobtrusive, as if it had always belonged there.

Beau hadn't moved. One arm still rested where it had been, his breathing steady, undisturbed. There was a time when I would have tried to name a moment like that—assign meaning to it, decide what it was supposed to represent and where it might lead. That instinct didn't feel present now. The moment didn't ask for anything beyond attention—even that felt optional.

I slipped out of bed carefully and crossed the room

without waking him. The floorboards shifted lightly underfoot as I moved toward the kitchen, the quiet of the cabin holding in a way that made even small movements feel deliberate. By the time I stepped onto the porch with a mug of coffee, the air had settled into the cool edge of morning, the landscape still working its way into focus.

A thin layer of fog hung low between the ridges, softening the distance and muting the edges of the mountains. The world felt suspended in that early hour, not fully awake, not entirely still, as if it had paused somewhere between the two.

Behind me, the door opened.

"You disappeared," Beau said, his voice still rough with sleep.

"I didn't go far."

He stepped out beside me and leaned against the railing, his shoulder brushing mine in the same easy way it had the night before. We stood there without speaking for a while, the quiet holding without effort, the kind that didn't ask to be filled.

"This almost makes me forget what day it is," he said after a moment, glancing out over the horizon.

"Almost?"

He nodded, his attention lingering on the mountains before shifting back toward the cabin. "Give it a minute."

I followed his gaze briefly, then returned to the view. "How long do you get before it catches up?"

"Not long," he said. "There's a stop in town late this afternoon, then Knoxville tomorrow. After that, more of the same."

The answer didn't feel heavy. It didn't need to be. It was simply what came next, stated without resistance or emphasis, as if acknowledging it was enough.

We finished our coffee in the same quiet we had started it

in, letting the morning move around us without trying to hold onto it longer than it was meant to last. When we stepped back inside, the shift was immediate. The stillness didn't disappear, but it no longer defined the space.

Beau's phone lit up first, a series of notifications stacking on top of one another before he had even set his mug down. He glanced at the screen once, then again, his expression changing in small, nearly imperceptible ways as he scrolled.

"Claire?" I asked.

"Yeah," he said, already moving toward the living area. "And about five other people."

He answered one call, then another, pacing once across the room before stopping near the window. His voice stayed even, controlled, but the rhythm had changed—shorter responses, more listening, the kind of focus that pulled him back into a world that didn't exist in the quiet of the cabin.

I stayed where I was, watching as the space adjusted around him. The room hadn't changed, but the way it was being used had, the stillness replaced by a kind of forward motion that didn't need to be visible to be felt.

After a few minutes, he ended the call and set the phone down on the table, though it didn't stay there long before lighting up again.

"Everything alright?" I asked.

He nodded once, picking the phone back up, scanning another message before setting it down again. "Yeah. Last night got more traction than they expected."

"That's not a bad thing."

"No," he agreed, leaning back slightly against the edge of the table. "It's not. There's been some noise that comes with it."

"What kind of noise?"

He considered the question for a moment, as if deciding

how much of it was worth repeating. "Online, mostly. People pushing back. Some of it a little more pointed than usual. Enough that Claire's already talking about adjusting security for the next few events."

The words settled into the room with a weight that hadn't been there a moment before, quiet but unmistakable.

"And you?" I asked. "What do you think?"

He met my gaze, steady, unchanged. "I think it comes with the job," he said. "You say something clearly, people are going to react to it. We'll take the precautions we need to—make sure everything's where it should be. That part's manageable."

"And the rest of it?"

He held my gaze for a second longer before answering. "The rest of it doesn't change anything."

There was no hesitation in it. No edge of defensiveness or doubt. It landed the same way his answer had the night before— calm, certain, already decided.

"Of course it doesn't," I said.

A small smile crossed his face, brief but genuine, before his attention shifted back to the phone as it lit up again. He picked it up and stepped away, already moving back into the rhythm of whatever came next.

I stepped out onto the porch once more, letting the cooler air settle in around me as the morning carried on without interruption. The fog had begun to lift, the mountains emerging in a rising symmetry, their peaks appearing with a sudden, quiet deliberation.

Inside, Beau's voice carried faintly through the open door, steady and assured, answering questions that didn't seem to have simple answers. The peace hadn't disappeared—it had thinned, making room for something else.

NINETEEN

"There's always been a rainbow hanging over your head." — Kacey Musgraves

Back in Nashville, the apartment was tranquil the way it usually was on weekday afternoons—the kind of peace that came from routine rather than environment. Papers were spread across the coffee table in front of me, a red pen resting loosely in my hand as I worked through a stack of drafts that had begun to blur together somewhere around the third page. I had read the same paragraph twice without retaining any of it.

From the other room, Beau's voice carried just enough to register, low and steady, the cadence familiar even when the words themselves were not. He had taken the call a few minutes earlier, stepping into the bedroom without much explanation beyond a brief glance in my direction.

I hadn't thought much of it at the time.

Now, something in the tone had shifted.

"…I understand," he was saying. A pause. "No, I hear you."

I set the pen down on the table, not because I had decided

to stop working, but because the words in front of me had stopped making sense.

Another pause.

Then, quieter, more measured: "How credible?"

The question landed differently.

I leaned back slightly, my attention no longer on the papers in front of me. The conversation continued, Beau's voice still controlled, still even, but there was a weight to it that hadn't been there when the call started.

"Alright," he said after a moment. "And you're coordinating with local?"

A longer pause this time.

"Yeah," he added, almost as an afterthought. "We'll be there."

The room fell quiet again.

Not immediately—there was the faint sound of movement, the shift of something being set down, a hand brushing against fabric—but then the silence held in a way that felt more deliberate than it had been before.

I didn't move.

A few seconds passed before Beau stepped back into the living room, his phone still in his hand, his expression composed in a way that would have looked unremarkable if I hadn't been listening for the change.

"Everything alright?" I asked.

He nodded once, already crossing toward the kitchen. "Yeah," he said. "Just logistics."

"That didn't sound like logistics."

He glanced over his shoulder, a faint smile pulling at the corner of his mouth. "You've started analyzing tone now?"

"It's kind of what I do."

"That explains a lot."

He set the phone down on the counter, then leaned back against it, arms crossing loosely. For a moment, it looked like he might leave it there—let the conversation pass without expanding on it.

He didn't.

"Sheriff's office in Clarksville," he said. "They flagged some chatter around the event later this week."

"What kind of chatter?"

He shrugged, but it wasn't dismissive. More like he had already sorted through it once and didn't feel the need to do it again out loud. "Online stuff. Messages. Nothing specific enough to act on, but enough that they wanted to make contact."

"And?"

"And they'll have a presence there," he said. "Coordinate with our team. Make sure things are covered."

The explanation was clean and measured. It fit neatly into the kind of language designed to keep situations from expanding beyond their edges.

"And you're fine with that?" I asked.

He met my gaze without hesitation. "It's not unusual," he said. "You say something clearly, people respond. Some of them louder than others."

"That's one way to put it."

"It's the accurate way."

I studied him for a moment, the steadiness of it, the lack of visible concern. It wasn't that he was ignoring it. He had already accounted for it, filed it into a category that didn't require anything more than attention.

"You don't think it's worth reconsidering?" I asked.

"The event?"

I nodded.

He shook his head. "No," he said. "If anything, it means

people are paying attention."

"That's not always a good thing."

"Maybe not," he replied. "But it's part of it."

There was no edge to it. No defensiveness. Just the same quiet certainty he had carried through the debate, the same sense that the decision had already been made and revisiting it wouldn't change anything.

He pushed off the counter then, crossing back into the room and reaching for the stack of papers on the table.

"You're behind," he said, flipping through the top page. "This is unlike you."

"That's because I've read the same paragraph three times and still don't know what it says."

"Sounds like a problem."

"It is."

He set the paper back down where he'd found it, his hand lingering there for a second before he looked back at me.

"You'll catch up," he said.

"Eventually."

A small smile crossed his face, brief but familiar.

"Don't overthink it," he added.

I almost laughed at that.

"I'll try," I said.

He nodded once, satisfied enough with the answer, and moved toward the bedroom again, already pulling his attention back to whatever came next.

I watched him go for a moment longer than I needed to. Then I picked the pen back up. The paragraph in front of me hadn't changed.

The following week settled back into something recognizable.

By Monday morning, campus had filled in again, the quiet

of spring break replaced by the usual movement of students crossing the quad, conversations overlapping in the hallways, the steady return of routines that had only paused, not disappeared. It felt as though the days in the mountains had been set slightly apart from everything else, contained in a way that made them easier to revisit than to place.

I was back in the classroom by mid-morning, standing at the front of the lecture hall with a set of notes I had reviewed often enough to rely on without reading. The room gradually quieted as students filtered in, the last few conversations tapering off as the hour began.

"History," I said, once the room had settled, "has a way of flattening decisions that were anything but simple when they were made."

A few students looked up from their laptops.

"We tend to look back and assume outcomes were inevitable," I continued, pacing slowly across the front of the room. "That people knew what they were doing would lead to a particular result. But most of the time, that isn't how it works. Most of the time, decisions are made with incomplete information, competing pressures, and a limited understanding of what comes next."

I paused, letting the thought settle.

"The clarity we assign to those moments usually comes later," I said. "After the fact. Once the consequences are already in place."

The words lingered longer than I expected them to. I moved on without acknowledging it.

After class, I gathered my notes more slowly than usual, stacking papers that didn't require stacking, checking for things I already knew were in place. A couple of students lingered near the front, one of them hesitating before stepping closer.

"You watched the debate, right?" he asked.

"I did."

"What did you think of it?"

"I think he was clear about what he believes," I said.

The student nodded, considering that.

"Yeah," he said. "That's kind of what stood out. Most people don't answer like that."

"No," I replied. "They usually don't."

He lingered a second longer, then gave a small nod and stepped back. The others followed, the room emptying out in its usual, unremarkable way.

Back in my office, the quiet returned in a different form— less open than the cabin, more contained. The walls held the sound in a way that made everything feel closer, more immediate. I sat at my desk and opened my laptop, scanning through emails that had accumulated over the past couple of days.

Most of them required little more than a response.

A few didn't.

I worked through them steadily, the rhythm familiar enough to require little thought. At some point, my phone buzzed against the desk, the name on the screen enough to shift my attention immediately.

Colt.

I answered, leaning back slightly in the chair. "You caught me between emails," I said.

"That sounds about right," he replied. "Figured I'd try my luck."

"Your timing's decent," I said. "What's going on?"

"I was looking at the map this morning," he said. "Clarksville's not far. Close enough that I don't really have a reason not to come down."

"For the event?"

"For the event," he confirmed. "And to see you. Might as well do both at once."

"You don't need to justify it."

"I know," he said. "But it makes it sound like I planned something."

"That would be new."

"Let's not get ahead of ourselves."

There was a brief pause, easy and familiar.

"How've you been?" he asked.

"Good," I said. "Better, actually."

"Better how?"

I thought about it for a moment. "Less in my own head," I said. "More present."

"That's a change."

"Feels like one."

He let that sit for a second. "You sound different," he said. "In a good way."

"I think it is."

"Good," he replied. "I was hoping it would be."

Another pause, lighter this time.

"So, I'll come down Saturday," he added. "We'll find somewhere after, catch up properly."

"Alright," I said. "Text me when you get close."

"I will."

We hung up without needing to stretch the conversation any further.

The office felt quieter after that, though nothing about it had changed. I closed the laptop and leaned back in the chair for a moment before reaching for the stack of papers again.

By Friday, the week had begun to narrow toward the weekend.

Beau called that evening, the sound of his voice carrying

the familiar background noise of a campaign moving around him.

"You still planning on making the trip tomorrow?" he asked.

"Yeah," I said. "Heading out mid-morning. Colt's coming down too."

"That's good," he said. "It'll be nice to actually spend some time with him."

"You've met him."

"Briefly," Beau replied. "That was more of an introduction than anything else."

"That's fair."

"I'll be there most of the day," he continued. "Walkthrough, a couple meetings, then the event."

"Sounds like you're keeping a light schedule."

"Trying something new," he said.

I smiled. "Let me know how that goes."

"Don't hold your breath."

There was a brief pause, not uncomfortable, but aware of itself.

"I'm looking forward to it," he said, more quietly.

"Yeah," I replied. "Me too."

"Drive safe."

"I will."

The call ended without ceremony.

Saturday came quickly after that.

The drive to Clarksville felt shorter than it should have.

The route was familiar enough—long stretches of highway that cut cleanly through the space between Tennessee and Kentucky, the landscape shifting in gradual, almost imperceptible ways as the miles passed. It wasn't a difficult drive, and it didn't demand much attention beyond what was already required to stay on the road. Even so, I found myself checking the time more often than necessary, as if the act of arriving carried more weight than the distance itself.

By the time I reached the outskirts of town, the signs of the event were already visible. Campaign placards lined portions of the road leading in, volunteers stationed at intersections guiding traffic with an efficiency that suggested this was not their first time doing it. The closer I got, the more the movement began to concentrate—cars slowing, people gathering in small clusters, the general shape of something organized taking form.

The venue sat just beyond the main stretch of town, an open space that had been partially sectioned off with temporary barriers and rope lines. It was larger than the stop in the mountains, more structured, more deliberate. There was an energy to it that felt contained but not restrained, the kind of anticipation that builds when people arrive expecting to be part of something rather than simply observe it.

Security was present, though not in a way that drew immediate attention. A few uniformed officers near the perimeter, others positioned closer to the stage, their presence steady but unobtrusive. It didn't feel excessive. It didn't feel alarming. It felt like something that had been accounted for.

Still, I noticed it.

I parked a short distance away and made my way toward the entrance, moving with the flow of people already filtering in. Conversations overlapped as I passed—fragments of recognition, disagreement, curiosity—each one carrying its own version of what the day meant.

Inside the barrier, the space opened up more clearly. The stage had been set at the far end, framed by campaign signage and flanked by staff moving in quiet coordination. Volunteers circulated through the crowd, answering questions, directing people where they needed to go. It was organized, but not rigid.

There was room for movement, for interaction, for the kind of unpredictability that came with people gathering for something they believed in—or at least wanted to understand.

I spotted Beau before he saw me.

He stood near the side of the stage, speaking with two members of his team, his posture relaxed but attentive, the same steady presence he carried into every room. Even at a distance, there was something about the way people oriented themselves around him—subtle, but consistent. Conversations adjusted when he entered them. Attention followed without being asked.

For a moment, I stayed where I was, watching.

There was nothing performative about it. No shift in demeanor depending on who he was speaking to, no visible calculation in the way he moved through the space. The same clarity he carried onto a debate stage, the same ease he brought into quieter conversations—it was all there, intact, unaltered by the setting.

It would have been easy to think that kind of consistency came without effort.

I knew better.

As if he felt it, Beau glanced up, his gaze moving across the crowd before settling on me. The recognition was immediate, the change in his expression small but unmistakable. He said something quick to the people beside him, then stepped away, closing the distance without hesitation.

"You made it," he said, the words carrying a familiarity that didn't need emphasis.

"I said I would."

He stopped in front of me, close enough that the space between us felt unnecessary, his attention settling fully in a way that made the noise around us recede slightly.

"I wasn't sure what your timing would look like," he said.

"Traffic can get unpredictable out here."

"It wasn't bad," I replied. "I got here earlier than I expected."

"Good."

There was a brief pause, not empty, but full in a way that didn't require anything additional to define it. He reached for me without hesitation, his hand settling at my side, grounding in its familiarity before pulling me into a brief, steady embrace.

It was not a dramatic gesture. It didn't need to be.

"You've been here a while?" I asked as we stepped back.

"Most of the morning," he said. "Walkthrough, a couple meetings. The usual."

I nodded, glancing briefly toward the stage before returning my attention to him. "Looks like a bigger crowd than the last stop."

"It is," he said. "Different kind of turnout here."

"Because of the debate?"

"That helped," he replied. "So did everything that came after."

The phrasing was neutral, but it carried enough weight to make the meaning clear.

I studied him for a moment, the steadiness of it, the way he had already absorbed whatever response had followed that night and placed it where it belonged.

"You alright with it?" I asked.

"With the attention?"

I nodded.

He considered the question for a moment, not because he didn't have an answer, but because he was deciding how to frame it.

"I'm alright with what I said," he replied. "The rest of it comes with that."

It wasn't deflection. It wasn't avoidance. It was the same answer he had already given, in different forms, without needing to adjust it for the setting.

Before I could respond, a voice called his name from across the space. One of the staff members gestured toward the stage, a silent reminder of what was coming next.

Beau glanced in that direction, then back at me.

"I've got a few more things to handle before we start," he said. "Don't go anywhere."

"I won't."

He nodded once, as if that settled something, then hesitated for a fraction of a second longer than necessary.

"I'm glad you're here," he added.

The words were simple, but they carried more weight than anything else he had said.

"Me too," I replied.

He held my gaze for a moment longer, then stepped back, already turning toward whatever was waiting for him on the other side of the space.

I watched him go, the movement of the crowd closing in around him as he returned to it, the rhythm of the event continuing without pause.

Around me, the energy of the room built gradually, conversations rising and falling as more people filtered in, the anticipation taking shape in ways that were difficult to name but easy to feel.

Nothing about it suggested anything out of place.

Nothing about it suggested that anything would be different from what it was supposed to be.

And still, there was something in the way the space held itself—something just beneath the surface of it—that refused to settle entirely into that expectation.

I couldn't have said what it was.

Only that I noticed it.

Colt found me before I saw him.

"Figured I'd beat you here," he said, stepping in from the side with the kind of ease that made it seem like he had always been part of the space.

I turned, the familiarity of it settling quickly. "You're early."

"Traffic wasn't bad," he replied. "Either that or I finally planned something right for once."

"That would be new."

"Let's not make a habit of it."

He glanced past me, taking in the layout of the event—the stage, the movement of staff, the clusters of people forming and reforming as more arrived.

"This is bigger than I expected," he said.

"It is," I replied. "More attention after the debate."

He nodded once, as if that confirmed something he had already assumed.

"And he's handling it alright?" Colt asked, his tone casual enough that someone else might not have noticed the intention behind it.

"He is," I said. "Same as he was at Christmas."

Colt let out a faint breath through his nose, something close to agreement. "Yeah," he said.

We stood there for a while, not speaking, the quiet between us shaped more by familiarity than absence. Around us, the event continued to take form—more people arriving, conversations overlapping, the general movement tightening as everything edged closer to beginning.

Colt shifted his weight slightly, crossing his arms as he continued to take it in.

"You look different," he said after a moment.

"You've said that already."

"I know," he replied. "Still true."

I didn't respond to that.

A ripple of movement near the stage pulled our attention forward. Beau had stepped back into view, now flanked by two members of his team, his focus already narrowing toward what was about to begin. Even at a distance, there was a shift in him—not a change, but a sharpening of purpose that seemed to draw everything else into alignment around it.

Colt followed my line of sight.

"He's in it now," he said.

"Yeah."

There wasn't any curiosity in his voice. No need to assess or question. Whatever he had taken from that week at Christmas had stayed with him.

"He was like that then too," Colt added. "Just… smaller room."

I glanced at him, surprised enough by the observation to register it.

"That's a fair way to put it."

Colt nodded once, then looked back toward the stage.

"And you're alright with all of this?" he asked.

The question wasn't about the event.

"I am," I said.

He held my gaze for a second longer, then gave a small nod, like that was enough.

"Good," he said.

The crowd had begun to settle more fully now, people moving closer to the front, conversations tapering into something more focused. The sound shifted with it—not quieter, but more contained, anticipation replacing the loose movement from earlier.

Beau stepped toward the stage, pausing briefly at the base as someone handed him a microphone. He said something to the person beside him, then turned, his gaze moving out across the crowd.

For a moment, it passed over us.

Then it stopped.

The recognition was immediate. Even at that distance, there was no mistaking it—the brief shift in expression, the smallest easing at the edges of something that had been held in place.

Colt noticed it.

"He always finds you," he said.

I didn't answer.

Beau turned back toward the stage a second later, the moment passing without needing to be acknowledged further. The event moved forward, the structure of it taking over where individual interactions left off.

Colt exhaled lightly beside me.

"This is something," he said.

"It is."

Neither of us said anything else.

We didn't need to.

The crowd settled in stages rather than all at once.

Conversations thinned out near the front first, people shifting closer to the stage as if proximity might sharpen what they were about to hear. The movement carried outward from there, small adjustments rippling through the space until the earlier looseness gave way to something more focused. By the time Beau stepped fully into position, the energy had tightened into expectation.

He didn't rush into it.

There was a brief exchange with someone off to the side—final adjustments, a nod, the kind of small coordination that disappears once the microphone is live. Then he turned forward, his attention settling across the crowd in a way that felt deliberate without being rehearsed.

From where I stood, I could see the moment it shifted.

Not in him—he had already been there—but in the room itself. The noise lowered without being asked to, the last few conversations fading out as people oriented themselves toward him.

He began without preamble.

"I know most of you didn't come out here today for a long speech," he said, his voice carrying cleanly across the space. "So, I'll try not to give you one."

A few scattered laughs moved through the crowd, enough to ease the edge without breaking the focus.

"I came out here because I think we've gotten used to accepting things that don't make much sense," he continued. "Not because we agree with them, but because they've been that way long enough that they start to feel normal."

He paused, not for effect, but to let the sentence settle into something people could recognize.

"I've spent the last few weeks talking to people across this part of the state," he said. "And I keep hearing the same thing, over and over again. People are working. They're doing what they're supposed to do. They're showing up, putting in the time, trying to build something steady."

He shifted slightly, his gaze moving across the crowd.

"And still, it doesn't quite add up."

There was no rise in his voice, no push for reaction. The words were steady, measured, offered without pressure.

"You can call that an economic issue," he said. "You can

call it policy. You can call it a lot of different things depending on what you want to focus on."

Another brief pause.

"But at a certain point, it stops being theoretical."

The crowd held.

"It becomes about whether the systems we rely on are actually working for the people they're supposed to serve."

I watched the way people responded—not loudly, not dramatically, but in small shifts of posture, in the way attention settled more firmly rather than drifting. Some nodded. Others stayed still, listening in a way that suggested they were deciding what they thought in real time.

Beau didn't press them.

"I'm not interested in telling anyone that the answer is simple," he said. "It isn't. And anyone who says it is probably hasn't spent much time looking at it closely."

A few quiet reactions moved through the crowd again, more acknowledgment than agreement.

"But I do think we can be honest about what isn't working," he continued. "And I think we can decide whether we're willing to leave it that way just because changing it might be difficult."

He let that sit, not filling the space that followed.

"I'm not asking you to agree with me on everything," he said. "That's not how this works. I am asking you to pay attention. To ask questions. To decide for yourself whether the way things are set up right now is actually serving the people it's supposed to."

There was a clarity to it that didn't rely on volume.

"That's the responsibility," he added. "Not mine. Not yours alone. All of ours."

He stepped back slightly, not as a signal that he was

finished, but as a shift in stance that marked the end of the thought.

The applause came gradually.

It started in pockets, then spread outward, building into something broader without ever tipping into spectacle. There were people who didn't join in, who remained still, their expressions harder to read at a distance. But they were fewer, and they were quieter.

From where I stood, the sound mattered less than the shape of it.

It wasn't unanimous.

It wasn't meant to be.

Beside me, Colt let out a breath that sounded almost like a low whistle.

"He doesn't try to sell it," he said.

"No," I replied. "He doesn't."

"That's why it works."

I didn't answer that.

Beau stepped away from the microphone as someone else moved in to close out the formal part of the event. The structure began to loosen again, the edges of it softening as people shifted from listening to moving, conversations picking back up in smaller clusters.

Onstage, Beau was already being pulled into something else—staff, local organizers, a quick exchange that looked like it would lead into several more.

For a moment, the space felt exactly like it was supposed to.

Ordered. Controlled. Moving forward in a way that made sense.

If there was anything else beneath it, it didn't show itself.

The transition offstage was quieter than I expected.

There was movement, of course—staff stepping in, quick exchanges, someone guiding Beau toward the side—but it lacked the urgency that had filled the space before he spoke. The structure held, but the pressure of it had eased, replaced by something more routine.

I moved closer with Colt as the crowd began to shift, slipping through the edges of it without much resistance. By the time we reached the side of the stage, Beau had already stepped down, his attention briefly pulled in two directions before settling.

He saw me first.

For a moment, everything else seemed to fall slightly out of focus—not gone, but less immediate, less pressing than it had been a second earlier. He closed the distance without hesitation, one hand finding my side as he pulled me into him.

It wasn't quick.

Not drawn out either. Just steady, certain, the kind of contact that didn't need to announce itself to mean something.

"You made it through," I said quietly.

He let out a breath against my shoulder, something that felt closer to release than exhaustion. "I told you I would."

"I know."

He stepped back slightly, his hand still resting where it had been, like neither of us felt any need to move it yet. Then he glanced past me, registering Colt.

"Good to see you," Beau said, extending a hand.

"You too," Colt replied, taking it. "Hell of a crowd."

Beau gave a small nod. "Yeah. Bigger than I expected."

Colt stepped back easily, not lingering in it, the exchange complete without needing anything more.

Beau's attention returned to me, settling in again with the same steadiness.

"You okay?" he asked.

"I should be asking you that."

"You can," he said. "Answer's the same."

I studied him for a moment, the steadiness of it, the way nothing about his expression suggested anything unsettled beneath the surface.

"You were good out there," I said.

He shook his head lightly, not dismissing it, but not fully accepting it either. "I said what I needed to say."

"That's not the same thing."

"It is to me."

There was a quiet in that, not disagreement, but definition.

Behind him, I could see the movement beginning to shift again—people gathering closer to the front of the stage, the rope line taking shape as volunteers guided the flow of the crowd into something more organized.

Beau glanced over his shoulder, tracking it for a second before looking back at me.

"They'll want me out there for a few minutes," he said.

I followed his gaze, then returned to him. "Of course they will."

He hesitated—not visibly, not in a way that anyone else would have noticed, but enough that I felt it in the space between us.

"I won't be long," he added.

"I'm not going anywhere."

That earned the faintest hint of a smile.

"Good," he said.

There was a beat of something unspoken there, something that might have stretched into more if the moment had allowed it to. It didn't.

A staffer approached, speaking quietly but directly.

"They're ready when you are."

Beau nodded once. "Alright."

The staffer stepped back, already turning to coordinate something else.

Beau looked at me again, his hand finally dropping from where it had rested, though the absence of it felt more noticeable than the contact had been.

"Stay close," he said.

"I will."

He held my gaze for a second longer, as if confirming it, then turned toward the rope line, stepping back into the structure of the event without hesitation.

I watched him go, the crowd already beginning to shift toward him, the distance closing quickly as people moved forward with outstretched hands and expectant expressions.

From where we stood, it still looked like it was supposed to.

Like everything was continuing exactly as it should.

The rope line formed quickly.

What had been a loose edge of the crowd tightened into something more defined, volunteers guiding people forward in a slow, steady progression. Hands were already reaching out before Beau had fully stepped into it, voices overlapping in short bursts—names, thanks, brief attempts to hold his attention for a second longer than the moment allowed.

From where I stood, it was difficult to follow any one interaction for long.

Movement kept interrupting the line of sight. Shoulders shifting, people stepping forward, others leaning in from angles that didn't quite align with the structure that had been set. It wasn't disorderly. It just wasn't still.

Beau moved through it easily.

He met each person where they were, offering just enough to make the interaction feel complete before moving on to the next. A handshake held a fraction longer than expected. A brief exchange. A nod that carried acknowledgment without slowing the pace.

It worked because it always had.

Beside me, Colt shifted slightly, adjusting his position to see past the people in front of us.

"You weren't kidding," he said quietly. "They all want a piece of him."

I didn't respond. My attention stayed fixed forward, tracking Beau's movement as best as I could, though it came in pieces more than a continuous line—one moment clear, the next partially obscured, then visible again as the crowd shifted.

A woman stepped forward, gripping his hand with both of hers, saying something I couldn't hear. Beau leaned in slightly, listening, responding with a few words that didn't carry this far. She nodded, stepped back, replaced immediately by someone else.

The rhythm held.

It was predictable in a way that made it easy to stop questioning it.

A few feet to the right, someone moved more abruptly than the rest—not enough to draw immediate attention, but enough to register as different. A shift that didn't quite match the pace of everything around it.

Then something changed.

Not in a way that announced itself. There was no single moment that separated before from after. It was a break in rhythm more than anything else. A disruption that didn't immediately resolve into meaning.

The crowd tightened suddenly, the space compressing in a

way that made it harder to see. A voice rose—not loud enough to carry clearly, but sharp enough to cut through the rest.

Beau disappeared from view. For a second, I thought it was just the movement of people closing in, someone stepping forward too quickly, security adjusting to it. That kind of thing happened. It resolved itself.

This didn't.

The movement didn't return.

Instead, it ruffled again—faster now, less coordinated. Someone stepped back into someone else. A hand came up, not in greeting but in reaction. Another voice, louder this time, though the words still didn't land.

"What—"

I took a step forward without realizing it, then another, trying to find a line of sight that would hold long enough to make sense of what I was seeing.

It didn't.

There were too many bodies between me and where he had been. Too many angles, too much motion. The space refused to resolve into anything clear.

"Hey—"

I didn't know if I said it or someone else did. A surge moved through the crowd, not outward, but inward—people pressing toward something they couldn't fully see, others pulling back at the same time, the two motions colliding in a way that made everything feel briefly unstable.

Security pushed in from the sides, the shift in their movement sharper than anything else around it.

That was when I knew something was wrong.

Not what.

Just that it was.

"Move—"

A hand caught my arm—Colt's—and then released just as quickly as we both tried to push forward at the same time.

"I can't see—" he said, though I wasn't sure if it was to me or to himself.

Neither could I.

For a moment, the crowd parted just enough to offer a fragment—Beau's shoulder, someone's arm across him, another figure moving in close—but it didn't hold long enough to make sense of.

Then it was gone again.

Voices overlapped, louder now, urgency cutting through what had been controlled only seconds earlier. A command from somewhere behind the line. Another from the side. None of it formed into anything I could follow.

I pushed forward again, harder this time, the resistance immediate.

"Let me—"

The words didn't finish.

Someone stepped in front of me, not aggressively, but firmly enough to stop the movement. A hand came up, directing, blocking, holding the line in place as the space beyond it shifted further out of reach.

"Sir, you need to—"

"I'm with—"

It didn't matter.

The words didn't land anywhere that changed what was happening.

Beyond him, the movement had become tighter, more contained. Not calmer—just more controlled in a way that suggested something had already been decided.

I tried to see past him again, to find something that made sense of it, but there was nothing to hold onto.

Only fragments.

Motion.

Sound that didn't resolve into meaning.

And the absence of where Beau had been.

The shift from chaos to control happened without warning.

One moment, the crowd was pressing inward, voices overlapping, movement breaking in too many directions at once. The next, there were hands where there hadn't been before—firm, directive, cutting through the space with a kind of authority that didn't leave room for hesitation.

"Step back—"

"Clear the line—"

"Give us space—"

The words carried differently than everything else had. Not louder, but sharper. Defined.

Someone moved between me and the rope line again, this time not just blocking, but redirecting.

"You need to come with us," he said, already guiding rather than waiting for a response.

"I'm with him," I said, the words landing without impact.

"I know," he replied. "That's why you need to move."

Colt was at my side again, closer now, his hand catching my arm as the crowd shifted around us.

"What's going on?" he asked.

"I don't know."

The answer felt insufficient the moment I said it.

We were moved along the edge of the space, away from the center of it, the noise behind us continuing but no longer surrounding us in the same way. It didn't disappear. It just became less immediate, like something happening at a distance I couldn't measure.

I tried to look back.

It didn't help.

The view was already obstructed—bodies, movement, the same fragments that hadn't resolved before refusing to resolve now. For a second, I thought I saw something—someone being lowered, a flash of color that didn't belong—but it was gone before I could be sure of what it had been.

"Keep moving," the voice said again.

We reached the edge of the secured area, where a cluster of campaign staff had already gathered. Claire stood among them, her posture rigid, her attention fixed somewhere past us, toward the center of the event.

She didn't look at me.

Not at first.

"Where is he?" I asked.

No one answered immediately.

"He's being taken care of," someone said finally, though the words felt like they had been chosen for function rather than meaning.

Taken care of.

It didn't explain anything.

Another voice cut in, more urgent. "We need to get them to the vehicles. Now."

A hand pressed lightly at my back, guiding again. Not forceful, but insistent.

Colt stayed close, matching each step without needing direction.

"They're bringing an ambulance around," someone said behind us. "We'll follow."

Follow.

The word landed, but it didn't settle.

The parking area looked different than it had when I

arrived. Not physically changed, but redefined by movement—people repositioned, vehicles idling where they hadn't been before, doors already open in anticipation of something that had yet to fully arrive.

We were directed toward one of the campaign SUVs.

"Get in," the same voice said.

I didn't remember opening the door.

Only that I was inside, Colt beside me, the space closing in as the door shut with a weight that felt heavier than it should have.

Outside, the movement continued.

A siren cut through the air before the vehicle even started moving.

Not distant.

Close.

Approaching.

I turned toward the sound without thinking, my hand already on the door handle before I realized what I was doing.

"Wait—"

Colt's hand closed over mine, stopping it.

"Just—" he started, then stopped himself, like he didn't have anything better to offer.

The ambulance came into view a second later, moving faster than anything else around it, the lights reflecting off the surrounding cars in sharp, intermittent flashes.

I couldn't see inside.

The back doors were already closed.

Someone moved past the front of our vehicle, speaking quickly to the driver, pointing toward the road.

"Stay with them," I heard. "Don't lose it."

The engine turned over with a low, reluctant thrum that seemed to pull at the sudden silence of the parking lot. The ambulance pulled away first, its lights cutting sharp, rhythmic gashes into the dusk, and we followed—tethered to it by nothing more than the dwindling distance between us. The drive didn't feel like movement; it felt like a suspension of time, the road unspooling beneath us without ever leading anywhere.

I tried to track where we were going—I couldn't. Every turn felt the same as the last.

"How far is the hospital?" Colt asked, his voice lower now, controlled.

"I don't know."

Neither of us said anything after that.

The ambulance didn't slow until it had to.

When it did, it turned sharply into a drive that opened into a wider space—emergency entrance, people already moving before the vehicle had fully stopped.

Our driver pulled in behind it.

The doors opened before I was ready for them to.

"Stay here," someone said.

I was already out of the car.

The ambulance doors swung open ahead of us, a rush of movement following—paramedics, equipment, a shape between them that I couldn't see clearly enough to understand.

I tried to move closer.

A hand stopped me again.

"Give them space."

"I need to—"

"Not right now."

The words held.

Not forcefully.

Just enough.

The stretcher moved quickly, disappearing through the doors before I could catch anything more than fragments—

fabric, motion, something red that didn't belong.

Then it was gone.

The doors closed behind it.

The space outside the entrance settled into something quieter, though the movement hadn't stopped.

We were directed inside.

The shift from outside to inside was immediate—fluorescent lighting, controlled temperature, the sound of footsteps echoing differently against the floor. A waiting area, already partially occupied, though it didn't feel like it belonged to anyone in particular.

"Have a seat," someone said.

I didn't remember sitting down.

Only that I was.

Colt next to me.

His hand still resting on my arm.

Somewhere across the room, the campaign team had gathered, their voices low, contained, forming a separate center of gravity that didn't quite intersect with where we were.

No one said anything to us.

Not yet.

Time did not move the way it was supposed to.

It passed—there was no denying that—but it did so without shape or sequence, each minute folding into the next without distinction. The clock on the wall marked it in steady, measurable increments, but nothing about it felt measurable.

Colt hadn't moved. He sat beside me, one hand resting against my arm in a way that didn't call attention to itself but never fully disappeared either. Every so often, his grip would tighten slightly, then submerge again, as if reminding himself I was still there.

Across the room, the campaign team had gathered into a

loose formation near the far wall. Claire stood at the center of it. She hadn't sat down. Not since we arrived. Her posture remained upright, controlled, her attention fixed somewhere beyond the room itself, as if the act of staying still required more effort than anything else she could have been doing.

A set of doors opened down the hall.

Not the ones we had come through. Further in. More restricted.

The shift was subtle at first. A few heads turned. The low conversations across the room thinned, then stopped.

A doctor stepped through.

There was nothing outwardly remarkable about him—no visible urgency, no sign of distress beyond the kind that belonged to the setting itself. He looked toward the group near the wall, then past them, his gaze moving across the room until it found us.

"Family?" he asked.

The word landed strangely.

Colt's hand tightened again.

I stood before I realized I was doing it.

"Yeah," I said.

The answer came out more certain than it felt.

The doctor nodded once, acknowledging it, then stepped closer—not fully into the space, but near enough that the distance between us no longer felt accidental. Claire moved in beside him, her attention fixed, controlled, waiting.

He spoke.

The words were clear.

I heard them.

But they didn't settle.

They moved through the space without attaching to anything I could hold onto, each sentence complete on its own

and disconnected from the next. I followed the shape of them—
the pauses, the tone, the careful pacing—but not the meaning.

Across from me, Claire didn't respond right away.

She stood there for a moment longer than anyone else, as
if she were waiting for something to be corrected, or clarified, or
taken back.

Then she sat down.

Not slowly. Not carefully. Like whatever had been holding
her upright had simply given way.

The room shifted.

Not all at once. Not in a way that could be named. Just
enough that everything felt slightly out of alignment, like
something fundamental had been removed and nothing had
replaced it.

Beside me, Colt's hand tightened again. I didn't look at
him.

The doctor said something else—I couldn't follow that
either. I stayed where I was, still standing, my attention fixed
somewhere between him and Claire, waiting for something to
resolve into something else. It didn't. No one corrected it. No
one interrupted. There was a terrible stillness to it, as if the world
had forgotten how to turn. Across the hall, the doors had already
closed again. Nothing moved behind them, and they didn't open
again.

I had spent years telling my students that history makes its
sense in hindsight—that meaning comes later, once the outcome
is already fixed in place. Standing there, I understood something I
hadn't before. There is a moment before that—brief,
disorienting—when everything has already changed, and nothing
has caught up to it.

TWENTY

> "Happiness, not in another place but this place…not for another hour, but this hour."
> — Walt Whittman

The room did not change all at once.

It adjusted.

Voices returned in low, uneven fragments, conversations forming in places that had been silent only moments before. Someone crossed the room with purpose. Someone else stopped mid-step, as if unsure where they were meant to go. The shape of it reassembled without ever returning to what it had been.

I sat down at some point. I didn't remember doing it. Colt was still beside me, his hand resting against my arm in the same steady way it had been, though I couldn't have said how long we had been there or how much time had passed since the doctor had spoken.

Across the room, Claire hadn't moved from where she had sat.

People had gathered around her now—closer than before, their voices lowered, contained. Someone crouched slightly to speak to her at eye level. She nodded once, then again, the motion controlled but distant, like she understood without fully engaging.

No one looked in our direction—not directly. The separation wasn't intentional. It was structural. The room had divided itself into centers—family, campaign, everyone else—and we existed somewhere between them without quite belonging to either.

The doors down the hall opened once more—this time, the reaction was immediate. Movement shifted toward it, subtle at first, then more defined. A nurse stepped through, followed by another, both speaking quietly to someone just out of view. The attention in the room narrowed—not in volume, but in focus.

Beau's parents came through a few seconds later. I recognized them before I fully registered why. His mother moved first, her pace measured but unsteady in a way that suggested she was holding it together through effort rather than instinct. His father stayed just behind her, one hand hovering at her back without quite making contact, like he was ready to steady her without interrupting whatever momentum she had. His sister followed, her expression fixed in a way that made it harder to read than either of theirs.

The room shifted again. Claire stood this time, crossing the space between them without hesitation. Whatever distance had existed before disappeared as the two groups met, the quiet of their exchange carrying more weight than anything that had been said out loud earlier.

I didn't move. I watched it happen from where I was, aware of the way the moment belonged to them in a way that it didn't belong to anyone else. Colt's hand tightened slightly against my arm, then settled again.

"They just got here," he said quietly.

I nodded, though I wasn't sure if the motion registered.

Beau's mother said something to Claire—too low to hear, but urgent in its shape. Claire responded immediately, her voice just as quiet, her posture still controlled, though something in it had shifted—less rigid now, less performative.

Beau's father turned slightly, his gaze moving across the room in a way that felt like he was trying to locate something that wasn't visible.

A nurse stepped closer to the group, speaking in a tone that suggested instruction more than explanation. They moved together after that, not quickly, but with purpose, disappearing down the same hallway the doctor had come from.

The doors closed behind them. The room settled again. Not into stillness. Into waiting. I leaned forward slightly, my hands resting against my knees, my attention fixed on the hallway even though there was nothing left to see. It felt like something else should happen next. Another update. Another movement. Something to interrupt the way everything had stopped without actually stopping. Nothing came. Beside me, Colt shifted slightly in his seat.

"You want me to go check?" he asked.

I shook my head. "No." The answer came automatically. He didn't push it.

We stayed where we were. Across the room, the campaign staff had begun to move again—quiet coordination, small conversations that carried the weight of decisions already being made. Phones came out. Someone stepped toward the exit. Another followed.

The world outside the room was already moving forward.

Inside, it hadn't caught up. I sat there, watching the hallway, waiting for something that didn't seem to know it was supposed to come. The noise followed us back inside, though it changed as soon as the doors closed behind us.

Outside, it had been sharp, pressing forward, layered with questions that didn't wait for answers. Inside, it settled into something lower, more contained, the urgency still present, but no longer spilling over itself. Voices carried down the hallway in fragments, footsteps moving quickly in one direction or another, each person already shifting into whatever came next.

I didn't stop walking. I wasn't sure where I was going, only that standing still no longer felt possible. The hallway stretched out ahead in the same sterile repetition—doors, lights, turns that looked identical no matter how many times you passed them. People moved around us, some purposeful, some uncertain, all of it blending into a kind of motion that didn't require attention to follow.

Colt stayed beside me. He didn't try to direct it. Didn't ask where we were going. Just matched the pace, close enough that I was aware of him without needing to look.

We reached the exit without either of us saying anything. The air outside felt different this time. Cooler, sharper, carrying none of the weight that had settled inside the hospital. The press had shifted further back now, held at a distance by a loose perimeter that hadn't been there before. A few cameras still turned in our direction as we stepped out, but the attention had already begun to scatter, moving toward the next update, the next angle, the next version of the same story.

The campaign vehicles were still parked along the curb. Engines idling. Doors opening and closing as people moved in and out, voices low, purposeful, already organizing what came next in a way that suggested the moment itself had begun to pass, even though nothing about it felt past. I slowed slightly. Colt did the same.

"You heading back?" he asked.

I nodded, though the motion felt disconnected from any

real decision. "Yeah."

"I'll ride with you."

The offer came easily. Naturally.

I shook my head.

"You don't need to."

He didn't respond right away.

"Nate—"

"I'm fine," I said, the words coming out steadier than they felt. "You should get back."

"To what?"

"To the baby," I said, meeting his gaze for the first time since we had stepped outside. "To home. You've got something that still needs you there."

He held my eyes for a second longer, like he was deciding whether to push.

"You don't think I should be here?" he asked.

"I think you've done enough," I replied. "And I appreciate it all."

That wasn't the reason—we both knew it, but it was the one that made sense to say. Colt exhaled slowly, his attention shifting past me for a moment, toward the movement around the vehicles, before returning.

"You sure?" he asked.

I nodded. This time, it felt more like a decision. "Yeah."

He studied me for another second, then gave a small, reluctant nod.

"Alright," he said. "Call me when you get back."

"I will."

"Don't disappear."

"I won't."

He stepped forward then, pulling me into a brief embrace—firm, grounding, the kind that didn't linger but didn't need to.

"Drive safe," he said.

"You too."

He pulled back, his hand landing briefly against my shoulder before dropping away. Then he turned, moving toward his car without looking back. I watched him go until he disappeared into the movement of everything else. For a moment, I stood there, the sounds of the street settling into something distant, less defined. Then I turned in the opposite direction.

The apartment felt unfamiliar when I stepped inside, though nothing about it had changed.

The same books lined the shelves, the same papers sat where I had left them, a stack of drafts still spread across the coffee table in the exact arrangement I had abandoned earlier that week. Even the air carried the same stillness it always had, undisturbed, contained. There was no visible sign that anything had shifted beyond the fact that I had returned.

I closed the door behind me and remained there for a moment, my hand resting against the handle, as if I hadn't fully committed to being inside. The quiet settled quickly, heavier than it should have been, pressing in now that there was nothing left to interrupt it. I found myself waiting for something—a notification, a voice, the sound of movement from another room—but nothing came. There was a defiance in the way the chair stayed angled toward the window, refusing to acknowledge the vacancy.

I moved further in, the steps automatic, guided more by familiarity than intention. The living room opened up in front of me, unchanged and intact, but without the context that had made it feel complete before. The papers on the table caught my attention first, not because they mattered in that moment, but because they were still there, waiting in a way that suggested they expected to be picked back up where I had left off.

I didn't go to them. Instead, I sat down on the edge of the couch, leaning forward slightly, my elbows resting against my knees as the room held itself around me. My phone was already in my hand before I registered picking it up, the screen lighting as I moved it, revealing a list of missed notifications that had accumulated without being answered. Messages, calls, alerts— each one a small indication that time had continued to move somewhere outside of where I had been.

One name stopped me.

Marcia.

The missed call sat there, time-stamped from earlier in the day, from a moment I couldn't clearly place. I tried to remember whether I had seen it and ignored it or simply hadn't noticed at all, but the distinction didn't matter. The call existed either way, waiting in the same way everything else in the room seemed to be.

I pressed it.

The line rang only once before she answered, her voice coming through quickly, tightly controlled in a way that suggested she had been expecting it.

"Nate?"

"Yeah."

There was a brief pause on the other end, not empty, but measured, as if she were deciding how to approach something that didn't have a clear way in.

"I saw it," she said. "On the news."

"I figured you might."

Another pause followed, shorter this time, but heavier.

"Is it true?" she asked.

The question held there, uncertain in a way that made it

feel almost deliberate, like she was allowing space for a different answer even if she didn't expect one.

"Yes."

The word settled between us with more permanence than anything else that had been said.

"I'm so sorry," she said.

"I know."

I leaned back slightly, my gaze drifting across the room without settling on anything in particular. The papers were still there. The room around me was a still-life of a life—lives—interrupted.

"How are you?" she asked.

"I don't know," I said after a moment. "It doesn't feel like anything yet."

She let that sit.

"I wish I were closer," she said. "I'd be there if I could."

"I know you would."

"If you need me, I can stay on the phone," she added. "Or we can just… not talk. Whatever you need."

I considered that for a moment, the quiet of the apartment settling more firmly around me as I did.

"I think I'm alright," I said. "I just… needed to hear your voice."

"I'm here," she said. "As long as you need."

"Thank you."

"Of course."

The call lingered for a moment after that, neither of us speaking, neither of us quite ready to end it. Eventually, the silence became something we both accepted, and the line went quiet.

I lowered the phone and set it down on the table beside me, the motion deliberate, as if placing it somewhere specific mattered more than it did. The moment held its breath, a brief pause in the historical record. I leaned forward again, my hands resting together, my attention drifting briefly back to the papers before slipping away from them just as quickly. The words didn't hold. They didn't connect. They simply existed on the page; separate from anything I could engage with.

When I finally rose, it wasn't a choice so much as a surrender to the weight of the silence; staying put had begun to feel like holding back a tide. As I moved toward the door, the room remained anchored in its own unblinking stasis, a landscape that would endure, perfectly intact, long after I had closed the door.

The air outside had cooled since I'd last stepped into it. It wasn't cold, not in a way that demanded attention, but it carried a sharpness that hadn't been there earlier, something cleaner, less forgiving. The street was quieter than I expected, the usual rhythm of the city still present but muted, as if it had settled into a lower register without fully stopping.

I didn't have a destination in mind.

I just started walking anyway.

The movement came easily, more instinct than decision, my body falling into a pace that didn't require direction. Sidewalks passed beneath me in steady intervals, intersections appearing and disappearing without much distinction between them. I registered the shapes of things—buildings, streetlights, the occasional car passing—but none of it held long enough to become meaningful.

It felt less like going somewhere and more like being carried. Time moved differently out here. Not slower, not faster. Just less defined. The distance between one block and the next blurred together, the repetition of it smoothing out any sense of progression. I could have turned at any point. I didn't.

By the time I realized where I was, I had already stopped.

The Capitol stood in front of me, unabridged, its outline fixed against the darkening sky in a way that felt both familiar and distant at the same time. The steps stretched upward in clean, deliberate lines, the structure itself unmoved by anything that had happened beyond its view.

I hadn't planned to come here.

That was the first clear thought that settled.

The second was that I wasn't surprised I had.

I remained where I was for a moment, taking in the stillness of it, the way the building held itself with the same quiet certainty it always had. There was no movement beyond what belonged to the space itself—no crowd, no urgency, no indication that anything had shifted beyond the fact that I was standing there.

I had spent years studying places like this.

Not the buildings themselves, but what they represented. The decisions made inside them, the way those decisions carried outward, shaping lives in ways that rarely traced cleanly back to where they began. I had understood it as a system, something that could be observed, analyzed, taught.

Standing there, it felt different.

Not larger.

Just closer.

The events of the day hadn't reached this place in any visible way. There were no signs of it, no markers to suggest that anything had changed beyond the boundaries of where it had happened. The building remained what it had always been— steady, unmoved, waiting for whatever came next to pass through it and become something else.

I tried to connect the two.

There was the man from the stage, his voice still echoing

with a familiar, practiced clarity—and then there was this: the unblinking geometry of the structure in front of me. It would persist, unmoved and indifferent, long after the life of that afternoon had been folded into the broader, quieter fabric of history.

The connection didn't resolve. Not fully. It lingered somewhere just out of reach, like something I would have understood more easily at a distance, once time had done whatever it does to moments like this. I remained there for a while, though I couldn't have said how long.

The city moved around me in small, quiet ways—cars passing, a door closing somewhere down the block, the distant sound of something I couldn't place. None of it disrupted the stillness of the space in front of me.

What I didn't know—what I couldn't see yet—was what came next. And standing there, I realized I had nowhere in particular to go.

TWENTY-ONE

"Life can only be understood
backwards; but it must be
lived forwards." —Søren
Kierkegaard

The service began before the room had fully settled. People were still finding their seats, conversations tapering into quiet acknowledgments as they moved down the rows, programs folded and unfolded in absent hands. The space carried a kind of restraint that felt practiced but not rehearsed, as if everyone present understood the shape of the moment without needing to be told how to hold it.

I arrived early. Earlier than I needed to, though I couldn't have said why. The front of the room had already begun to fill, Beau's family gathered near the first few rows, their presence anchoring everything else around them. I took a seat a few rows back—close enough to feel part of it, far enough to avoid becoming the center of anything I wasn't prepared to become part of.

Elijah found me before the service started. He didn't say much when he sat down beside me, only nodded once in acknowledgment, his presence settling into the space without disruption. There was something grounding in it, the familiarity of someone who understood the weight of the moment without needing to define it.

"How are you holding up?" he asked quietly after a moment.

I considered the question, aware of how easily it could expand into something I didn't have the language for yet.

"I'm here," I said.

He nodded, like that was enough.

Daniel stepped forward a few minutes later, the shift in the room immediate but subtle, conversations falling away not because they had to, but because there was nothing left to say that belonged to that moment anymore. He stood at the front without rushing into it, his gaze moving across the room as if taking account of everyone there before beginning.

"Thank you all for being here," he said, his voice steady, carrying without strain. "I know this is not a place any of us expected to be, at least not like this."

The words settled easily, not heavy, but deliberate.

"There's a passage in Ecclesiastes," he continued, "that speaks to moments like this better than anything I could offer on my own." He paused briefly, then read, his voice softening just slightly as he did.

"To everything there is a season, and a time to every purpose under the heaven: A time to weep, and a time to laugh; A time to mourn, and a time to dance."

The room held still around it.

Daniel closed the Bible gently, letting the words remain where they had landed before continuing.

"It's easy to hear something like that and think it's asking us to move from one thing to the next," he said. "That there's a point where mourning gives way to something lighter, something easier to carry."

He glanced out across the room again, his expression steady.

"But I don't think that's what it's saying," he continued. "I think it's reminding us that both can exist at the same time. That grief and gratitude, loss and love, can occupy the same space without canceling each other out."

I felt Elijah shift slightly beside me, not enough to draw attention, just enough to register.

"Beau lived in that kind of space," Daniel said. "He believed deeply in what he was doing, but he never lost sight of the people around him in the process. He made room for both— for the work, and for the relationships that gave that work meaning."

The words carried differently now. Not heavier—closer.

"He didn't wait for the right moment to care about people," Daniel added. "He did it in the middle of everything else, even when it would have been easier not to."

A quiet movement passed through the front rows, small enough that it didn't break the stillness, but present enough to be felt.

I didn't look directly at Beau's family, but I was aware of them in a way that didn't require it—the way the space seemed to hold around them, the way everything else oriented itself in relation to where they sat.

Daniel paused again, letting the room settle.

"There's another passage," he said, "that I've come back to a lot over the past few days."

He opened the Bible again, his voice steady as he read.

"The Lord is close to the brokenhearted and saves those who are crushed in spirit."

The words didn't resolve anything. They weren't meant to.

"They don't take away what's been lost," Daniel said. "They don't answer the questions we wish we had answers to. But they remind us that we are not carrying it alone."

I felt that differently than I expected to. Not as comfort— not yet. But as something that held, even if I didn't know what to do with it.

Daniel closed the Bible again, his attention returning fully to the room.

"Beau's life was not defined by how it ended," he said. "It was defined by how he lived, and by the way he chose to show up for the people around him, day after day, without hesitation."

He paused, just long enough.

"That kind of life doesn't disappear," he added. "It changes shape. It moves forward through the people it touched."

The words lingered. I didn't try to hold onto them. I wasn't sure how.

Beside me, Elijah remained still, his presence steady in a way that made the moment feel slightly less uncontained than it might have otherwise. For a while, nothing else seemed to move.

The service ended without a clear break. There was no moment where it felt finished, no single point where the room shifted from listening to something else. Instead, it eased out of itself—people remaining seated a little longer than necessary, conversations beginning in low tones that didn't quite rise above the weight of what had just been said.

I stayed where I was at first.

Not because I was waiting for anything in particular, but because standing up felt like it would require a kind of participation I hadn't fully returned to yet. Around me, the rows began to thin, people stepping into the aisle, pausing to speak quietly with someone beside them before moving on.

Elijah stood after a moment, glancing down at me. "I'll be around," he said, his voice low, as if the room still required that kind of restraint.

I nodded. "Thank you."

He didn't linger. He didn't need to. His presence had already done what it was meant to.

I remained seated a few seconds longer, then stood, the motion slower than it needed to be, as if I were still adjusting to the idea of moving through something that had already passed.

The front of the room had begun to gather.

Beau's family stood near the aisle, receiving people in a steady line that moved forward without urgency. Each interaction was brief—hands held, shoulders touched, words spoken quietly enough that they didn't carry beyond the space they occupied. It wasn't rehearsed, but it had a rhythm to it, the kind that forms when there isn't another way to move through something.

I approached more slowly than the others. Beau's father saw me first this time. There was a moment where his expression shifted—not dramatically, but enough to register recognition— and then he stepped forward, closing the distance before I had fully reached them.

"Nate," he said, his voice steady, extending a hand that I took without thinking.

"I'm glad you're here."

The words were simple, but they carried something more than acknowledgment.

"I wouldn't be anywhere else," I replied.

He nodded once, his grip firm, then released it, his hand resting briefly against my shoulder before he stepped back. There was no need for anything more than that.

Beau's mother followed. She didn't speak immediately when she reached me, her hand finding mine in the same way it had outside the hospital, though the motion was gentler now, less urgent. For a moment, she simply held it, her expression softening in a way that felt less like grief and more like recognition.

"He talked about you," she said quietly. "More than he probably let on."

The words settled differently than anything else had that day. I felt them more than I understood them.

"I know how much you meant to him," she added.

I tried to respond, but nothing that came to mind felt equal to it.

"Thank you," I said finally, the words inadequate but the only ones that would come.

She nodded, her hand tightening slightly before she let it go, her attention already beginning to shift toward the next person waiting in line.

Beau's sister stood just beside her, her posture more controlled, her expression composed in a way that suggested effort rather than ease. She met my eyes for a moment, then stepped forward, pulling me into a brief embrace that was firm without lingering.

"I'm glad he had you," she said quietly.

I nodded, unable to offer anything back that didn't feel incomplete.

The line moved.

I stepped aside, the space closing behind me as the next person moved forward, the rhythm continuing without interruption.

For a moment, I remained where I was, the movement of the room continuing around me, each interaction folding into the next in a way that made it difficult to separate one from another.

A voice behind me broke through it.

"Nate."

I turned.

Senator Frazier stood a few steps away, her presence composed in the way I had come to expect from her, though there was something quieter about it now, less defined by the role she usually occupied. She didn't extend a hand immediately, didn't move into the kind of formal greeting that might have belonged in another setting.

"I'm very sorry," she said.

"Thank you," I replied.

She stepped closer then, her tone lowering slightly, not private, but intentional.

"He believed in what he was doing," she said. "That doesn't change because of this."

I nodded, though I wasn't sure what agreement would have meant in that moment.

"He also believed in people," she continued, her gaze steady. "In the idea that when something matters, someone steps forward."

The words didn't linger long enough to feel like a statement. They settled, then moved on.

"I'm glad you're here," she added, echoing something I had already heard, though it carried a different weight coming from her.

I didn't respond right away. I was still numbed by the setting. She seemed to understand that, her expression softening just slightly before she gave a small nod.

"Take your time," she said. Then she stepped back, allowing the moment to pass without pressing it further.

I remained there for a second longer, the noise of the room returning in pieces, less distinct than before. Around me, people continued to move. Conversations formed and dissolved. The shape of the space shifted again, slowly emptying, though nothing about it felt finished.

***

The campus seemed to exist outside of time, a curated version of a world I no longer recognized. Students moved between buildings in the same steady patterns, conversations carrying across walkways, the rhythm of it all continuing without interruption. There were small acknowledgments—lowered voices in passing, a glance held a second longer than usual—but nothing that altered the shape of the day in any visible way. Classes met. Offices opened. The system held. I walked through it without slowing.

The familiarity of it made the difference more noticeable, not less. Every step followed a path I had taken dozens of times before, each turn leading exactly where I expected it to, the predictability of it standing in quiet contrast to everything that had happened outside of it.

Professor Reynolds' office door was open when I arrived. He looked up as I knocked lightly against the frame, his expression shifting as he registered who it was.

"Nate," he said, standing almost immediately. "Come in."

I stepped inside, closing the door behind me as he moved around his desk, the formality of the space softening slightly in the way he approached the moment.

"I'm glad you came by," he said. "I was going to reach out, but I wasn't sure—"

"It's alright," I said. "I needed to be here for a bit."

He nodded, like that made sense.

"Of course," he replied. "Take a seat."

I sat across from him, the chair settling into the same position it always had. Books lined the walls behind him, papers stacked neatly along the edge of his desk, everything arranged with the same order it always carried.

"I don't want to make any assumptions," he said after a moment, his tone measured, careful. "But I did want to check in. See where you're at."

I nodded, though I wasn't sure how to answer.

"We can adjust your schedule," he continued. "Classes, responsibilities—whatever you need. There's no expectation that you come back into this at full capacity right away."

"I appreciate that," I said.

He leaned back slightly, his attention steady, not pressing, but not pulling away either.

"That said," he added, "you don't have to step away entirely if you don't want to."

The distinction landed more clearly than anything else he'd said.

"This place," he continued, gesturing lightly around the office, "can be… grounding, for some people. Structure has its uses."

I glanced toward the window, the movement outside continuing in the same steady rhythm it had held since I arrived.

"I'm not sure yet," I said.

"That's alright," he replied. "You don't need to be. There's no timeline on this," he added. "No decision you have to make today."

I nodded again, the motion feeling more like acknowledgment than agreement. We sat in the quiet for a moment, the kind that didn't demand to be filled.

"I did want to say," he continued, his tone shifting slightly, less administrative now, more personal, "what you've been doing here—it matters. Your work, your teaching… it's had an impact."

I let that sit, not fully engaging with it, but not dismissing it either.

"I know things like this can change how you see that," he said. "Or whether it feels like enough."

The words landed closer to something I hadn't put language to yet.

"I don't expect you to have an answer for that right now," he added. "But when you do—whatever direction that takes— you'll have support here."

"Thank you," I said.

He nodded once, the conversation settling into something that didn't need to continue further.

"If you need anything," he said, "you know where to find me."

"I do."

I stood, the motion signaling the end of it more than either of us saying it outright. As I reached the door, he spoke again.

"Nate."

I turned.

He hesitated for just a second, like he was deciding how to say it. "People like him don't leave things the way they found them," he said. "What he started… it tends to carry on."

I nodded, then stepped back into the hallway. The movement of the building picked up around me again almost immediately—students passing, voices overlapping, the same steady rhythm continuing without interruption. For a moment, I stood there, letting it move around me, the familiarity of it settling in a way that felt both grounding and distant at the same time.

My office looked the same as I had left it. The door opened without resistance, the lights coming on in a steady, familiar hum that filled the space before anything else could. Books lined the shelves in careful order, papers stacked along the desk, a half-finished set of notes still spread across the surface where I had stopped working days earlier. Nothing had been disturbed. Nothing suggested that anything had shifted beyond the fact that I had been gone.

I stepped inside and closed the door behind me, the sound quieter than I expected, as if the room absorbed it before it could fully register. For a moment, I remained there, letting my eyes adjust not to the light, but to the stillness of it—the way everything held its place without question, without interruption.

The notes on the desk drew my attention first. They sat exactly where I had left them, ordered and intentional, a structure waiting to be reentered. I moved toward them slowly, my hand brushing against the edge of the desk as I stopped in front of it, looking down at the page as if it might have changed in the time I had been away.

The heading remained at the top in my own handwriting: Historical momentum and institutional response. I read it once, then again, the words familiar enough to recognize but distant enough that they didn't immediately connect to anything beyond themselves. When I had written them, they had felt complete. Not just as an idea, but as something I understood—something I could explain, teach, organize into a framework that made sense of how events moved from one moment into the next.

Now, that clarity didn't hold in quite the same way. It wasn't that the words were wrong. The structure was still there, the logic intact, each point leading into the next with the same coherence it had before. But standing there, looking at it now, I was aware of how much of it depended on distance—on the ability to step back far enough to see events as part of something larger, something that could be ordered after the fact. This wasn't that—not yet.

I pulled the chair out and sat, my attention still fixed on

the page as I read through the outline again, slower this time, as if the meaning might settle differently if I gave it more time. The arguments were still there. The transitions still worked. It was the same work I had been doing for years, the same way of thinking that had always felt stable, reliable in a way that didn't require me to question it too closely. But it no longer felt sufficient—not in the way it had before.

There was something missing from it now, something I hadn't accounted for when I first wrote it—something that couldn't be understood from a distance, or organized into a sequence that made it easier to explain. I sat with that for a while, the pen resting loosely in my hand without being used, the page in front of me lacking any meaning no matter how long I looked at it.

Eventually, I closed the notebook, not abruptly, but with a kind of quiet finality that felt less like finishing something and more like stepping away from it. The room settled again around the motion, holding itself in the same order it always had, as if it expected me to return to it in the same way I always had.

For a moment, I considered that. How easy it would be to stay here, to pick up where I left off, to continue moving through something familiar enough that it didn't require me to confront what I couldn't yet make sense of. The structure was here. The expectations were clear. Everything about it still worked in the way it was designed to. But standing there, I was aware of the distance between that version of things and where I was now— not measured in time. In something else.

I pushed my chair back and stood, the movement slower than it needed to be, as if I were giving myself a chance to reconsider before it was complete. The apartment held its own stony composure, offering nothing in response. I turned off the light and stepped out into the hallway, closing the door behind me with the same silent ease.

The building continued on around me, steady, uninterrupted, students moving through it in the same patterns, voices carrying just enough to suggest normalcy without demanding attention. It all remained intact, exactly as it had been. But it no longer felt like something I could stay inside.

TWENTY-TWO

"We live in time—it holds us
and molds us—but I've never
felt I understood it very well."
— Julian Barnes

The line outside the Bluebird stretched farther than usual.

It wasn't loud. There was no sense of anticipation in the way people typically gathered before a show—no bursts of laughter, no raised voices carrying down the sidewalk. Conversations stayed low, contained, as if everyone had arrived with an understanding they didn't need to articulate. A few people held drinks from the bar next door, untouched longer than they normally would be. Others stood with their hands in their pockets, shifting their weight from one foot to the other, eyes fixed somewhere ahead rather than on each other.

I took my place near the back.

No one asked why I was alone. No one needed to. The kind of night this was didn't invite introductions, and it didn't require company to be felt.

By the time I stepped inside, the room had already filled.

The Bluebird had always felt smaller than it actually was,

the tables close enough together that even quiet conversations carried, the stage set low enough that the line between performer and audience never fully existed. Tonight, it felt smaller still—not crowded, but condensed, as if everything had drawn inward to hold the weight of what had brought people there.

A single microphone stood at the center of the stage.

No band. No backdrop. Just a stool with a guitar resting against it and a sign near the center: *Remembering Beau.*

I found a seat along the side wall, close enough to see clearly but far enough that I wouldn't be noticed if I didn't move. The table in front of me remained empty, a glass placed at the corner as if someone had meant to return to it and never had. I rested my hands against the edge of the table, grounding myself in something physical as the room settled into a quiet that didn't feel imposed so much as shared.

The lights dimmed slightly, though not enough to obscure anything.

A man stepped onto the stage, his presence acknowledged not with applause but with a kind of collective stillness that replaced it. He adjusted the microphone once, glanced out across the room as if taking account of it, and then let his hand rest briefly against the body of the guitar before lifting it into place.

"This one's for Beau," he said.

No elaboration. No introduction.

He didn't need one.

The first notes came softly, the kind of sound that doesn't fill a room so much as settle into it. The guitar carried the melody in a way that felt deliberate, unhurried, each chord given enough space to exist fully before the next replaced it.

I recognized the song almost immediately.

Not because I had been expecting it, but because it belonged to this place in a way that made it feel inevitable once it began.

The voice that followed wasn't strained, wasn't reaching for anything beyond itself. It stayed grounded, steady, the words delivered with a kind of familiarity that made them feel less like a performance and more like something being remembered out loud.

"Won't you tell me how you've been…"

The line settled into the room, moving through it without resistance.

I felt it before I had time to think about it.

Around me, no one shifted. No one interrupted the quiet that had formed around the sound. It held, stretching just enough to make the absence of everything else more noticeable.

The next verse came, carried in the same steady tone.

"Wish I could say I'd see you again…"

Something in my chest tightened at that—not sharply, not all at once, but in a way that made it difficult to ignore.

I kept my eyes on the stage, though I wasn't really looking at anything in particular. The performer remained still, his focus fixed somewhere just beyond the front row, as if the song existed slightly outside of the room even as it filled it.

I hadn't let myself think about that part of it.

Not directly.

There had been too much movement in the days since— too many conversations, too many moments that required presence without allowing space for anything beyond it. Even alone, my thoughts had stayed contained, circling around the edges of what had happened without fully settling into it.

The song didn't allow for that distance.

It moved through it.

"It's the good Lord's will, I reckon…"

The words came without emphasis, delivered in the same

quiet steadiness as everything else, but they carried differently this time. Not as explanation. Not as comfort. Just as something stated plainly, without argument.

I let out a slow breath, realizing only then that I had been holding it. The room remained still. Not silent—the music filled it—but still in the way that mattered. No one reached for their phones. No one spoke. The usual small movements that filled spaces like this—the shifting of chairs, the quiet clink of a glass against the table—had faded into something almost imperceptible.

It felt like being held in place. The song continued, moving forward without hesitation, each line building on the last without asking anything from the people listening to it. It didn't explain itself. It didn't try to resolve anything it brought up. It simply existed. And for the first time since the hospital, I stopped trying to stay ahead of it. I didn't think about what came next. I didn't try to place any of it into something that made sense. I just sat there, letting the sound move through me in a way that didn't require anything in return.

By the time the last note faded, the room didn't react immediately. There was a pause—brief, but noticeable—where no one moved, as if the ending hadn't fully arrived yet or no one was ready to acknowledge that it had. Then, slowly, the applause came. Not loud, not overwhelming. Just enough to fill the space that had been left behind.

I didn't join it right away.

My hands remained where they were, resting against the edge of the table, the feeling of the wood grounding me in a way that the rest of the room didn't.

Eventually, I stood.

Not because the moment had ended, but because staying felt like it would require something I didn't have.

The room shifted as I moved toward the door, the sound of the next performer stepping onto the stage beginning to rise behind me, the rhythm of the night continuing in the way it always did.

Outside, the air felt cooler. Sharper. I stepped onto the sidewalk and paused, the noise of the city settling back in around me in pieces—the passing of a car, a voice from further down the street, the low hum of something I couldn't place.

For a moment, I stayed there, the sound of the music still lingering somewhere just beneath everything else.

The stillness followed me inside. It settled differently than it had before, not as something waiting to be filled, but as something already present, already shaped by everything that had come before it. The apartment held itself the same way it always had—the same books along the shelves, the same papers on the table, the same small details left exactly where I had last seen them—but none of it felt untouched anymore. It felt like it had been waiting.

I didn't turn on the lights right away.

The dimness from the street filtered through the windows just enough to outline the room, softening the edges of things without obscuring them completely. It gave the space a kind of distance, as if I were looking at it from somewhere slightly removed rather than standing inside it.

For a moment, I stayed near the door, letting my eyes move across what was already familiar, taking in the shape of it without fully engaging with any one part. Then my attention shifted.

The box sat where I had left it, near the corner of the room, half-tucked beside the chair as if it had been placed there temporarily and never moved again. It wasn't marked. There was nothing about it that suggested importance beyond the fact that it didn't belong to me.

I hadn't opened it. Not because I had decided not to, but because there had always been something else—something more immediate, more necessary—that had kept me from it. Even when I had noticed it before, it had existed at the edge of my attention, acknowledged but deferred. That wasn't possible now.

I moved toward it slowly, lowering myself into the chair beside it, the fabric of the cushion giving slightly under my weight as I leaned forward. The box remained closed, its edges worn just enough to suggest it had been moved more than once before it ended up here.

For a moment, I rested my hand against the top of it. Not opening it—just acknowledging it. The room held still around me, the faint sounds from outside continuing in the background, distant enough that they didn't interrupt the moment but present enough to remind me that time was still moving somewhere beyond this space.

I opened it.

The contents weren't arranged in any deliberate order. Papers stacked loosely, some clipped together, others folded or marked in ways that suggested they had been revisited more than once. A notebook sat near the top, its cover bent slightly at the corner, a pen tucked into the spiral as if it had been left there mid-thought.

I lifted it first.

The pages inside were filled with handwriting I recognized immediately—not because I had seen these words before, but because I knew the rhythm of it. The way the lines leaned slightly forward, the way certain words were pressed harder into the page than others, as if they had carried more weight when they were written.

I turned a few pages without reading.

Then stopped.

The sentence caught my attention before I had fully processed it.

"I'm lucky to have a very smart historian in my life."

I read it again, slower this time, the words settling differently now that I wasn't moving past them.

There was no date at the top of the page. No indication of when it had been written or what context had shaped it. It didn't read like a finished speech. The lines were uneven, some rewritten, others crossed out entirely, ideas trailing off before they could fully form.

It was a draft. Unpolished. Unresolved. I kept reading.

"I think we can learn a lot about our future by understanding our history. We know that hate, division, classism, poverty—and leaders who do not listen—always lead to something broken."

The wording shifted slightly between lines, the phrasing adjusted in places, as if he had been searching for the right way to say it and hadn't quite landed yet.

"When we look at history, we don't just see what went wrong. We see how to do better. To be better. For our future."

The pen marks deepened at that part, the indentation visible even where the ink had faded slightly.

I felt something tighten in my chest. I closed my eyes for a moment, the words remaining there even without the page in front of me, repeating in a way that felt less like memory and more like something still in motion.

He had written this before the debate—before the threats. Before any of it had taken the shape it ultimately would.

I opened my eyes again, my focus returning to the page, to the lines that followed, though they didn't form a complete thought. A sentence started, then crossed out. Another attempted beneath it, unfinished. The structure of it was there, but the ending hadn't been decided.

My hand remained on the page, my thumb resting lightly against the edge as if I might turn it, though I didn't. The room felt smaller now. I read the first line again.

"I'm lucky to have a very smart historian in my life."

The words landed differently this time. Not as a compliment. As something else. Something that hadn't been meant only for the page. My vision blurred slightly before I realized why.

I exhaled slowly, the breath uneven in a way I hadn't felt since the hospital, my hand tightening slightly against the notebook as if holding onto it might steady something that had already begun to shift.

For days, everything had felt contained—structured into moments I could move through without fully stopping in any one of them. Even at the funeral, even at the Bluebird, there had been something holding it together, something allowing me to remain present without being pulled under by it.

That distance had vanished. There was no longer a buffer, no academic shield between me and the truth of it. The words hummed in the air like a broken neon sign on Broadway— flickering, unfinished, a message mid-sentence that refused to resolve. For the first time, I allowed the pressure beneath the surface to break. It wasn't a flood, but a slow, steady leak— enough to finally admit that the silence had weight.

I lowered my head slightly, my hand still resting against the page, the sound of my own breath the only thing that broke the quiet of the room. The rest of the box remained open beside me, its contents untouched, waiting in the same way the notebook had before I opened it.

I didn't reach for anything else—not yet.

Morning came without much distinction from the night before. The light filtered in gradually, soft at first, then settling more fully across the room, touching the edges of things that hadn't been moved. The notebook remained where I had left it, open on the table, the words no less present for having been read.

I hadn't gone back to bed. At some point, I had moved from the chair to the couch, though I couldn't have said when. The hours between had passed without structure, measured less by time than by the steady awareness of the space around me and the weight of what sat within it.

The knock at the door came mid-morning. Not urgent. Not hesitant. Just firm enough to be heard without disrupting anything beyond what was necessary.

I stood, crossing the room with a kind of quiet awareness that felt different from the night before, less uncertain, though not settled. When I opened the door, Daniel stood on the other side, his presence unshifting in a way that felt intentional.

"Hey," he said.

"Hey."

For a moment, neither of us moved to say anything more. Then he stepped inside, his gaze shifting briefly across the room before returning to me, taking in what had already been understood without needing to ask.

"I figured I'd come by," he said.

"I'm glad you did."

He nodded once, then moved further into the apartment, not with hesitation, but with a kind of quiet respect for the space he was entering. His attention settled on the table, where the notebook still lay open, exactly where I had left it.

"That his?" he asked.

"Yeah."

I stepped closer, my hand resting lightly against the edge of the table as he approached. He didn't reach for the notebook immediately. Instead, he stood there for a moment, looking at it as if recognizing what it represented before engaging with it directly.

"Do you mind?" he asked.

I shook my head. "No."

He picked it up carefully, not delicately, but with intention, as if aware that the act of holding it carried more weight than the object itself. His eyes moved across the page as he read, his expression steady, not shifting in any obvious way, though I could see the moment settling in him as it had in me.

The room remained quiet while he read. When he finished, he didn't close it right away. He let the page remain open for a second longer, his hand resting lightly against the margin before lowering it back onto the table in the same position he had found it.

"He was working through something," Daniel said.

I let out a quiet breath. "Yeah."

"He didn't have it all figured out yet."

"No."

There was no disappointment in that. No sense that something had been left incomplete in a way that needed to be corrected.

Just recognition.

Daniel's attention shifted back to the page, then to me.

"That's not a finished speech," he said. "It's something he was still building."

The word landed more clearly than the rest.

Building.

I nodded, though I hadn't put it in those terms myself.

"He believed in it," Daniel continued. "You can see that

much."

"Yeah."

"But it wasn't meant to stay on paper," he added, his tone even, not pressing, not leading.

I didn't respond right away.

The thought settled into the space between us, not as a suggestion, but as something that didn't require agreement to exist.

Daniel didn't fill the silence that followed.

He didn't need to.

Instead, he moved slightly, resting his hand against the back of the chair, his presence grounding in a way that felt familiar but no longer directional.

"You don't have to know what to do with it yet," he said after a moment. "That's not what this is asking of you."

I glanced back at the notebook, the lines still visible, without change, though they felt different now, less like something left behind and more like something still in motion.

"It doesn't feel finished," I said.

"It isn't," Daniel replied. "Not in the way you're thinking."

I looked at him then.

"What do you mean?"

He held my gaze for a second, his expression steady.

"I mean it didn't end with him," he said.

The words didn't carry weight in the way I expected. They didn't land heavily or demand anything from me. They simply existed. And because of that, they settled deeper. I exhaled slowly, my attention drifting back to the page, to the lines that had felt incomplete only minutes before. The lines were still incomplete, but now in the way an almost-finished map still gives some direction.

Daniel stepped back slightly, giving the space room again,

his presence still there but no longer centered in the moment.

"I'm here," he said, not as an offer, not as a reassurance, just as a statement of fact.

"I know."

He nodded, his attention lingering for a moment longer before shifting toward the door.

"I'll let you sit with it," he added.

There was nothing more to say.

Not yet.

The door closed softly behind him, the sound settling into the room without disrupting the quiet that remained.

I stood there for a moment, the notebook still open on the table, nothing about the words glowing in it had changed, but they were no longer distant and muted.

For the first time, they didn't feel like something left behind.

They felt like something waiting.

The apartment settled again after Daniel left, the quiet returning without resistance, but not in the same way it had before. It no longer felt like something I was moving through alone. The notebook remained open on the table, the page unchanged, the words still present in a way that made it difficult to step too far away from them, even without looking.

I stood there for a while, not reading, not turning the page, just aware of it in the same way you become aware of something that has shifted without fully understanding how.

After a moment, I reached for my phone.

The contact list opened without thought, my thumb moving instinctively before I had fully decided on it. Colt's name sat near the top. I pressed it.

The line rang longer than I expected.

Then clicked.

"I was just about to call you," he said.

"Hey."

There was a brief pause on the other end, not empty, but attentive in a way that felt familiar.

"You good?" he asked.

"I don't know," I said.

That seemed to be enough for him.

"Alright," he replied. "What's going on?"

I leaned back against the counter, my eyes drifting toward the table where the notebook sat open, the page still turned to the same place.

"I found something," I said. "Some of his stuff."

"Yeah?"

"Yeah."

I hesitated for a moment, then continued.

"It's a draft. Something he was working on. A speech, I think."

There was a shift on the other end—not in what he said, but in how present he became.

"What kind of speech?" Colt asked.

I glanced back at the page, the lines still clear even from a distance.

"The kind he was giving," I said. "About everything. About what he thought he could build."

"Alright."

I let out a slow breath, my hand resting against the edge of the counter.

"He mentioned me in it," I added.

That landed differently. I could hear it in the silence that followed.

"What do you mean?" Colt asked.

I swallowed slightly; my gaze still fixed on the notebook.

"He wrote—" I stopped, then tried again, more carefully. "He said he was lucky to have a historian in his life. That we can learn from the past. That it tells us how to do better."

There was a pause on the other end—longer this time.

"That sounds like him," Colt said finally.

"Yeah."

Another pause.

"You think he meant you to see it?" he asked.

The question caught slightly.

"I don't know," I said. "It wasn't finished."

"That doesn't mean it wasn't meant for something."

I didn't respond right away. The words sat there, not heavy, not pushing, just present.

"I keep reading it like it's incomplete," I said. "Like something's missing from it."

Colt let out a quiet breath.

"Or maybe it's not done yet," he said.

I looked back at the notebook, the lines remained steady, the page still open in the same place. The thought settled in differently than it had when Daniel said something similar.

"You thinking about something?" Colt asked.

There it was.

Not direct.

But close enough.

I hesitated.

Not because I didn't know.

Because saying it out loud would make an absurd thought an absurd proposition.

"I don't know what I'm thinking," I said. "But it feels like… there's something there."

Colt didn't interrupt.

"Then don't rush it," he said. "You don't have to have it

figured out right now."

"I know."

"But if it's there," he added, "you're not gonna be able to ignore it for long."

That felt true in a way that didn't need to be argued.

I nodded slightly, even though he couldn't see it.

"Yeah."

There was a brief shift on the line, something moving in the background on his end—a door, maybe, or a voice further away.

"I've got to get back," he said. "But call me when you figure out what that is."

"I will."

A pause.

"You alright?" he asked.

I looked back at the notebook again, the words still resting where they had been, but no longer feeling as distant as they had earlier.

"I think so," I said.

He let that sit for a second, then responded.

"Alright."

The line clicked shortly after, the quiet returning again, though it no longer felt the same as it had before. I remained there for a moment, the phone still in my hand, the room unchanged around me. Then my attention shifted back to the table. The notebook hadn't moved, but something about its unfinished story had.

The next few days didn't move all at once. They settled into something slower, less defined, the kind of time that doesn't announce itself as passing but accumulates quietly in the background. The apartment remained mostly the same. The notebook stayed where I had left it, open at first, then eventually closed—not put away, just no longer resting in the center of the room like it had been that morning.

I found myself returning to it in pieces. Not sitting down to read it through, not trying to make sense of it all at once, but moving through it the way you revisit something that hasn't fully revealed itself yet. A line here. A phrase there. The unfinished parts lingering longer than the rest, not because they demanded attention, but because they didn't resolve.

Daniel's words stayed with me. Colt's, too. Not in a way that pushed me toward anything immediate, but in a way that made it harder to return to the version of things that had existed before all of this. The idea that something had been left unfinished didn't feel as distant as it had at first. It felt closer.

At some point, I stopped reading and started considering. Not what it meant, but what it required. The difference was subtle, but it rattled everything around it. I didn't decide anything that day—or the next. But the thought didn't leave.

It followed me through the stillness of the apartment, through the moments where I tried to focus on something else, through the spaces where I might have set it aside before. It stayed just close enough that ignoring it would have taken more effort than acknowledging it.

So, I didn't ignore it—I made another call.

***

The building didn't stand out.

Set back slightly from the street, it carried the same quiet functionality as the others around it—brick, glass, a small plaque beside the door identifying it as a district office rather than anything more formal. There were no cameras, no visible security beyond what might have been expected anywhere else. If not for the name on the sign, it could have belonged to any number of offices that handled work most people never thought about directly.

Inside, the air was cooler. A receptionist looked up as I entered, her expression shifting into something polite but attentive as she recognized my name when I gave it. There was no delay beyond what was necessary. A brief exchange, a nod, and then I was directed down a short hallway, past closed doors and muted voices that didn't carry far enough to make out.

Senator Frazier's office door was open. She stood when I stepped in, the motion immediate but unhurried, her attention settling fully on me in a way that suggested this moment had already been accounted for.

"Nate," she said. "I'm glad you came in."

"Thank you for meeting with me."

"Of course."

She gestured toward the chair across from her desk, and I took it, the space between us defined but not distant. The office was orderly without feeling staged—papers arranged in deliberate stacks, a few framed photographs along the wall, a bookshelf lined with policy reports and materials that looked like they had been used rather than displayed. It felt like a place where decisions were made quietly, without needing to announce themselves.

She didn't sit immediately. For a moment, she studied me—not in a way that felt evaluative, but attentive, as if taking in something she already understood in part. Then she sat, her posture settling into something steady and unforced.

"How have you been holding up?" she asked.

The question was familiar by now, but it didn't feel automatic coming from her.

"I've been managing," I said.

She nodded once, accepting the answer without pressing further.

"I was sorry I didn't get a chance to speak with you longer at the service," she said. "It was… a difficult day."

"It was."

The pause that followed didn't ask to be filled. It held just long enough to acknowledge what didn't need to be repeated.

"He believed in what he was doing," she said after a moment. "That much was clear. And he wasn't careless about it. He understood what it meant to take a position like that—what it asked of him, and what it might cost."

I nodded slightly, recognizing the weight of that in a way that felt more immediate now than it had at the time.

"He also understood people," she continued. "Not just in theory. In practice. That's harder to come by than most realize."

Her attention remained steady, though her tone never shifted into anything directive. It stayed observational, grounded in what had already been true rather than what might follow from it.

"What can I do for you?" she asked.

The question was direct, but it didn't feel like an opening being offered so much as a space being acknowledged. I leaned back slightly, my hands resting together, the answer forming in a way that didn't feel rehearsed.

"I've been going through some of his things," I said. "Notes, drafts… things he was working on."

Her expression didn't change, but her attention sharpened almost imperceptibly.

"He had ideas that weren't finished yet," I continued. "Not in a way that felt incomplete. Just… still moving towards a finish line."

"That sounds like Beau," she said.

I let out a slow breath, my gaze drifting briefly toward the window before returning to her.

"I keep coming back to it," I said. "Not because I think I understand all of it. But because it doesn't feel like it was meant to end there."

She held that for a moment, not interrupting, not stepping in to shape it into anything more defined. When she spoke, it was with the same measured tone she had used from the beginning.

"That's makes sense," she said. The phrasing was deliberate—acknowledging without directing.

"What are you thinking?" she added.

I hesitated, not because I didn't have an answer, but because saying it out loud would give it a kind of form it hadn't fully taken yet. My attention drifted briefly to the edge of her desk, to the small, ordinary details that grounded the room in something practical, before returning to her.

"I don't know exactly what this looks like," I said. "But I don't think I can step away from it."

She didn't respond immediately. The silence that followed didn't feel like hesitation, but consideration—something being weighed without urgency.

"From the future he was working for," she said quietly, not as a question, but as a way of giving the thought language without fixing it in place.

"Something like that," I replied.

She nodded once, her gaze steady.

"He didn't think small," she said. "And he didn't leave much room for the people around him to think small either. That was part of what made him effective." A faint shift in her tone, just enough to register. "You're not him," she said.

"I know."

"But you're not starting from nothing either. You understand something about what he was trying to do—something that isn't easy to step into from the outside."

The words didn't push. They didn't assign anything. They simply recognized what was already present. I didn't respond right away. I didn't need to.

"There will be people who move toward this," she continued after a moment. "That's how these things go. The space doesn't stay empty for long."

Her attention didn't leave mine.

"What matters is how people understand what it asks of them," she paused. "And what they're willing to give back."

The phrasing stayed with me, not as instruction, but as something that didn't require explanation to make sense. I leaned forward slightly, my hands still resting together, the thought settling into something that felt less like a question and more like a recognition.

"I'm not trying to step into his place," I said. "That's not… I could never replace him."

She gave a small nod. "I don't think anyone could."

"But I don't think what he was building should disappear either," I added, the words quieter now, but more certain.

For a moment, neither of us spoke. The room remained steady around us, unchanged in any visible way, the same order holding in place as it had when I walked in. But something within it had shifted—not outwardly, not in a way that could be pointed to, but in the way the conversation had settled into something that no longer needed to be defined to be understood.

Frazier held my gaze for a second longer, then nodded once, almost imperceptibly.

"Alright," she said, a small smile crossing her face.

No emphasis. No conclusion. Just acknowledgment.

"We can keep talking," she added after a moment, her tone returning slightly to the practical without losing the steadiness that had carried everything before it. "And maybe we think through what he would've done in your position."

"I'd appreciate that."

She studied me briefly, then allowed the moment to pass without extending it further.

"Good," she said, standing to shut the door to her office.

The conversation moved on from there—not into anything decisive, not into anything that would have marked a clear beginning, but into something brewing. Something that suggested movement without announcing it.

My office was quiet when I stepped back into it. Not empty—there were still signs of use, books pulled slightly from their places, a stack of papers left at the corner of the desk—but quieter in a way that felt removed from the rhythm the building usually carried. It was late enough in the day that most of the movement had already passed, the hallway outside reduced to the occasional sound of a door closing somewhere down the line.

My desk remained as I had left it. The same notes, the same outline, the same half-formed structure waiting where I had set it aside days earlier. For a moment, I stood there, taking it in, aware of how easily I could step back into it the way I had before—pick up where I left off, follow the same logic, complete the argument in the same way I had planned. But something in it no longer held in quite the same way.

I moved closer, setting my bag down beside the chair before pulling it out and sitting, my attention settling on the page before of me. The heading was still there, written in my own hand, unchanged.

Historical momentum and institutional response.

I read it once, then again, letting the words settle without immediately moving past them. They still made sense. The framework remained intact, the structure of the argument clear in a way that didn't require adjustment. But it felt incomplete. Not because anything was missing from the outline itself, but because of what it assumed—distance, perspective, the ability to observe movement without being part of it.

That distance wasn't there anymore.

I reached for the pen, not with hesitation, but with a kind of quiet certainty that felt different from the last time I had sat in this chair. The page didn't resist. It didn't ask to be rewritten entirely. It simply waited.

I didn't start at the beginning. Instead, I moved to the margin, just beneath the heading, where there was space enough to add something without disrupting what had already been written.

For a moment, I considered the phrasing. Not in the way I might have before—searching for precision, for something that could be defended or explained—but in a way that felt closer to recognition. Then I wrote—

> *Momentum exists apart from the people who carry it.*
> *It is not sustained by structure alone, nor does it end*
> *when a single voice is removed from it. When it is*
> *built on something enduring—on ideas that take*
> *hold beyond any one moment—it moves forward, even*
> *when its origin no longer remains.*

I paused, the pen still in my hand, reading the lines back not as a conclusion, but as something that had been there all along, waiting to be articulated. It wasn't a departure from the argument—it was the part I hadn't accounted for.

I leaned back slightly, my gaze drifting across the rest of the page, the outline now shifting subtly in relation to what had just been added. The structure still held, but it felt less contained, less dependent on the distance I had once relied on to make sense of it.

For the first time, it didn't feel like I was explaining

something from the outside. It felt like I was inside of it. I let out a slow breath, setting the pen down against the desk, the sound soft but distinct in the quiet of the room.

The paper wasn't finished. Not completely. But it no longer felt incomplete in the same way. It had somewhere to go now. And now, so did I.

TWENTY-THREE

"What is remembered is not what happened, but what survives." — Anne Carson

The room wasn't large—it didn't need to be.

A handful of rows had been set up facing a small platform at the front, the kind used for community meetings or local announcements, nothing about it suggesting scale or significance beyond the people who had chosen to be there. A few cameras stood along the side wall, unobtrusive but present, their lenses angled forward with a quiet expectation that something worth recording would happen, even if it hadn't yet taken shape.

Near the front, Senator Frazier stood speaking quietly with someone from the campaign, her attention steady, her presence enough to anchor the space without needing to draw it. The conversations moved low through the space, measured and contained, rising and falling without ever fully settling into anything distinct. People spoke in pairs or small clusters, their attention split between each other and the front of the room, where the podium stood waiting in a way that felt less like preparation and more like inevitability.

A few signs leaned against the side wall, stacked neatly but not yet distributed, their design simple and direct—the name in bold, the office printed beneath it: United States Senate.

Colt found me first. He didn't say anything right away—just stepped in close and pulled me into a brief, steady embrace, one hand firm against my back like he was making sure I was still there.

"You good?" he asked when he pulled away.

I nodded.

He studied me for a second longer, then gave a small, almost imperceptible nod of his own. "Alright," he said. "Go on."

Daniel was just behind him. He didn't hesitate—just wrapped his arms around me, quick but certain. When he stepped back, his hand lingered briefly at my shoulder.

"Faith's not really about knowing," he said quietly. "It's about moving anyway."

I let out a quiet breath I hadn't realized I'd been holding.

"I know," I said. When I stepped back, the room came into focus again.

I remained near the side of the platform, just outside the center of it, aware of the movement around me without needing to engage with it directly. A few people passed by, offering brief nods of acknowledgment, the kind that didn't require recognition to be returned. Someone adjusted one of the chairs in the front row, the legs scraping lightly against the floor before settling again. A staffer moved through the space with a clipboard, speaking quietly to someone near the entrance before disappearing back into the edges of the room.

The details registered, but they didn't hold. My attention stayed fixed on the podium. It was simple. Unmarked. A microphone fixed at the top, angled slightly downward, as if it had last been adjusted for someone else and left that way without much thought. Nothing about it that suggested permanence. It wasn't a stage meant for spectacle. It was a place to speak—and to embrace possibility.

I had seen versions of this before—from the audience, from backstage. Always separated from it—by position, expectation, the understanding that my role was to observe rather than participate. Even when I had been close to it, it had never felt like something I was meant to step into. That distance wasn't there anymore.

A voice near the front called out something I didn't catch, followed by a subtle shift in the room as people began to settle more fully into their seats. Conversations tapered, not abruptly, but with the kind of quiet coordination that didn't require instruction. Chairs filled. Movement slowed. The space began to orient itself toward the front without needing to be told to.

I remained where I was for a moment longer, aware of the weight of the moment without feeling the need to define it. It didn't feel like a beginning. It didn't feel like an ending either. It felt like something already in motion, something I had stepped into rather than arrived at.

The notebook had stayed with me. Not physically. I hadn't brought it. But the words had become ingrained in me. They had settled somewhere beneath everything else, no longer separate from it, no longer something I had to return to in order to find again. They were there the way memory is—not always visible, but present enough to shape the way everything else is understood.

Claire glanced in my direction, then toward the podium, offering a small, almost imperceptible nod. I returned it without thinking. The movement toward the front didn't feel deliberate. It didn't feel hesitant either. It felt like the next step in something already decided, even if I hadn't named it that way at the time.

The room settled as I reached the podium, the quiet shifting into something more focused, more attentive, without losing the steadiness it had held from the beginning. Faces turned. The small, incidental movements that had filled the space before gave way to stillness, not imposed, but shared.

For a moment, I stood there without speaking. Not searching for words. Not waiting for the right moment. Just aware of where I was—how I had gotten there and what it meant to stand in a place I had once only observed from a distance. My hand rested lightly against the edge of the podium, the surface cool beneath my fingers, grounding in a way that didn't distract from the moment but anchored it. I looked out across the room before I began.

"The history of our future…"

The words carried more quietly than I expected, not lacking in strength, but measured, as if they didn't need to reach beyond the room to be understood.

For a moment, I let the rest of the sentence form without rushing it, the rhythm settling into place in the same way everything else had—gradually, without force.

"…is something we build together. Not all at once. Not perfectly. But in the choices we make, and in what we choose to carry forward. Not because we're certain. But because what we carry forward matters."

I paused, not for effect, but because it felt natural, the words already spoken settling into the room in a way that didn't require anything more immediate to follow them.

Out across the audience, no one moved. Not because they were waiting. Because they were listening. I felt it then—not as pressure, not as expectation, but as something shared, something that extended beyond the moment without needing to be defined by it.

For years, I had taught that history required clarity—distance and time.

Standing there, it became clear that clarity doesn't always come first. Sometimes it follows. Sometimes it must be built. Historians may know how things end—but not while they're still unfolding.

I let that settle—not as a conclusion, but as something still taking shape.

And I moved toward it.

More from *Fletcher Hopkins*

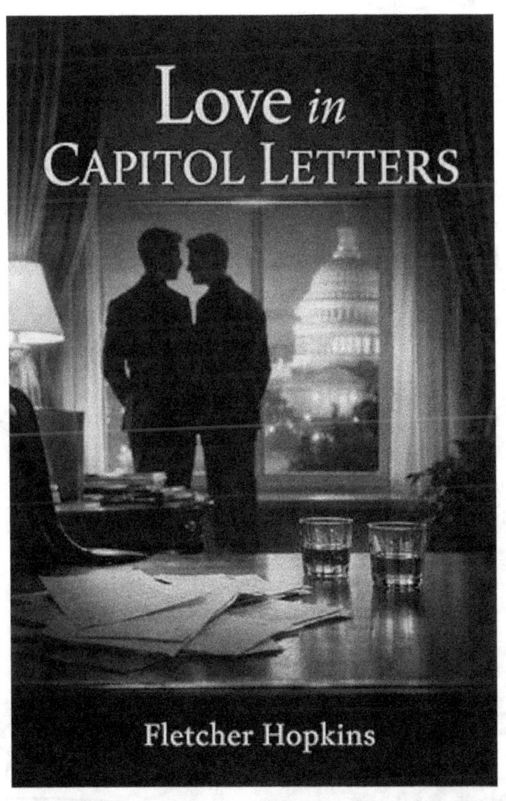

A secret love in the world's most powerful city.
Years of distance did nothing to ease the
feelings between this Congressman and the
newly appointed White House counsel.
Emotionally intimate in the midst of power,
politics, and fear

We all have a claim to our future. When historians some day look back at the history of today, you should be able to say *you* played a part in it.

Not everything that shapes a future happens on a stage. Some of it happens quietly. Privately. Without recognition.

If this story meant something to you, consider taking part in the real one.

Register or check your status

If something felt familiar...

If parts of this book felt familiar in a way that was difficult or uncomfortable, you're not alone.

You deserve to feel safe. You deserve to be treated with respect. And you deserve support—whether you're ready to reach out or not.

If you want to talk to someone, there are people who will listen without judgment and at your pace.

— Fletcher Hopkins

National Domestic Violence Hotline (U.S.)
1-800-799-7233
www.thehotline.org

www.ingramcontent.com/pod-product-compliance
Lightning Source LLC
Chambersburg PA
CBHW050741180726

48003CB00018B/52